Blanche

❦ AMONG THE ❦

Talented
Tenth

Also by BarbaraNeely:

Blanche on the Lam

Blanche

~ AMONG THE ~

Talented Tenth

BARBARA NEELY

ST. MARTIN'S PRESS   NEW YORK

BLANCHE AMONG THE TALENTED TENTH. Copyright © 1994 by BarbaraNeely. All rights reserved. Printed in the United States of America. No part of this book may be used or reproduced in any manner whatsoever without written permission except in the case of brief quotations embodied in critical articles or reviews. For information, address St. Martin's Press, 175 Fifth Avenue, New York, N.Y. 10010.

LIBRARY OF CONGRESS CATALOGING-IN-PUBLICATION DATA

Neely, Barbara.
    Blanche among the talented tenth / Barbara Neely.
        p.   cm.
    ISBN 0-312-11248-3
    1. Afro-American women—Maine—Fiction.
    2. Women detectives—Maine—Fiction.   3. Women
domestics—Maine—Fiction.   I. Title.
PS3564.E244B55   1994
813'.54—dc20   94-12802
                                                            CIP

First Edition: September 1994

10 9 8 7 6 5 4 3 2 1

For those most responsible: Ann, Bernard, Jeremiah.

Acknowledgments

All thanks and praises to:

All the sisters, dark, light, and in between, who tried to help me get it right, including: Maxine Alexander, Taifa Bartz, Donna Bivens, Rhonda Celester, Demita Frazier, Charlena Gilbert, Hattie Gossett, Marsha Morris, Beverly Smith, Barbara Taylor, and April Taylor;

The All Girls Writing Group: Lynn Burbridge, Shelley Evans, Linda Mizell, and most especially, the irreplaceable Kate White whose editing and critical advice I value beyond measure;

The other midwives and mamas: Michael Denneny, Keith Kahla, John Clark, and Barbara Elovic for their assistance; Lisa Dodson for the word on bops on the head; Jeremiah Cotton, Roz Feldberg and Peter Hardie for their careful read; Mimi Hersh for those writerly lunches; Karen Lombard for the writer-friendly medical examiner; Kate Maddes for GP; Miz Mama, Vanessa, Bryan, Rasheen, Taifa, Tyrone, Gloria, and Chanel for providing the ballast; Sarah McMahon for information and articles on Maine; Long's Christine Megos for her jewelry expertise; Katherine Hall Page for leading me through the labyrinth; Pam Rodgers for her supportive postcards; Sharon Rosen for suggesting Maine; Nancy Ryan and Barry Phillips for the perfect soupçon of inspiration; Renee Scott, for her historical research; LeVar Small for the right word; Charles Tolbert for his professional advice and general encouragement; Phyllis Wender for her wisdom, friendship, and advice.

"The Talented Tenth of the Negro race must be made leaders of thought and missionaries of culture among their people. . . . The Negro race, like all other races, is going to be saved by its exceptional men."

—W.E.B. Du Bois, "The Talented Tenth"

Chapter One

∽

The size sixteen shorts slipped easily over her hips. Blanche gathered the excess material at her waist and admired the contrast between her deep black skin and the nearly colorless cloth. She turned and looked over her shoulder at her substantial behind. A comfortable fit. She bought her pants and skirts at least a half size too large to give herself room to move and breathe and eat. She used to buy larger clothes because she thought they made her look slimmer. That was back when she'd believed she needed to be a woman-in-a-boy's-body to be attractive, even though big butts were never out of style in her world. Nowadays, all she wanted was the strongest, most flexible body she could maintain. She was hoping to be using it for at least another forty-two years.

She took off the shorts, folded them and packed them in the open suitcase on her bed. Clothes would be important at Amber Cove. Black people, even well-off black people, seemed to believe in looking good. She'd cleaned and cooked for plenty of rich white people who dressed like they got a kick out of being mistaken for a homeless person. No black people she'd ever known or worked for played that stuff. She'd once asked a black psychologist whose house she'd cleaned on Long Island about black people's attachment to clothes. She'd told Blanche it probably was partly due to African peoples' belief in body adornment in a spiritual way, and partly because, consciously or unconsciously, black people in America hoped clothes would make them acceptable to people who hated them no matter what they wore. She hadn't said which reason carried the most weight. In either case, Blanche knew Taifa would be mortally embarrassed if Mama Blanche didn't look just so. It wasn't an attitude the child got from her, but Blanche had made sure that the sand-beige, washable silk skirt and shirt, the off-white linen dress and slacks with matching jacket and Bermuda shorts, the pastel floral print sundress and the dressy, pale blue halter dress with its bolero jacket all had designer tags and were all so conventional and, originally, so expensive, they would undoubtedly meet with Taifa's approval.

She checked her list. Everything was packed except her robe, slippers and sponge bag. She gathered those last items. Outside, the scream of a police siren was quickly followed by the squeal of brakes. As the sound died out, someone drove down her street with their radio pumped up to maximum volume. The bass made her floor vibrate. She sighed and waited for the tiny silence that comes after a loud noise, before the regular, pushed-aside noises move back in. She breathed in the silence and let it ease some of the tension in her neck and shoulders. Was she ever going to get used to the sounds of city life again? She'd lived in Harlem for more than fifteen years; surely it was not as noisy here in Boston as it was there. But between New York and Boston, she'd been spoiled by living back home in North Carolina. It hadn't taken her a full day in Farleigh to grow re-accustomed to the sounds of birds singing and wind moving through the pine trees. Her readjustment to noise was taking longer. She'd been living in Roxbury—as this part of black Boston was called—for over a year. It would be good to be out of town, in the green world, by the sea, even if Amber Cove wasn't a place she'd choose to visit if the choice were hers to make. She folded her robe, packed it and tucked her slippers in the suitcase. She turned to the phone a millisecond before it rang. She put the receiver to her ear and started speaking before her caller had a chance to say a word.

"You found that Amber Cove article didn't you? It's about time!"

"What kinda way is that to answer the phone, girl! I coulda been one of your customers or a wrong number."

"Ardell, don't I always know when it's you? Now tell me what the article says."

"Why you got so much attitude, girlfriend?"

Blanche felt her face flush. "I'm sorry, Ardell." She sat on the bed next to her suitcase. "You know how packing can get on my nerves."

"Hummm," Ardell said. "I think you got more to worry about than how many pairs of drawers to pack."

Blanche waited for Ardell to go on.

"I got a bad feeling about this trip."

"Why?" Blanche wanted to know.

"Hummm. Well, this article on the place got a picture with some folks sittin' on a terrace by the ocean. I swear, I can smell the money just looking at this picture. And all the people in it could be models for the after pictures in a skin-lightener ad, even the men. Anytime you get this many light-skinned black people together at least half of them are going to be light-skinned folks who *act* light-skinned. On top of that, I think the man who built the place made his money . . ."

Blanche could hear Ardell flipping magazine pages.

"Wait a minute. Let me find it." Ardell turned more pages.

Blanche knew what Ardell meant. It wasn't natural for a picture of black people in a public place to all be the same complexion, unless somebody wanted it that way. But then, folks in Amber Cove were rich. The women who were mistresses of the few rich black homes where she'd cleaned or cooked didn't look like her, regardless of their husbands' complexions. She assumed there must be some black-black rich women in the country, but she'd never seen one; so she wasn't expecting to find her eggplant-black self mirrored at Amber Cove. But color wasn't the only way she'd be different. She doubted anyone in the Amber Cove picture had, like her, worked four parties to raise the money to spend two nights at the Inn. She could have stayed in the Crowley's cottage—they'd taken the children out on their new boat and wouldn't be back until Sunday. She'd move into their place next week, after they left the children in her care and went off for their ten days alone. When she'd turned forty, she'd promised herself as many little treats in life as she could afford, since the big ones were well beyond her reach.

"I can't find the part I'm looking for." Ardell's voice had that distracted lag that goes with reading and talking at the same time. "About the man who started the place, I mean." Ardell went back to turning pages.

Blanche waited with as much patience as she ever could. She was curious about Amber Cove. She'd never heard of the place until her kids were asked to spend their summer there. Her mind slipped backward a few months:

"You know Miss Christine said she'd love to have us, Mama Blanche!" Taifa's voice was as clear in Blanche's head as it had been when Taifa spoke three months ago, including that touch of wheedling in her tone that Blanche couldn't stand. But it was the little girl's eyes that had held her.

"This is really important to you, isn't it, Sugar Babe?"

Taifa had jerked her head up and down at an alarming rate. She'd been so focussed on what she wanted, she hadn't even reacted to Blanche's use of her now-despised nickname.

"And what about you?" Blanche had put her hand on Malik's shoulder.

"Casey's dad's got a new boat and he's going to teach me how to sail! If you let us go."

And, of course, she had agreed. How could she have refused them an opportunity for a summer by the sea, especially

since they'd made it clear they didn't want to spend the summer in North Carolina with their grandmother? "Wack," is
what they'd called that idea.

Blanche looked at the clock by her bed: It was after ten. Her
bus left at quarter to midnight and she hadn't finished dress-
ing. She was about to point this out, when she heard Ardell
clear her throat. Blanche shifted the phone to her other ear.

"OK, here it is." Ardell's voice took on a reading-aloud
tone:

" 'Many people are surprised to learn of a black resort on
the coast of Maine. In fact, the Maine coast is rich in black
history. Many runaway African slaves passed through Maine
on their way to freedom in Nova Scotia. When slavery offi-
cially ended, some of them, and/or their children, migrated
down into Maine . . .' OK, wait, this is about blacks in the
state . . . "Now, wait a minute." Silence again.

"Ardell, please! I got a bus to catch."

"OK, OK. Let me see . . . All right, listen to this, 'Amber
Cove was built in 1898 by Josiah Coghill, a black tycoon who
made his fortune on Coghill's Skin Lightening Creme, Coghill's Silky Straight, a lye-based hair straightener for black
men, and related products. The Coghill Mansion, now Amber
Cove Inn, was built after Coghill was refused admittance to a
wealthy white resort on Cape Cod. Coghill built spacious
cottages on the Mansion's extensive grounds and sold them
to friends and business associates, thereby creating his own
exclusive summer resort. The Coghill Mansion became
Amber Cove Inn in 1939. In its early days, guests at the Inn
had to be related to or recommended by one of the Amber
Cove cottage owners. In 1968, Amber Cove dropped this
exclusive policy. The Inn continues to be owned by members
of the Coghill family. Most of the cottages are also still owned
by descendants of the original owners'. See what I mean?"
Ardell added.

"I guess there won't be a lot of guests sittin' around talkin'
about how beautiful black is." The sarcasm in Blanche's voice
was sharpened by memories of past rejections and jeers be-

cause of her blackness and the knowledge that in black America, "exclusive" very often related not only to wealth or social position, but also skin color.

"Call 'em up and tell 'em you can't come," Ardell said.

Blanche saw herself getting on the phone, making up some lie, listening to Christine Crowley be nice about having to find someone to keep her kids and Blanche's for the ten days Blanche had promised to stay with the children while Christine and David got some time alone on their new boat. "No, it's too late for that. And it's only fair. They'll have Taifa and Malik for practically the whole summer."

"Yeah, but it ain't like you asked them to do it."

Blanche thought about the freedom the Crowleys were giving her. "Even if it was their idea, I gotta do something for 'em besides buy 'em a vase. You know how it is, Ardell."

Blanche slipped her hand in the side pocket of her suitcase and took out a small bundle wrapped in one of her grandmother's handkerchiefs. "And I got something to do there, remember? That's why I'm leaving tonight instead of tomorrow night." She held the phone between cheek and shoulder and untied the handkerchief to make sure she'd tucked Madame Rosa's instructions inside.

"Hummm. That's right. You need to get that dream business figured out. And you don't have to socialize with those people."

Blanche could hear the edge in Ardell's voice and knew what caused it. They were the same in that way—more angry about what hurt their friends than their friends sometimes were, certainly for longer. Blanche still didn't speak to Rose Carter because she once called Ardell a crazy bitch. And distance had no effect on their closeness. They still talked to each other on the phone at least three times a week, even though Blanche was in Boston and Ardell down in Farleigh, NC.

Blanche glanced at the clock again. "Anything else?"

"Yeah. Here's another picture. Of the Inn itself. Like a big old white plantation without pillars. Right on the ocean. Cottages look nice, too. Big, with porches. They only show the outside. Pretty."

Blanche didn't try to visualize the place. She could tell it would be different from the black resorts where she'd stayed before—places with erratic plumbing, rickety furniture and greasy but abundant food. In those spots the evenings rang with shouts and laughter from bid whist and tonk tables while B. B. King's voice slid from the sound system to float on the bar-b-que-scented air. She had no such high hopes for a place where a couple of doctors had a summer cottage.

"Well, I better get moving if I'm going to make this bus."

"Hummm. There ain't a place in the world I'd ride ten hours on a bus to reach. I hope it's worth it," Ardell told her.

"Me, too." She put her sponge bag in the suitcase and closed it. "If nothing else, I get to the sea, get some of my stuff worked out, maybe."

"Well, kiss Taifa and Malik for me, and tell them Aunt Ardell said not to give you no mess."

"Yeah." There was a heaviness in Blanche's tone.

"They're good kids, Blanche."

Both women were silent. Given how she'd gotten the money to send them to Wilford Academy, it would have been better all around if she hadn't had the wherewithal. But as soon as she'd realized those white folks in North Carolina were going to pay her for not putting their nasty business in the street, she'd known she'd use the money to buy Taifa and Malik the best education she could. She wanted them to have every opportunity and advantage a first-rate education could provide. But whatever they parlayed their educations into, she didn't want them to develop any dumb ideas about a lawyer or a doctor being a better person than someone who hauls garbage.

Blanche wondered if Ardell was thinking of the heated disagreements they'd been having recently about the children and how they were changing. Blanche was considering taking them out of Wilford Academy, where she thought they were picking up hincty ideas. Ardell was positive the move wasn't necessary. Blanche hoped Ardell was right, that she was making a boil out of a pimple, but she kept remembering the look Taifa had taken to giving homeless people; and the way Malik laughed at how some people in the neighborhood talked. They were eleven and nine now. What would they be like at sixteen and fourteen? She'd been regularly asking the ancestors to please not let Taifa and Malik be up in Maine acting in ways that would make her ashamed. A recent phone call in which Taifa suggested Blanche should get her hair straightened before she came to Amber Cove had confirmed her concern. Taifa had whispered over the phone so as not to be overheard by Christine Crowley and her daughter, Deirdre, neither of whose hair required straightening in order to be kink-free. Blanche hadn't straightened her hair since she was nineteen and had yet to agree to allow Taifa to straighten hers. She remembered hanging up the phone and railing against her dead sister for getting cancer, for dying of it, for insisting Blanche take her children—for putting her in a position where she now loved them too much to even complain about having to put up with their bullshit, even if they could be a pain in the ass and a worry to boot.

"Blanche," Ardell's voice was firm. "You raised 'em decent. They'll be fine."

"Yeah, I know. Thanks, Ardell. And listen, I'm sorry about snapping you up earlier."

"If you didn't snap me up, how would I know it was you? Now you listen. It's gonna be OK. You been black long enough to handle whatever them fools at Amber Cove got to hand out."

"I ain't worried about handling it. I'm just damned sick of having to. For just once in my life, I'd like to get through a whole week without having to deal with some fool, white or black, who's got an attitude about the way I look."

"Hummm. Well, in this world, in this time, you got as much chance of that happening as you do of having a limousine come up through your toilet."

"Don't I know it?" Blanche agreed. "Everybody in the country got color on the brain—whitefolks trying to brown themselves up and hate everything that ain't white at the same time; black folks puttin' each other down for being too black; brown folks trying to make sure nobody mistakes them for black; yellow folks trying to convince themselves they're white."

"Hummm. It's a mess girl, but it's all the mess we got and it ain't no gettin' away from it."

Blanche sighed. "Yeah, I know. But it would be nice just for a week to have our color be like tonsils, or toenails, or something else nobody really gives a damn about. We don't even know what it would feel like, do we?"

They were silent for a few moments, trying to imagine a life as foreign to them as life in a monastery.

Ardell spoke first, in a cheery voice. "Well, hell, just 'cause this picture is full of light-bright folk, don't mean the place is color struck."

Before Blanche could comment, Ardell went on: "And who knows, maybe they'll be givin' away money up there and they'll give you a couple million to pass on to me."

People passing by her building probably heard Blanche laughing. When she stopped, Ardell went on:

"I know the kids and the trip ain't all that's buggin' you, Blanche." Ardell hesitated for a beat or two. "I saw Leo yesterday. He asked about you. He . . ."

"Ardell, you know it ain't really about Leo. Anyway, it's gettin' late. I gotta go. Be cool, girlfriend. I'll call you in a couple days."

As soon as Blanche hung up the phone, she trapped the Leo thing behind a door in her mind and propped a foot against it. There would be time for that when she got to the sea. She closed the suitcase and slipped on her long, wide skirt—much more efficient than pants in those little toilet stalls on the bus. She carried her suitcase down the hall and sat it near the door along with her folded poplin coat and her canvas bag. She was standing in the vestibule when the cab driver blew his horn.

Was there a special kind of light bulb that bus stations used that made gray-blue shadows puddle beneath people's eyes? As usual, the bus waiting room looked like the meeting place for the living dead. She took a seat about mid-bus, on the side opposite the driver. She put her suitcase on the floor under her feet and wedged her purse between her and the side of the bus beneath the window. On the floor under the window she set her zippered canvas bag of necessities of travel: food—a chicken sandwich with lettuce and tomato and garlic mayonnaise, a pear, a bunch of grapes, some apple juice, a chocolate bar and a plastic bottle of water; reading material—the latest copy of *The Amsterdam News* and Octavia Butler's *Dawn;* a flashlight, an inflatable pillow and toilet paper. She never trusted the bus company to provide the last after that time it hadn't. Fortunately, her girlfriend, Sherry, who worked for Amtrak had given her a box of small rolls of travel toilet paper. Now she reached down and unzipped her canvas bag. She fished out her inflatable pillow, blew it up and laid it on her coat on the seat beside her. She watched the other passengers get on.

Most of them were white kids in their twenties carrying backpacks or duffle bags, wearing saggy jeans and polo shirts. An ancient couple—like a pair of dried white raisins—got on and took seats in the back; a white man in a shiny gray suit with a large leather case that said "Salesman" sat near the front. A slick-haired man dark enough to pass for a person of color, if he wasn't one, took the seat in front of her. A couple took the seats directly across from Blanche: A pasty-pale girl dressed all in black and a deeply tanned young man who kept jerking his head up and back to fling his near-shoulder-length hair from his face. His clothes were worn but expensively cut. Her clothes were new and cheap. She had the skin of someone raised on fatback and Twinkies. His skin had the glow that comes from whole milk, fresh vegetables and plenty of protein. As soon as they were settled, they began necking with serious intent but little passion. Instead of reading a book, Blanche thought.

The bus wasn't full and it didn't look as though she was going to have a seat-mate. She likely wouldn't have had one even if the bus was close to full. One of the ass-backwards rewards of being black in America was that you were often the last person any white person sat beside on the bus, which meant she often had the added comfort of a double seat.

Once the bus reached the highway, there was little more to be seen out her window than a thick blackness with an occasional highway light or exit sign to break the dark into irregular charcoal pieces. She'd risen early and had a full day so that she would be tired enough to sleep through the bus ride. Now her body was ready for sleep, but not her brain. As usual, what she'd tried to lock out of her thoughts sprung free and ambushed her as soon as she'd relaxed her guard.

Leo's last phone call replayed in her mind. "If I thought for one minute that you were coming back, that you'd even consider . . . Blanche? Are you listenin' to me? Damn woman! Even now I can't get through to you!"

She hadn't denied it. Leo had never gotten through to her, that was the problem. They'd been a steady couple in high school and for a couple years afterward. Even in high school Leo had wanted to marry her. But all the married women she knew worked hard in somebody else's house, field or plant and came home to take care of a full-grown man and a houseful of kids who seemed to think her labor was their due. Blanche had other ideas. After she left Farleigh for Harlem, she'd see Leo when she went to Farleigh to visit her mother. She'd looked forward to seeing him, too. It was always extra-good to have sex with a man you trusted as much as she trusted Leo. When she'd moved back to Farleigh a couple years ago, Leo made it clear that he still wanted to marry her. She could see now how she'd let him believe that someday he might throw her down and hogtie her. She'd had sex with him practically every day for the first two months she was there, until she began to settle in and he began to get on her nerves. They still had sex after that, but more rarely. The cost in argument about getting married and giving the children two parents was too high. But that hadn't interfered with Leo's plan, which from the beginning was bound to fail. He thought she wouldn't marry him. He refused to understand that she simply could not marry. There'd been two other men who'd tried to marry her. Both times she'd been overcome by the same feeling she'd first experienced at the age of twelve, while stuck in a small elevator for three hours. She'd been comfortable with her decision to remain single for the rest of her life. Until this thing with Leo.

By the time she'd left Farleigh for Boston, she'd grown nearly deaf to his complaints about being tired of waiting for her. She'd forgotten about distance and change. Two months ago, Leo had proven how tired of waiting he was by marrying Luella Johnson. How could a man who'd been attracted to her marry meek little Luella? Unless, of course, what the man wanted was someone to call wife, period. She hadn't gone to the wedding. She'd felt like a person whose insurance policy had been cancelled. It hadn't felt wise to travel. It was one thing to choose to be on her own and another to have no choice. The ninety-nine times she'd said "no" to Leo's proposals didn't count. She'd never rejected him, only marriage. But he had actually ended their relationship. He had finally and completely said "no" to her. The stab in her chest that accompanied the thought lessened a little in moments like now, when she accepted that the pain couldn't be avoided. She shifted about in her seat and adjusted her inflatable pillow. The couple across the aisle had fallen asleep all in a tangle. From the lack of voices around her, everyone else might be asleep, too. She closed her eyes and listened to her own breathing become intermingled with and then indistinguishable from the hiss-bump, hiss-bump of the bus's tires.

The dream dropped over her like a gunnysack. She struggled against it, telling herself she was just dreaming, just dreaming. But of what? The moment she opened her eyes it disappeared. She knew it was the same dream because she woke from it with the same empty feeling and tears in her eyes. Her fingers ached from clutching the armrests of her seat. She'd had the dream at least four nights a week since Leo got married, although she was positive that the dream wasn't actually about him. When it became clear that the dream was going to be a regular thing, she'd taken the necessary trains from Boston to Harlem to see Madame Rosa. Madame Rosa told her she was at a major crossroad in her life and the dream was trying to tell her something about the change that was coming.

"Go to Mother Water. Honor and praise her, tell her about this dream. Ask her for its meaning, for the memory of it. She will answer you before you leave that place. There are connections she wishes you to make there."

Madame Rosa told her to wear light-colored clothes and white cotton underwear, to burn white candles and go away from Boston—to a place with the initials A.C. (which Blanche had assumed meant Atlantic City because she knew Madame Rosa was partial to the casinos)—to perform the ritual Madame Rosa described and let the sea wash away her worries. It wasn't until she returned home that she realized that A.C. was as much Amber Cove as Atlantic City.

Blanche hoped Madame Rosa knew what she was talking about.

She drifted into a deep and dreamless sleep. When she woke, the day had taken over from the night.

Chapter Two

～

The ocean was never this blue at Rockaway, or Atlantic City. The sky was not this big or the trees as deeply green in those places either. She'd never seen a place so beautiful north of the Mason-Dixon Line. There was a peaceful quiet about Amber Cove, even though she could hear the deep rumble of sea against rocks. It was as though the spot had gathered to itself all those small, deep silences between waves.

Amber Cove Inn was smaller than she'd expected—a white three-storied central building with black shutters and trim. There were newer-looking, one-storied wings extending out from either side of the Inn. She glimpsed some cottages among the trees. Pine trees covered the area on the other side of the road and dotted the Inn's grounds.

She paid the cab driver and carried her own bag through the front entrance into a cool, slightly dim lobby. The lobby ended in a glass wall that separated it from the bar on the right and from the dining room to the left of it. Both looked out on to the terrace and the grounds and sea beyond.

The lobby smelled of the sea and was furnished with deep,

high-backed rattan chairs and love seats painted white with flower-patterned cushions. The rugs, over tiled floors, were rich in reds and blues that had mellowed with age. Occasional tables, a couple of lamps, some book and magazine racks, and three ancient Moroccan hassocks gave the place a used feel. And it was currently in use.

At the far end of the room, a slim, white-haired, high-yellow woman with a mass of gray curls sat with a pencil in her right hand and a small sketch pad propped against her thigh. She looked up at the arrangement of flowers and leaves across the room, then down at her work with quick movements of her head and hand. The way she sat—straight, with her back not touching the chair—reminded Blanche of a tapestry she'd once seen of Old Queen Somebody or Another at her needlework. This woman, too, appeared totally absorbed in whatever she was drawing, but she had an air of awareness, as if she could see through her pores, which made Blanche sure her own entrance had not gone unnoted.

Blanche looked around the lobby again. Despite the quiet and calm, there was an echo in the air of something not so serene. Something unpleasant had happened here, and not too long ago. She was sure she was right. She was good at sensing buildings, picking up the mood and personality of place. She thought of this sixth sense as a skill she'd developed from years of cleaning and cooking in houses, apartments and offices of all types.

Behind the unattended check-in counter was a closed door with OFFICE printed on it. Blanche tapped the service bell. The door to the office opened and out stepped a slight, light-skinned, thirtyish man with delicate hands and a puffy bottom lip. His black-on-white name badge said, ARTHUR HILL, MANAGER. His large, dark eyes widened when he saw Blanche. The full tilt smile that had automatically sprung to his face drooped, then dissolved when he raised his eyes to stare at her unprocessed hair. Without a word, he placed his hands on the counter, leaned slightly forward and played his eyes over her luggage, shoes and clothes in a way that said who made her clothes and how well she'd whiteified her hair were major issues for him. In the case of someone as black as her, were her clothes and the condition of her hair even more important to him? *Something* had to compensate.

Arthur Hill, Manager, sucked on his bottom lip and squinted at her in a way that said she was definitely a problem. However, he seemed satisfied that she was at least wearing labels of which he approved and that her small suitcase was, indeed, real leather. He pressed his lips tightly together, then allowed them to turn up slightly at the corners.

"Good morning. How may I help you?" Frost filmed his eyes.

Blanche gave him a look cold enough to freeze hell. She held him with her frozen gaze until his shoulders drooped and he pumped up his smile. She wondered how he'd react if he knew her clothes had been marked way, way down by the time she'd acquired them at Filene's Basement, that her luggage had been bought hot in a neighborhood bar, and that she made her living the same way his grandmama likely did?

"Good afternoon, young man," she mimicked the status-establishing tone she'd often heard rich white men use. She smiled at his confusion. Once she gave him her name and told him Christine Crowley had made her reservation, his smile was back in full bloom, although it never got warm enough to thaw his eyes. Some things were not to be forgiven, no matter whose friend she was.

Blanche filled in the card he slid toward her. A chubby white boy with wavy brown hair and a wide grin came running when Arthur Hill, Manager, gave the bell on the counter three rapid taps.

"Enjoy your stay," Arthur Hill told her with as much insincerity as could be packed into three words. Blanche rolled her eyes at him and sucked her teeth in disgust before turning away.

The young man carried her bags across the lobby toward the arch on the right. As they passed near the sketching woman whose posture said "Do Not Disturb," Blanche could see that while the flowers across the room sprouted from a blue vase, the flowers in the sketch the woman was doing sprouted from the eye sockets, nose and mouth of what looked to Blanche like a cross between a human skull and an African mask.

Blanche followed the young man down a sisal-carpeted hall lined with pictures of fair-skinned men with muttonchops and women with patent leather hair. They all had grim, stingy eyes and collars that seemed to be choking them.

"This your first time at the Big House?" The young man asked her.

"The what?"

He explained that this was was the nickname for the Inn. He stopped before the last dark wooden door in the wing. It had a brass number seven screwed to it. He pointed out the spacious bathroom, crossed the room and opened a door that led to a common porch that ran the length of the wing. It was dotted with porch chairs and ended just a few feet past her door with a screened door and three steps down to the grounds.

The young man's eyes lit up with pleasure at the size of his tip. Being a woman in service, Blanche believed in generous tips.

When he'd gone, Blanche walked around the spacious room. She ran her hand along the arm of the oversized wicker armchair with its matching footstool, the old-fashioned iron bedstead painted blinding white, the bureau under the gilt-framed mirror, the little writing desk in its own alcove. She slipped off her shoes and sat in the armchair, massaging the corn on her left baby toe. She almost convinced herself to take a nap, but she knew the impulse had more to do with wanting to avoid thinking about her welcome to Amber Cove than with a need for rest.

She rose, stretched and opened her suitcase. She was still fighting the irritation left over from her encounter at the check-in desk. She felt like she was paying dearly to be someplace she wasn't going to like. She wasn't one for dismissing her feelings; she always got into trouble when she did. Like the way she'd tried to ignore that Republican vibe Malik and Taifa were bringing into her house. Now she had to do something about it. At least she'd be able to use this time to get some information. She wanted to see Taifa and Malik on their friends' turf. She wanted a glimpse of how and why being among people who had everything could make a child or a fool look down on those who didn't have a pot. She also wanted to see how Taifa and Malik behaved towards her on their friends' turf. Then maybe she could figure out what to do.

She changed into oversized shorts, a shirt and a pair of the world's oldest Keds. While she was prepared to dress to accommodate Taifa and the other guests when the child arrived, Taifa wasn't here now. She picked up her sunglasses and tucked her room key in her pocket. She left her room by the outside door. She walked to the end of the porch and stepped down onto a stone path. She stood still for a moment, looking at the ocean. Madame Rosa called the ocean, Mother Water. Blanche liked that—it explained who it was that beckoned to her from the waves whenever she was within hailing distance of the sea.

The path branched off in three directions—one toward the three cottages nestled among flowers and trees off to her right; another out toward the beach in front of her; the third along the beach side of the Inn. On the way to the Inn, the bus had passed a small village that she could just see in the distance to her right, beyond the cottages. She took the path that led to it. Her legs needed a brisk walk after all that bus; and she knew from previous trips that she had to get her postcards bought immediately, or they weren't likely to ever get bought.

Amber Cove Village, the sign said. It could be walked end to end in five minutes. Its waterfront street sat on a log reinforced bluff. The houses, mostly white with black trim, seemed to run up the bluff, shouldering each other aside for narrow street space, making a pointy pattern with their steep

roofs and small, narrow windows. Three piers jutted out from
the waterfront street. She could see a few small, squat boats
out to sea. Flocks of sea gulls circled them. The pavement
under her feet felt gritty with sand, or salt. The buildings
along the waterfront were wide and low to the ground,
painted blue and pink and green with weathered wooden
signs hanging over their doors or in their windows—HAND
MADE HAMMOCKS, MAINE CRAFTS, STUART'S PHARMACY AND OLDE
TYME ICED CREAM PARLOR. At the far end of the street, CARMI-
CHAEL'S with greeting cards and sundries in the window. She
was already thinking about the kind of card she wanted to get
for Mama, Cousin Charlotte, Miz Minnie and . . . A loud
whistle blew as she was opening the door. She turned sharply
toward the sea, looking for the source of the sound. Her
elbow caught the woman who was just stepping out the door.
The woman's paper bag hit the ground and burst.

Blanche hurried across the pavement after the can that
rolled from the bag and snagged it. She scooped up the
remaining two boxes and turned to the woman she'd nearly
knocked off her feet.

"Sorry about that. I . . ."

The woman looked as though Blanche had caught her
farting at the dinner table. She brushed back her hair. Her
eyes flicked back and forth between Blanche's face and the
items Blanche was holding out to her. Blanche looked down
at the box of Rebirth Conditioner and Relaxer, the Straight
and Swingy Permanent Renewal Kit and the large can of
EverHold hair spray. She was surprised such black products
were available in this very white part of the world. Of course,
Amber Coveites probably spent a lot of money in this village.

The woman reached up and brushed back her hair again.
With her sandy blond hair and old ivory skin, Blanche had
thought the woman was white; a closer look revealed that
some of that lack of color was due to skillfully applied makeup
that made her face a shade or two lighter than her arms. She
had the kind of wavy and shoulder length, kink-free hair many
little black girls would kill their Barbie dolls for, even today.

But apparently she was getting some help with that. Blanche stared at the woman, caught in one of those moments in which the barrier between her and another human being seemed to momentarily drop; and she was able to see and understand with her gut, her heart and her bones. Poor thing, she thought. At the same time, she wanted to laugh at this silly woman made uncomfortable because someone she didn't know now knew she used chemicals to give her hair that white-girl look.

"Thank you." The woman snatched her purchases and hurried around the corner. Blanche wondered if she might actually be trying to pass for white.

She tried to imagine having that choice and taking it. She could picture herself a hundred shades lighter with her facial features sharpened up; but she couldn't make the leap to wanting to step out of the talk, walk, music, food and feeling of being black that the white world often imitated but never really understood. She realized how small a part her complexion played in what it meant to her to be black.

She chose cards with ocean and lighthouse scenes and went back to her room. She ate her chicken sandwich and a pear and drank some water. She fiddled around with her room, changing the angle of the armchair, moving the bed lamp closer to the bed and putting the ashtrays in a drawer. But she hadn't really had her fill of out-of-doors.

This time she took the path that skirted the beach side of the Inn and ran across the wide expanse of tree dotted lawn on the other side of the Inn.

There was a wide elevated, semicircular terrace on this side of the Inn. Stairs led down from the terrace to the lawn of deep green grass, flower beds and large, old trees. The terrace and the lawn near it were dotted with tables sprouting striped umbrellas from their middles, some chaises and chairs. A low stone wall separated the lawn from the rocky beach beyond. Blanche took a deep breath of sea-tinged air and tried to give her whole attention to the cause of that scent. The sight of the sea buoyed her. No matter what else happened the sea was there, and the trees and birds and flowers. She'd suck all the joy out of them that she could, despite the Arthur Hills and strange light-skinned women of the world. She walked diagonally across the grounds toward the beach.

A dark, portly man sat at a table on the lawn. He held a folded newspaper. An auburn-haired, freckled woman lay in a nearby chaise lounge reading a magazine. A tilted umbrella protected her from the sun. Neither of them looked up and Blanche didn't pass close enough to them to feel she needed to speak. Four or five other people lolled in umbrellaed chairs closer to the water. A woman jogged toward her in a shiny bright blue jogging suit, her male companion a few steps behind. Blanche nodded a "hello," first to the woman and then to the man. The woman had a blinking fit but recovered and returned Blanche's nod, although she didn't make eye contact. The man's lips lifted in a smile reminiscent of Arthur Hill's. Oh-oh. She hoped Ardell wasn't going to be proved right in her belief that well-off blacks were even more color prejudiced than the everyday folks who'd tormented Blanche all of her life. Of course, color wasn't the only thing operating in a place like this. There was also the close relationship between light skin and wealth—hadn't she read somewhere that light-skinned blacks made a dollar for every seventy-three cents dark-skinned blacks made? What else in a country that gave blue-eyed blondes the edge over other white folks? So folks here could dis her on two counts. She'd already discovered she couldn't pass for white, even in her imagination and she'd been around the well-to-do long enough to know that there weren't enough expensive clothes in the world to help her pass for money. It wasn't simply how a person dressed or talked that marked them, but how long they could sit without fidgeting and how easily they assumed they were at the top of whatever pecking order might be in place—traits that came from at least three generations of never having to be concerned about survival, and never coming in contact with need. She put on her sunglasses and walked slowly along the water's edge, keeping just out of the reach of the cold Atlantic. Madame Rosa had told her how to approach Mother Water. That would come tomorrow morning. Now sea gulls called to each other overhead; smaller birds she didn't recognize raced in front of her. She was glad for this time alone by the sea. She was eager to see her children, too. She still regularly longed to be her own, lone woman, but for now she was willing to have that need fulfilled by the occasional weekend when she left the kids with Cousin Charlotte, or times like now—of which there were an increasing number, she realized—when they were visiting friends from school. She took off her Keds and felt the weight of city living slip from her body like a heavy coat. This was where she needed to be, always needed to be: In the open, barefoot and totally sure that she, the sand, the water and the wind were one. She tried to remember this in the city, to live as though her life was not bounded by dirty streets, low pay, filthy air and dangerous traffic, to remember she was as much a part of this green and blue world as she was of her day-to-day grind, but it often required more optimism than she could muster. She took every opportunity she could to get out of Boston. She hadn't lived in the city long enough to know much about the place. What she had learned reeked of racism and political back-scratching in the white community. In the black community there seemed to be a lot of ministers mainly interested in being associated with City Hall or Harvard, and having their pictures in the paper. She'd met a couple good women and was beginning to think this was all the good she was going to find in Boston.

One of the worst things about the place was the way racist neighborhoods surrounded and claimed the city's beaches. She'd braved South Boston once, but the hostile air had diluted her connection to the sea so greatly it hadn't been worth her time, and the beach had been so dirty, it felt desecrated. She wondered if her recurring dream had anything to do with the frustration of being near the ocean but unable to communicate with it.

She walked the rocky beach until she reached a bunch of

boulders, some higher than a tall man, others half submerged and moss-covered—like shaggy dogs digging in the sand. She found a sunny, secluded spot among the rocks and sat down. A gold trail of sunlight made a sea path to the horizon. She cleared her mind of everything except what she could see before her. She leaned against the boulder behind her. The sun seeped into her veins. She felt it coursing through her like a shot of corn liquor—hot and burning in her chest, exploding its warmth out to the tips of her toes and fingers and the top of her head. The breeze evaporated the sweat beading on her forehead. She let her shoulders droop, then melt beneath the sun. She thought about people who worshipped the sun and saw how much sense that made. Her eyelids drooped. She willed herself to stay awake to enjoy the sun burning through her, but she was already half asleep. A woman's voice from the other side of the boulder brought her fully awake.

"She was a meddlesome, vicious bitch and I hope she's burning in hell as we speak."

"Carol, don't talk like that, please!" a man responded.

"Oh, have I shocked your sensibilities?" Carol said. "That's pretty funny under the circumstances."

A lighter flicked two or three times, then the smell of cigarette smoke before Carol continued. "Well, if Faith had had her way, you'd have plenty to offend your sensibilities. That bitch was about to tatter them beyond recognition."

"Don't talk tough, Carol. You know how I hate that."

"Honest to God, Hank! Try to stay in the real world." Carol's voice was sharp as Hank's was soft. It grew clearer and harder as she went on. "I can see why those white academic boys have you on the run! They'd have turned you into Jesse Owens once Faith got the word out. You must be as glad she's dead as I am. But even now you can't admit it!"

Blanche felt the mini-earthquake that statement caused.

"I'm sorry. I shouldn't have said that." Carol sounded as though she meant it. Blanche had a feeling she had a lot of practice saying it. Carol went on in a different vein, a more thoughtful tone: "Maybe none of this would have happened if we hadn't sat around for years watching Faith do to other people what she would have done to us, if . . ."

"If? There is no 'if,' Carol. It's too late for that." For the first time, there was heat in Hank's voice. "And I told you never to mention . . ."

"I only meant if she hadn't died, Hank. If she hadn't died. That's all I meant." Carol's voice was a damper for the fire in Hank's voice.

There was a long, tense silence in which the smell of ciga-rette smoke grew stronger. When Hank next spoke, all the anger was gone from his voice, replaced by what sounded to Blanche like tiredness beyond words.

"Let's not fight, Carol. Not now, not about this. It's all over now. Everything will be fine. Just fine. I'm going to make everything all right. I promise you."

Blanche felt, rather than heard the embrace that accompa-nied Hank's words. The two of them emerged from behind the boulders and walked hand in hand toward the Inn. Blanche pressed herself against the boulder and willed them not to turn around. When she felt it was safe, she leaned forward and took a look. Carol walked like a woman comfort-able in and in control of her body—something about the confident set of her shoulders and the way she swung her legs. Her hips were broad below her small waist. She wore a long skirt over a top that could have been a leotard. Her skin was a buttery yellow. A single thick braid hung to the middle of her back. Hank was just her height—no more than five ten. He was thick everywhere, from his block head to his large squared-off calves. While Blanche watched, he raised his arm and settled it across Carol's shoulders. She put her arm around his waist. They helped each other over the stone fence between the beach and the lawn. Blanche gathered this infor-mation in small bits, careful not to stare too long. When she took her final look, they'd disappeared.

Blanche took her time walking back to the Inn. She re-played the conversation she'd just heard and smiled. If this was the way people talked about each other here, even after they were dead, she might be in for a more interesting time than she'd thought. A real life soap! The only kind that held her interest. She wondered who the dead woman was and what put that quiver in Hank's voice.

There were three cottages on this side of the Inn, too. She could hear music coming from one of them. The couple she'd seen jogging earlier now jogged past her going in the opposite direction. Both of them developed a sudden interest in looking out to sea as they approached her.

"Don't worry, I'm not going to speak to you again!" Blanche hissed at them and laughed when they both jumped. As the sun moved toward setting, a cool breeze had blown up. She decided to check out the bar. She climbed the stairs to the terrace.

The woman who reminded her of Old Queen Somebody or Another was sitting on the terrace reading a book.

"Have you read this?" The woman asked as Blanche passed her chair. She held up a copy of *Deal with the Devil and Other Reasons to Riot,* by Pearl Cleage. "It's damned good!" the woman told her. "Good black feminist work!" She gave Blanche a sharp, direct once over. "Blanche White, isn't it?" She smiled at Blanche's look of surprise. "I looked at the register. I had to know the name of anyone who could put little Arthur in his place with a look and a change in tone. I'm Mattie Harris. I'd have spoken when you arrived, but I find it unwise to stop mid-sketch." The woman held out her hand. Blanche shook it with pleasure. She liked inquisitive people. She knew right off that she and this woman had that in common. She decided to show her respect with a gift of information.

"My children are staying with the Crowleys. I came up to give Christine and David a break."

"Ah, yes. Charming children. Good people, the Crowleys." Mattie paused. "Shall we have a drink? I could use a bit of chat." Mattie didn't wait for Blanche to reply. Despite her obvious years, she rose from the low armchair with a smooth grace and preceded Blanche to the bar. She carried a wooden walking stick with a silver snake winding round it. Two red stones glinted in the eye sockets of the head, which was also the handle. Mattie might as well have twirled it for all she used it for support. Mattie Harris. Hadn't she heard that name somewhere? They moved onto the bar and sat in leather club chairs around a low table.

The bartender picked up a bottle of liquor, a squat glass and a carbonated water dispenser before she approached them.

"Good afternoon, Miz Harris," There was genuflection in the young woman's voice. She let a few seconds pass between Mattie's acknowledging nod and asking Blanche what she wanted. She seemed to be having a hard time taking her eyes off Mattie's face. She poured Mattie a large drink and added a short spritz of soda. She added a twist of lemon peel before she went off to fetch Blanche's gin and tonic. She returned with Blanche's drink and a large sectioned bowl of peanuts, miniature pretzels and tiny fish-shaped crackers.

"What's your name, honey?" Blanche asked.

The young woman looked startled. "Glenda, ma'am, Glenda Morris." The smile reached her eyes.

"I'm Blanche White. Have one on me, Glenda."

"Thank you, Miss White."

"Blanche." Blanche winked at the young woman before turning back to her companion.

Mattie bowed in Blanche's direction. "An egalitarian, too."

Blanche wondered what the "too" was about.

Mattie picked up her glass, but her eyes were on Blanche. "You have the look of the Caribbean about you, Blanche. Are your people islanders?"

Ah, the third degree continues, Blanche smiled to herself. "You look like you might have steel drums in your blood too, Mattie. Are your people from the islands?"

Both women laughed.

"Sorry. Let's start again," Mattie suggested. "I sometimes forget that satisfying my curiosity isn't the major purpose of other people's existence." She raised her glass. "To the irony of the person who named you—although you must catch hell, Blanche White."

Blanche couldn't remember the last time anyone had spoken to her directly about the contrast between her color and her name. Giggles, shocked silences, stupid and disdainful looks, she was accustomed to all of that, but not this. She appreciated an opportunity to talk about it to someone who could differentiate between who she was and what her family had chosen to name her.

"Lots of people don't get it," she told Mattie. "People who consider themselves kind, hurry by it like it's an ugly birthmark. Some people just ain't smart enough to figure out how to hurt me with it. The rest get at least as good as they give."

"But how do you feel about it?" Mattie wanted to know.

Blanche thought about the changes she'd been through over her name—from hating it and vowing to change it, to wearing it as evidence that she honored her people's right to name their child what they chose, regardless of what other people thought about that choice. "It's my name," she said.

Mattie laughed. "I knew you were my kind of woman. I could tell by the way you deflated dear Arthur. There aren't many of our sort left, you know."

Blanche smiled and wondered whether this arrogant old girl would include her in "our sort" if they'd met while Blanche was cleaning the kitchen in somebody else's house. Blanche sensed someone heading toward them. She looked over her shoulder. It was Carol, from the beach. Hank wasn't with her.

Carol sank into the seat on the other side of Mattie and scooped up a handful of peanuts. "I don't know why I've let Hank drag me up here again! There is absolutely nothing like a dose of nature to turn me into a sedentary consuming organism. I need gasoline fumes and grit to throw me off my feed and keep me moving, otherwise I eat and drink myself into oblivion."

Mattie pushed the snack bowl toward her. "Carol, you've asked that question at least once a year every year for the last eight years." Carol grinned and popped some peanuts into her mouth.

"The usual, Mrs. Garrett?"

Carol smiled and nodded to Glenda, the bartender, then turned to look at Blanche. "Has Mattie been boring you with the good old days, when women were strong and men were conveniences?"

"That's not my point at all, Carol and you know it." Mattie tapped her walking stick on the floor for emphasis. "It just seems to me that young black women today have bought a mess of pottage with all this romanticism and need to find a soul mate in order to make a marriage. What every woman needs in a man, whether she knows it or not, is a good friend, a lover and a helpmate. In my day, women understood romance as a concept men developed to avoid life. *They* need it. Raw life makes men queasy and querulous, or worse, abusive. For us, husbands were for making children and building the community. Looks and sweet words didn't enter into it. My own marriage may not have contributed to the African-American community, but I assure you, it was not entered into out of any romanticism on *my* part."

"I heard love was supposed to have something to do with it." Blanche teased.

But Mattie responded seriously: "Yes, there is every once in a great, great while, love that is real and lasting but that is rare as to be very nearly holy."

I wonder who he was, Blanche thought.

"But don't confuse love with hormones, or a nesting instinct." Mattie went on. "Be clear-eyed. That's the important thing. Be in charge of yourself. Know what you're doing and why. Don't be fooled. And don't expect love with a capital *L*. It is, as I said, too rare."

Carol laughed. "I think you've generalized your particulars, darling."

Mattie waved her hand dismissively at Carol's comment. "Blanche White, this is Carol Garrett, our resident city slicker." She turned to Carol. "Carol, Blanche White.

Blanche is mother to the children staying with the Crowleys."
Carol leaned across the table and held out her hand. Her
dark, almond-shaped eyes scanned Blanche's face with interest. "Pleased to meet you, Blanche."

Blanche responded in kind and tried to remember how
she'd imagine the woman she'd heard talking on the beach
would look from the front. She'd pictured someone with
sharper features and a cooler gaze, a tighter mouth, not this
soft, round, almost plump face with its large, sad eyes. Carol
looked like the kind of woman older men called, "Baby-doll."
Not for any childishness on the woman's part, but for her
cuddly looks. And there was no childishness about this
woman. There was a weariness around her eyes, a set to her
mouth that was somehow opposite to her prettiness.

Mattie spoke before Blanche had time to reply. "Where's
that man of yours?" Mattie directed her question at Carol,
then winked at Blanche. "You've been in here almost five
minutes and there's no sign of him."

Blanche wondered what accounted for the sharp intake of
breath and two beats of silence before Carol spoke.

"We're not exactly joined at the hip, you know." Carol
tapped Mattie on the arm. "And who are you to talk? You'd
have your dear godson in your face every minute of the day,
if you could. Unfortunately for you, he's taking a nap."

Mattie nearly preened when Carol mentioned that Hank
was her godson, then went serious. "A nap? He's not still
brooding is he? I told him it's normal to be unhappy sometimes, even though we have no reason to be. You young
people think life is supposed to be a perpetual lark. It's not
as though he's ill. All that depression nonsense is behind him.
He mustn't indulge himself."

Carol's shoulders rose slightly, and she tightened her lips
in a way that said she didn't agree with Mattie but she didn't
say so.

"Do you have a doting spouse, Blanche?" Mattie's curiosity
gave her eyes a hungry look.

"Nope. What about you?"

"Oh, I'm too old for that! I should have been too young for it, as well. But that's done. Still, I've been lucky. I've been on my own now since I was fifty-seven. Twenty-two sweet, single years." She tapped her walking stick on the floor in time to each of her last four words.

Carol laughed. "Mattie! Blanche will think you were married to some battering bore. Your life with Carlton Syms was full of travel and meeting interesting people, and . . ."

Mattie interrupted her. "And raising two sons who are now much prouder of their Caucasian heritage than they are of anything else. And being the wife of the great professor." Mattie's voice grew heavy as she went on. "And enjoying the protection of a wealthy white husband in a world where most women who look like me might as well have bull's-eyes on their foreheads they're so endangered." She looked directly at Blanche: "Although, not as endangered as some. I was only in danger from myself. For thirty-five years, that's what I was, first and foremost, a danger to myself."

The bitterness in Mattie's voice struck both her listeners dumb.

Carol rattled the ice in her glass before she spoke. "Well, you've certainly made up for lost time."

Blanche knew from the way Carol stressed the word "you" that she was thinking more about her own life than Mattie's. There was admiration and some envy in Carol's tone. The term "School of Hard Knocks" leapt to Blanche's mind.

Glenda approached their table. "Ms. Harris, I know it's an imposition, but I wonder if you would . . . that is, I don't want to be a nuisance . . ." Glenda spoke all in a rush as if she were afraid she'd lose courage.

Mattie held out her hand. Glenda laid the book on Mattie's outstretched palm. A plain white cover with a crossed spear and shield stamped on it, overlaid with sharp black letters: *Woman as Warrior* by Mattie Harris. Blanche remembered where she'd seen Mattie's name before. It was in either *Ms.* or *Sojourner,* or some other women's newspapers or magazines that she always leafed through when she worked for Kathellen

McInnis. There'd been an article about Mattie. Dr. Mattie, as Blanche recalled. It had said that both her early and current artworks and her writings on education and women from the twenties through the forties were being rediscovered by art lovers and feminists, especially black ones. The article described Mattie as one of the foremost visionary feminist writers. Even before Blanche had remembered the article, she was already impressed by Mattie—a black woman of her age with her Diva-ness was bound to be interesting to a woman moving rapidly toward her own senior years. Now Blanche looked at Mattie with even more interest. She was eager to learn more about this woman. From the frank way that Mattie spoke about her life, Blanche was confident that she'd learn a lot more about her in time and she would be here ten days. Her stay at Amber Cove was definitely looking up.

When Mattie went off to the bathroom, Blanche turned to Carol.

"You and Mattie seem very close."

"Do we? I suppose we are in a way. Like bricks held together by the same mortar."

"You mean Hank?"

"Ummhumm." Believe me, without him, I'd be nothing as far as Mattie is concerned. Sometimes I think she likes me better because I can't have kids so she doesn't have to share Hank with any serious rivals."

Blanche covered her surprise with a sip from her glass. These folks didn't play around when it came to plain-speaking about each other, alive or dead.

"Of course, getting Hank away from Mattie would be no mean feat," Carol added, as if to cushion her previous comment. "And it's not just Mattie, most of the people here wouldn't acknowledge my existence if I wasn't connected to Hank. No poor unknown daughter of South Carolina share-croppers could achieve real insider status at dear old Amber Cove."

"I don't see sharecropper written on you nowhere." Blanche told her.

The pleasure in Carol's eye was balanced by the wry twist of her mouth. "Oh, I can play Miss Got-it-all as well as the next one. I've worked . . . I've known a lot of insider types, powerful types. You learn the moves."

Blanche nodded her agreement. She and Carol were similar in this. She had learned the manners, dress and forks of the rich from serving their dinners and cleaning their silver. Mattie was back before Blanche could ask Carol where a sharecroppers' daughter who wasn't in service acquired such skills. Blanche felt sure Carol wouldn't want to be asked in front of Mattie.

Other people had wandered into the bar while Mattie was away: A woman so thin she might have been crowned Miz Skinny entered followed by a dark, brown-skinned man Blanche had seen reading the newspaper on the lawn. A young man stood at the bar with a beer in his hand. Next to him, a slim man stood facing a tawny, shapely woman with shoulder-length hair. She wore a tight creamy sheath. Her eyes were elaborately made up and gold bracelets clinked with her every move. She sat wide-legged, the man's hand was on her thigh. The jogging couple strolled in. They ordered orange juice and took it out on the terrace. A middle-aged couple in tennis whites so sparkling and keenly pressed they could not have been on the courts came in after the jogging couple went out. As more people gathered, there was a tension in the air that Blanche associated with her earlier sense that something unusual had happened here. She watched people mill, speak, split off and regroup. Their faces wore expressions on the somber side. There was a good bit of head shaking. Another couple entered the bar. They looked ready for a night at the clubs—he in a gray sharkskin suit, she in a purple silk minidress. The were hardly in the door before the woman spoke.

"Well, I for one am not going to shed a tear for the evil bitch. It's just too bad somebody didn't get the satisfaction of killing her."

"Baby, please. Keep your voice down." Her companion

tried to lead her toward a table, but the woman was still having her say. "Bunch of hypocrites!" She looked around the room. "I heard ya'll talking about her!" The woman's companion actually pulled her toward a table and pushed her onto a chair from which she glowered around the room.

"What's that all about?" Blanche asked Mattie, who fiddled with the head of her walking stick before she answered.

"Faith Brown. She and Al J.'s cottage is the last one beyond that wing of the Inn." Mattie gestured in the direction of the wing where Blanche was staying.

"Why's she taking on so?" Blanche wanted to know.

"No, she's not Faith. Faith is the person she's talking about. She managed to electrocute herself in her bathtub last night."

"Last night? Here? How?" Blanche couldn't help but flick a look at Carol who was so still she might have been holding her breath.

"Dropped her radio in the tub while taking a bath. Rather odd way to die in this day and age, don't you think?" Mattie picked up her glass and sipped some rum. "Of course, a nasty shock seems an especially appropriate death for Faith."

Mattie didn't elaborate. Carol's face was as closed as a triple-locked door. Mattie went on talking:

"I remember Faith when she was child. Her family is one of the founding members of this place, you know. I don't think she was ever a nice person, even though her parents were perfectly decent, as I recall. Could she have been born a bitch, do you think?"

Blanche's face must have registered her surprise. Mattie gave her an amused look. She leaned over and patted Blanche's arm.

"I am old, my dear, but I am not nice. The closer I get to death, the more convinced I become that there's no more sense in respecting the undeserving dead than there is in honoring the undeserving living. Still, there are the deserving living to consider. Poor Al J." she added after a few moments.

"Any children?" Blanche asked.

"That was a part of the problem. She wanted children, or rather sons, desperately. She had at least three miscarriages. Considering the kind of influence she was likely to have on a child, it's just as well she couldn't manage it." Mattie finished her drink.

"Did they both summer here as children?"

Mattie laughed. "If only, my dear! There wouldn't have been such a flap if Al J. had been one of this set. No. Faith's mother almost had apoplexy when Faith bought her new beau up for the weekend. I remember it like yesterday, one of the advantages of advanced age.

" 'Black, poor, and uneducated,' is how Faith's mother described him. Al J. was a widowed postal worker with two kids and still going to night school trying to get an undergraduate degree at nearly forty. At the same time, I'm sure both Faith's parents were delighted to have someone take her off their hands. As I said, she was always mean-spirited. It's hard to understand what Al J. saw in her. Of course, there's love, I suppose."

The two waitresses setting tables in the dining room were like a signal for the guests to begin drifting away to prepare for the evening. Mattie announced that she wanted a hot soak before dinner, and the three women rose and left by the sliding door to the terrace. Blanche felt a change in the air around Mattie and Carol that she thought was due to the man walking across the terrace toward them.

He was tall and slim in a rounded kind of way. His skin was milk with a dollop of coffee, instead of the other way around. He was muscular without being gross with long, elegant hands and blue-green eyes. His medium brown hair had just a hint of a wave. There was a dusting of gray, like the first snowflakes, at his temples. Damn! Blanche thought, he probably gets anonymous pussy in the mail. She realized he was watching her watching him. She didn't look away.

"Hello Mattie, Carol." He spoke to them but continued to look at Blanche. Both women jumped as though they'd been goosed and almost in unison said, "Stu! How are you?" in overly friendly voices.

"Hello," he said to Blanche and held out his hand. "Robert Stuart," he said, not waiting for Mattie or Carol to introduce her. "Call me, Stu." He had a voice like honey and a smile that wrapped itself around her like silk.

Blanche took his hand and told him her name. The difference between what she was called and how she looked didn't seem to faze him. Blanche smiled up at him. While his pretty boy face wasn't all that interesting to her, he did have other physical attributes she liked—big hands with long, graceful fingers and the kind of lean hips that promised one of those pert, kissable behinds.

"This your first time at Amber Cove?" He looked as if whatever she said would be important to him.

Both Mattie and Carol expressed the need to hurry off and left Blanche wondering if there was something about this man that made them want to run.

Blanche began walking toward the terrace stairs. "First time in Maine," she told him.

Stu walked down the stairs beside her. "Are you enjoying it?"

Blanche wasn't sure she was, but she nodded in the affirmative. She was thrown off by the look he gave her. She hadn't expected to be cruised.

"And your husband? Is he enjoying it, too?"

Not subtle, but to the point. She liked that. "I don't have a husband."

His smile left no question as to how he felt about her answer. "I don't either," he said. "Have a wife, I mean."

Blanche stopped at the foot of the terrace stairs. "I thought you were headed inside."

"Was I? I guess I was. Just to see old Arthur. He'll keep." He continued to give her that soft-eyed smile. "Well," he held out his hand once more. "I hope to see you again very soon, Blanche." He trapped her hand between his large, warm palms. "Like at the dance tonight? I hope you're planning to come."

Blanche reclaimed her hand. "What dance?"

"You mean no one's told you about the famous Amber Cove Saturday night dance beneath the stars? The highlight of the month. Everyone comes. Live music, too. And right here on this very terrace."

Was he doing something with his eyes or did he look at everyone as though their face was something special to see?

"I hope you'll come, Blanche. I hope you'll save me a dance, or two, or three."

"Well, I may just do that. But how many dances you can claim will depend."

"On what."

"How well you dance." She shot him a quick wink. "Bye." She turned and walked toward her end of the Inn. She could feel him watching her and waved to him without turning around. He laughed. She smiled over her shoulder. He had the same golden glow whitefolks risk skin cancer to get. A dance. She'd never forgotten those dances in her teens where the girls would go in groups, assuming there'd be boys available for them to dance with. Being the blackest had usually meant being the last on the dance floor, rarely for a slow dance, and never with anyone who looked like Stu. In the sixties, women who looked like her became status symbols to be draped on revolutionary black arms like a piece of kinte cloth. Now she mostly saw black couples of the same color and darker men with lighter women. Be all that as it may, at tonight's dance there was at least one person who'd want to dance with her. She was surprised at how happy that made her.

Instead of going to her door, she walked around the end of the wing and looked across the grass to the three cottages nestled among the trees. The cottages were spread out and angled for maximum privacy. They looked alike, except for the different colored doors: one blue, one green, one yellow. They had identical deep, covered porches, each with a differ-

BLANCHE AMONG THE TALENTED TENTH   37

ent sort of porch furniture. The windows were open in the
cottage with the yellow door. Was that something by Miles she
heard coming from it? The windows in the green-doored
cottage were shuttered. The cottage with the blue door was
dark, its windows closed. There was a man approaching it. He
wasn't one of the guests she'd seen before, but she was sure
he was a guest. He looked quickly round, but didn't see
Blanche. He tried the door. It didn't open. He went to one of
the windows that opened on the porch, but didn't touch it. It
could be his cottage, she thought, but she doubted it. He
acted like a man visiting somebody else's wife. Maybe he was.
She watched until he went around toward the back of the
cottage. She didn't wait to see if he came back.

While she showered and changed, her mind slipped among
the questions that flowed from her afternoon:

Wasn't there something funny about the Inn holding a
dance the night after the death of somebody whose family
had owned a piece of the place forever? Maybe it was a way of
pretending death away; maybe it was a way of acknowledging
that life goes on. Or maybe it was like Miz Cooper who'd lived
across the street from Ardell. Miz Cooper was a sweet, quiet,
God-fearing, obedient little wife. Mr. Cooper was a real ty-
rant. He tried to stop the neighborhood children from walking on his pavement. He'd let the air out of people's tires if
they parked too long in front of his door. When Mr. Cooper
died, Miz Cooper came to the funeral in a red dress and a big
straw hat to match. Some people claimed they'd heard her
whisper, "I'm glad you're dead, you devil, you," as she leaned
over her husband's corpse. Blanche thought she'd said it all
with that dress. Maybe the dance was a similar message to
Faith.

Other questions slipped up to take first place. How would
her conversation with Mattie and Carol have been different if
they'd known she cleaned houses for a living? She didn't
entertain the possibility that there would have been no difference; she'd been around too long to believe that. Why was it
that the work a woman did in her own home was praised,

while doing the same work in someone else's home made you
a lesser being? Is that why she hadn't mentioned her occupa-
tion? Had she purposely not mentioned it? Was this how what
was happening to Taifa and Malik began, by being just a little
bit slow to be honest about who you were so that you could
fit in with people you thought might look down on you if they
knew just how very different you were from them? The last
question made her pause in buttoning her dress. "Watch
yourself, girlfriend," she told her reflection in the mirror.
"Just you watch yourself."

Chapter Three

~

Evening had settled in while Blanche was in her room. The sun was being hurried offstage by stars high in the sky. She walked slowly across the grounds toward the terrace. It was chilly enough for her to be glad of the shawl she'd slung around her shoulders. Maine might be as pretty as parts of the south, but it was missing that one major ingredient in her definition of a perfect climate, heat. The sea chuckled and beckoned to her. She stopped to spend a few minutes with it. She hadn't performed her ritual yet, but already she felt cleansed and calmed by the water beating out the rhythm of the planet on the rocky shore. She watched the sea and the gathering evening until her empty and complaining stomach pushed her toward the Inn.

From the terrace, she could see people seated in the dining room. She noticed that the dozen or so tables were arranged in two very separate groups—a cluster of six tables overlooking the terrace and the sea, and the other, larger group back against the lobby-side of the room. There was a wide aisle between the two sections. She slid open the screened door and stepped into a bee's hum of voices that died down as every head in the place turned in her direction.

For a moment, the whole room stared at her as though she were a horse in their bathroom. They were no more shocked than she. Had it been the same in the bar and she just hadn't noticed? No. Glenda was medium brown, but she wasn't a guest. There'd been the man with the skinny woman. He was nearly deep brown. But they weren't here. That leaves me, Blanche White, race representative, she laughed to herself, and was pleased to be able to find the humor in being the only guest present with any true color. She played with the fantasy of falling on one knee and belting out a chorus of "Mammy" to see if any of them fainted.

The name card on the table where she was seated said "Harris/White." Good. The company would be interesting no matter what the dinner turned out to be. The table was also well-situated for people-watching. She didn't intend to let these folks have all the fun. She started right in by checking the folks two tables away, only to discover neither of them was a stranger. The woman raised her hand and stroked her hair just the way she'd done in the village. Her evening makeup was a bit more pronounced. She averted her eyes from Blanche and spoke to the man seated across from her. Blanche gave him her full attention. He was the man she'd seen tiptoeing around that closed cottage. He was only slightly darker than his companion, with not a hair out of place. He looked like a man who was accustomed to having people do as he said, not the kind of man who needed to sneak around. What a lovely couple, she thought.

There were no other diners at the sea-side tables, although she could see name cards on all of them. There were no cards on the tables at the back, even though the jogging couple was sitting back there, as well as two women and a couple she hadn't seen before.

When Glenda returned to fill her water glass, Blanche asked her why name cards were on some tables but not others.

"We only use the name cards for the Insiders who own cottages and their visiting friends. They sit on this side of the room for dinner. We switch sides for lunch. It gets too sunny on this side." She jerked her head dismissively toward the non-card section. "Anyone can eat on the Outsider side. Except for Saturday night, it's usually Outsiders who are staying in the Inn."

"Good thing I'm well connected!" Blanche's voice was nearly drowned in sarcasm. Glenda didn't seem to get it. Blanche wondered if Glenda had ever considered where she would be seated if she came here for dinner. Poor little snob. But maybe her attitude was more a part of the job than the girl's own feelings. She was still young enough not to know the difference.

Mattie smiled and waved as she headed toward Blanche.

"Hello. I thought it might be fun to have dinner together, instead of you eating alone at the Crowleys' table. I'm sure Hank and Carol won't mind having dinner alone for a change."

Glenda hurried over and pulled out the chair across from Blanche.

"I hope you don't mind." Mattie sank into the chair and flipped her napkin into her lap without waiting for Blanche to respond.

Blanche smiled. These old Divas! They had that way of asking a question that was really a command put in such a way that no one even thought to disobey. Her mother was like that, and Miz Minnie and her Aunt Rose. Of course Miz Minnie was the all-time champion. Mattie reminded her of those women, except Mattie had had the good fortune of never having to do anything Mama and Miz Minnie would recognize as a day's work. This made Mattie all the rarer.

Glenda gave them hand-lettered menus and took their drink orders.

Mattie looked around. "This place never changes. I like that."

"How long have you been coming here?"

"Forever. Amber Cove has been my haven for many, many years. I would come down here to reclaim myself."

"But not your family?" Blanche made the question as light as possible.

Mattie gave her a piercing look. "You don't miss much, do you? You're correct, I did come here without my family. I've often wondered if Carlton ever regretted buying me a place here. It changed everything. Everything. The boys spent summers with my in-laws at their place on the Cape. Carlton holed up in his office. He worked as hard in summer as he did in winter, which is why he's dead. Carlton gave me the cottage for my thirtieth birthday. So I could, quote, be with my people, unquote." She chuckled as though this were both funny and sad.

Glenda brought their drinks, a basket of crusty rolls and a pie wedge of butter stamped with an entwined "AC." The same entwined monogram was on the handles of the silverware—which was clearly plated—and in gold script in the middle of the white porcelain plates.

They both decided to skip the shrimp toast or pate appetizers, as well as the vichyssoise or curried cream of pea soup. They both had the broiled catfish as opposed to the fettucine alfredo, or the grilled chicken breast in honey-mustard sauce.

"Salud." Mattie held her drink up to Blanche.

"To the best of people," Blanche countered.

Mattie's eyes lit up when Carol and Hank came in, or, rather, when she saw Hank. Mattie seemed fond of Carol, but it was Hank who put that gleam in her eye.

"So, you've deserted us for new company." Hank leaned down and kissed Mattie's upturned cheek. She reached for his hand and squeezed it briefly. From the look on Hank's face, Mattie's affection for him was returned.

"Don't kid me! I know you're delighted to have a private dinner with Carol!"

"What about me? Don't I have any choice in this?" Carol winked at Blanche. "Maybe I'd rather have dinner with

Blanche and leave you two to blabber on about the good old days."

"Ignore her, my dear," Mattie patted Hank's arm. "It'll only encourage her."

"Meow." Carol arched an eyebrow at Mattie.

"Hank, let me introduce you to Blanche White."

"Pleased to meet you, Blanche."

Blanche took Hank's hand. His hands and fingers were squared off like the rest of him. His small neat ears lay close to his head. His eyes were large and sad, but smiling now.

"I hope you're enjoying Amber Cove, Blanche." Hank looked right at her but seemed distracted—like a parent with a young child in the next room. Even so, he reminded her of Stu when he smiled as though Blanche's "yes" was the most delightful thing he'd heard all day.

Mattie was still beaming after Hank had gone. "He's quite wonderful, isn't he?" He's my godson, you know. He's coming up for a full professorship in the History Department at MIT next term. He'll be the first black full professor in the department." She didn't try to hide her pride. "His mother was my best, my dearest, dearest friend." Mattie's eyes went somewhere very far away for a moment. She sighed and looked around at the tables near her before she spoke again.

"I know everyone here," Mattie continued. "All of them have had places here since the beginning of Amber Cove."

Blanche noticed that "everyone" only included the people who owned cottages and sat on this side of the room.

"Most of their families have been coming here for generations—like the Tattersons." Mattie looked at the couple Blanche had been eyeing and had been eyed by earlier.

"Martin's great-grandfather designed this place. His grandfather was the first black man to serve in the Air Force Medical Corps. He's lawyer to everyone here, including Amber Cove itself." She chuckled at Blanche's surprised look.

"Oh, yes. Very clubby, very family. People may treat each other like dirt, but in the end, they hang together like bats in a cave."

"Is that good or bad?"

"Depends on what it is they hang together to do or not do."

"You said 'they,' not 'we.' "

"I'm not really an Insider." Mattie smiled at Blanche's nod of recognition at the term. "I see you've been given the distinctions," she said, then went on. "My people were genteel poor clerics. Educated, highly respected and respectable, but poor. They couldn't have bought Insider status here if they'd wanted to. Getting in because your famous white husband buys you in is good enough, but not as good as being born among the people who've traditionally owned cottages here, even if you're light-skinned."

"Well, something must have changed over the years, girlfriend, because you are clearly the big cheese now."

Mattie laughed. "Nothing like celebrity to up one's status in America, even among this set. Of course, being a fierce old bitch doesn't hurt." She paused and gave Blanche a curious little smile. "I don't believe anyone has ever referred to me as 'girlfriend' in that way before. I quite like it. Thank you."

They were both smiling when Glenda brought their dinner.

The blackened catfish was nicely spicy. The mixed greens were stir-fried to a turn and the hot, three-bean medley a nice change from potatoes. They ate in silence for a few moments. The door to the terrace slid back to admit the brown-skinned woman who'd loud-talked Faith in the bar and her male companion. She was quiet now and Blanche gave them both a good looking over. The man was of medium height with a pleasant, open face. He wore a lightweight tan suit with a chocolate brown shirt and tan tie. His wingtips were also brown and tan. The woman was both tall and quite attractive with large, slanted eyes and a full sensuous mouth. Her figure easily handled the hot pink, skintight Lycra halter dress that just covered her behind. Her pink sandals with their three-inch heels were the exact shade of her dress, as was her lipstick, the nail polish on her fingers and toes, and the flower tucked behind her ear. A black organdy shawl with fringes that swept the floor swung from her arms. Blanche thought about what her psychologist-employer had said about black people and clothes. It ain't just white folks we try to impress, she thought. Glenda seated the couple in the Outsider section of the room.

"Who are they?" Blanche asked Mattie.

"I don't know."

"Oh, I figured since they seemed to know Faith that you probably knew them, too." Blanche worked to keep the question mark out of her voice.

Mattie gave her a look that said she knew she was being pumped but didn't mind. "They didn't know Faith. Not in the way you mean. They just experienced her." Mattie told Blanche about the night Faith had made nasty remarks about the woman's clothes in a loud, ridiculing voice. Mattie screwed up her face as though the incident were an unpleasant smell. "But, believe me, that's hardly the worst thing Faith ever did. She was notorious for her delight in embarrassing other people. The Carsons haven't used their cottage since the summer Faith said those awful things about their daughter. Perhaps now that Faith's gone they'll give up looking for a buyer. The cottage has been in their family since it was built." Mattie's eyes and tone told of her indignation over the situation.

Blanche leapt right in, although she didn't expect much: "What did she say about their daughter?"

Mattie looked surprised for half a second, but was still in charge of herself: "Let's just say Faith's favorite sport was revealing other people's secrets before as large an audience as possible. The Saturday night dance was one of her favorite forums. I think that's why we were all determined to have tonight's dance go on. The first in decades without her venom spewing over the floor."

"What I don't understand is why ya'll put up with her mess." Blanche sucked her teeth. "In my neighborhood, Miss Faith would probably have gotten the cussing out of a lifetime, if not worse."

"If only we lived in your neighborhood! Here, we're all

afraid to raise our voices for fear of being called savages. We're all so intent on presenting ourselves as paragons of virtue and upholders of the race, we didn't dare tell Faith to stop acting like a bully. Faith collected secrets, you see. Everyone feared she might know about their particular fall from grace. If challenged, she might have blurted out one's own unsayable secret. Of course, there was also the nasty pleasure of watching others squirm. None of us was prepared to give that up, I'm sure."

"Didn't you say her cottage was down that end of the Inn?

Mattie chewed and nodded. "Blue cottage, the one with the blue door. The Tattersons own yellow cottage and green cottage is the Carsons. I told you about them."

"Oh yeah, Faith's other victims. Why'd she do it, I wonder."

"Faith was always jealous and mean-spirited, even as a child. She grew up to be a sad and insecure woman. Like many such people, she could be very cruel. But, of course, she wasn't half as clever a snoop as she thought. No one can figure out what Al J. saw in Faith, why he stayed with her. He's a perfectly nice man."

Blanche sucked her teeth again. "Women like her used to make me feel so bad, talking to me like I have a dust pan for a brain. Like I was born into this world to clean up after them and steal their possessions. Mistreatment is always worse from your own, I think." Blanche looked at Mattie and waited.

Surprise lifted the lines in Mattie's face. She leaned forward slightly. Her eyes searched Blanche's. "You're in service?

"Since I was nineteen."

Mattie fell back in her chair. "Well I'll be damned!" she chortled. She blinked at Blanche. "Does Arthur know?"

Blanche shrugged.

Mattie's eyes widened. Her lips were parted slightly. Blanche thought maybe she was trying to decide which question to ask first. People Blanche normally ran with would have simply asked what someone like her was doing in a place like this. Mattie probably thought such a direct question was rude.

Glenda stopped to see if everything was all right and to offer coffee and dessert. Mattie sent her away with the suggestion she come back later. Blanche gave her good marks for that. Ordering dessert would have been a perfect way to end their conversation.

"It's quite extraordinary, you know."

"For me to be here? Or for me to do domestic work?"

"How do you know the Crowleys?"

"Our kids go to school together."

"I see." Her frown denied her words.

Blanche was tempted to explain about the money her last North Carolina employer had paid for her silence and her decision to use that money to send her kids to private school, but she remembered Mattie's caginess about the Carson's daughter.

Mattie cast out another line: "Your work must be better paid than I realized."

Very good, Blanche thought. She didn't know if she herself would have known how to move on that one. She smiled a slow, sweet smile. "Let's just say I had a windfall," she told Mattie.

"Touché," Mattie laughed. "Touché." She raised her hand to summon Glenda. "Perhaps someday you'll tell me about it."

Damn! This old girl could do it to death! "Perhaps someday you'll do the same." she told Mattie with a smile.

When Glenda returned they both ordered the peach ice cream.

Blanche glanced around the room. "I swore I'd never eat in another segregated dining room but here I am. I guess that's why Mama always said, 'Never say never.' "

"Did I miss something, Blanche? I don't quite . . ."

"This Insider/Outsider business ya'll got going here. Don't it remind you of something?"

"It's really much better for everyone this way." Mattie's tone of voice was very similar to the one Blanche used when she was trying to convince the children that the punishment she was handing out was good for all concerned. Mattie went on.

"Occasionally there's a dish on the Insiders' menu that's not available to Outsiders. Think how people would feel if . . ."

Blanche laughed. "If that don't sound like the same kind of bull hockey reasoning white people used to keep us out of everything they wanted for themselves! Next you gonna tell me the Outsiders like it this way."

Blanche wasn't sure whether it was her words or her laughter, or both that got Mattie's back up, but the older woman's face went quite unfriendly for half a second before she could get her polite mask in place.

Mattie sniffed. "Really, Blanche, it's not the same thing at all. It's not as though we hold ourselves aloof from Out . . . other guests. It's just that those of us who have places here been coming here for ages. We know each other. We're comfortable together."

Blanche missed the rest of Mattie's explanation. She got caught up in Mattie's use of "we." Hadn't she just declared herself not an Insider? It was interesting to see where Mattie's Diva-hood broke down. The Divas Blanche knew would answer differently—maybe tell her it was none of her damned business, or that things were arranged just the way they liked them, thank you very much. If they were determined to discriminate against the Outsiders, they wouldn't try to make excuses or to make their behavior right. She hoped Mattie would do the same, but she didn't. She hoped Mattie's silence was due to sheer cussedness, and not the belief that the Insiders were right. Hank and Carol rose to leave. They waved on their way out. Mattie dabbed at her lips and laid her napkin on the table. "I think I'll have a bit of lie down before the dance." She picked up her walking stick and rose from her chair. She gave Blanche the frosty smile of someone not accustomed to being declared wrong. Blanche gave her a long, appraising look. That Old Queen Somebody or Another shit could be carried too far.

Blanche lingered over her coffee. Her thoughts turned from Mattie's behavior to what Mattie had said about Faith's putting people's business in the street. Had Faith been planning an exposé for tonight? Would it have been about Carol and/or Hank? She was still amazed that a bunch of people would let one person screw them around, secrets or no secrets. It reminded her of WCP—Whitefolks' Curdled Passion—a kind of lumpy roiling stew on which the lid was always kept, until the pot exploded. At which point, the kind of people Blanche worked for usually had a migraine; visited their therapist; went off to Aspen for R&R; or retired into a whiskey bottle or a coke spoon. She wasn't accustomed to black people who let things fester and go unsaid. In her world, people got in each other's faces and talked loud about each other's bad behavior. But it looked like she'd been wrong about the Whitefolks part of WCP. Maybe Curdled Passion had more to do with believing in a white bread world than being white—in believing that emotions were nasty habits that needed to be hidden, if not destroyed.

She left her table and went to her room. She undressed and watched herself part and repart her hair five times before she got it the way she wanted it. She could pretend her excitement was all about looking forward to an evening of interesting talk and music but she knew it was mostly about that man. She liked the way he looked in her eyes and not at her breasts, even though he was clearly making moves on her. She liked that something soft in his eyes. She even liked the sense that she was missing something about him. Like a partly blurred photograph, she could make out the outlines, but felt sure she was missing some important detail. That was part of what made him interesting. That and those lean hips, broad shoulders and soft strong hands.

She lifted her arms, aware of her breasts, heavy and tender. When Leo married, she'd decided to be celibate. That way, her lack of a sex life wasn't about the loss of Leo, it was about choice. Even if she hadn't decided to just say no, despite her horniness, she wouldn't have sex with a man she'd just met.

Long before AIDS there'd been enough VD around for her to practically want to know the names of every person a potential sex partner had been with before she decided to get it on. If ever there was a time for a strictly monogamous relationship, this was it. If that's what a person wanted. She still thought there were too many complications, with the kids, and her irregular work hours. And your attitude, she heard Leo say in her mind. She wished she'd taken a little more advantage of Leo, although she doubted that memories of orgasms past would satisfy her now.

She slipped the pale blue halter dress over her head and turned to the mirror. She'd always liked her big, broad shoulders, now they gleamed against the blue halter. She decided against any jewelry. She looked fine. Just her and the dress. Go, girl! she told her reflection in the mirror.

The music reached out for her when she stopped outside. She made herself walk slowly toward the terrace. A night like this was not to be rushed by. She stepped off the path and walked across the grass. Mother Water was wearing her silver party outfit and whispering something slow and sexy to the moon. She was glad she'd come to Amber Cove, if only to stand right here, right now.

Multicolored Chinese lanterns ringed the terrace. The band was against the glass wall separating the terrace from the dining room. The terrace was magically turned into a dance floor with a rim of small tables and chairs. The band of middle-aged white men with a black drummer wore shiny, royal blue satin pants with matching bow ties and white ruffled shirts. They were playing "Moon River" and sounded as hokey as they looked. But like all live music, the making of it on the spot somehow lessened its faults, that and the sound of the sea that snaked through it. She only recognized a few of the couples on the dance floor. The jogging couple laughed as they danced by; the woman who dead Faith had dissed was dancing with her partner. They were both dressed as they'd been at dinner. He moved with the light, easy grace of a good dancer enjoying himself. She danced as though her feet hurt. Judging from her three-inch heels, they probably did. The hot couple who'd been fondling each other in the bar had shifted their activities to an upright position on the dance floor.

Blanche crossed the terrace and went inside. Carol's husband, Hank, was sitting at the end of bar, the only other customer. He sat with his head bowed over an old-fashioned glass that he was using to make interlocking wet rings on the bar. Blanche took a seat one over from him and looked at him until he turned his eyes away from his liquor glass and glanced at her.

"Hey, how you doin', Hank?"

He snorted and returned his gaze to his glass. He lifted it and sipped. He put the glass down and began moving it around. "How'm I doing? Now that's a good question." He chuckled low and deep in his throat. "How'm I doing? How am I doing?" He laughed again.

Uh-oh. What had she walked in on? She started easing down from her stool.

Hank held up his hand. "No, no, please. Don't go. Please." He looked in her eyes for the first time. Blanche almost raised her arm to ward off the haint that stared out at her. The term "living dead" floated across her mind.

"Would you like a drink?" He signaled the bartender—a white male in his thirties that Blanche hadn't seen before.

"So how are you finding your stay at old AC? You like it here, Blanche?" he asked after her gin and tonic arrived.

"It sure is beautiful."

"That's not what I mean." He turned his ghostified eyes on her again. He finished his drink and told the bartender to fetch him another. "What I mean is, are *you* having a good time. Are you getting along? Are you . . ."

"You can't get this many people together without somebody being nasty."

"That's true," he agreed. "But there is nasty and then there is nasty. Some people are eternal world champions. Even after death that make your life hell. Now that's what you call a real, first-class, A-number-one . . . well, you know what I mean. And there are plenty more like her in the world. Although, I'm sure my other nemeses would take umbrage, on the basis of gender, at being referred to as first-class, A-number-one, et ceteras." When he turned toward her this time, he looked as though he really saw her. "Of course, life is an A-number-one bitch, so what can you expect from people?"

Blanche only looked at him. A part of her wanted to ask why it was a man's world until things went bad and life was a bitch, but she was more interested in the haint.

"Whose world are we talking about exactly?"

Hank snorted again. "*Life*, Blanche. *Life*. All of it. Every damned bit of it from the water we can't drink to drive-by shootings."

The haint had more substance than she'd assumed. She tested her drink and ordered another slice of lemon before she responded to Hank:

"I think life is more like that coat I bought last year," she told him. "That coat looks just like a plain old poplin rain-coat, but it's got five or six big pockets in the lining plus a secret outside pocket I didn't know was there until I put my hand in the outside pocket I could see. That may not mean much to you, since men's clothes always come with good pockets, but for me, it means I don't always have to carry a rip-off ad, otherwise called a handbag. I was so glad I decided to try that coat on instead of making up my mind just by looking at it! Course, it cost more than I'd planned to pay. But that's why they call it life, ain't it?"

Hank laughed his first real laugh since they'd begun talk-ing. "Did Carol send you in here?" He seemed both genu-inely suspicious and truly amused.

"Why? You need a keeper or something? You want a refill on that glass?"

Over Hank's shoulder, Blanche watched Stu walk up the stairs onto the terrace. Too old to be led around by my hor-mones, she told herself and tried to return her attention to Hank, but her consciousness of Stu was like a small cool breeze whisking Hank's words away and raising goose bumps on her arms. Damn! Be careful, girl, she cautioned herself once again. She watched him looking slowly around, as though searching for someone and felt a thump of satisfaction knowing she was likely that someone. She fought the urge to wave. Maybe I should have had a cold shower, she chided herself.

Hank interpreted her sudden interest in the terrace in another way. "Would you care to dance?" Said in just the tone he'd probably learned in Jack and Jill.

Blanche wanted to say no. She wanted to tell Hank that whatever it was that was eating his ass up, he could handle it. Life was generally not larger than the liver. She was positive of that. But it was too late. They were already out the door.

Stu grinned and waved to Blanche. His smile disapperaed when he looked at Hank. Hank's response was no more friendly.

"Friend of yours?" He held Blanche like a man who knew his duty was to lead, but didn't care for it much.

"You likely know him better than I do. I met him this afternoon."

Hank turned Blanche around so that he was no longer facing Stu. "His father was my godfather."

Blanche was conscious that Hank had skipped right over Stu to his father. "Don't sound like you two were childhood friends."

Hank shrugged. "You know how it is with kids. I guess he was jealous. Maybe I would have been too, if my Dad always wanted some other kid hanging around. Of course, I didn't understand that back then. And now . . ."

Stu was beside them on the dance floor almost before the music stopped. "You're here." He grinned, then turned to Hank. The grin disappeared. "Hank. Long time." Stu offered his hand. Hank professed it was good to see him, but Blanche wasn't convinced.

"My dance," Stu announced to Hank as the music began again.

Hank turned to Blanche. The haint was clearer now, more in control. "You take care of yourself, Blanche. Don't lose that coat. Mine's feeling a bit too big for me."

"It can be altered, you know," she called after him. He didn't turn around.

"What's that all about?" Stu stood with his arms in dance position, waiting for her to join him. Blanche didn't move. Stu stepped back.

"I'm sorry. I forget myself. It's just that I . . ." He broke into a sheepish grin and shook his head, as though either at a loss for words, or too embarrassed to say them. He looked both appealing and sincere. "May I please have this dance?"

Trainable. She held out her arms to him. He took her hand and slid his other arm around her waist. His body eased into the music. He held her like a man who knew what to do on the dance floor, and elsewhere. The band was playing "Since I Fell for You." Neither of them spoke. Blanche could feel the heat building between them and decided it needed a bit of banking.

"So, Hank was a part of your growing up?" Lame, but it was all she could think to say; and she was interested in that bad vibe she'd picked up between Stu and Hank.

"Yeah, but not Carol. I met her for the first time when Hank married her."

When she'd asked Hank about Stu, he'd talked about Stu's dad instead. Now Stu was telling her about Carol instead of Hank.

"He told me he was close to your dad. His godson did he say?"

Stu's spine stiffened slightly. "My dad liked him a lot. So, are you enjoying yourself here?" he added.

Blanche wondered if he really thought she could be so easily turned away from a subject, unless, as in this case, she was prepared to let him pretend to lead. She learned an awful lot about men that way. She'd learned to steer clear of the real lead junkies—the ones who always had to make the decisions, as well as those so accustomed to having the women do the hard parts, they expected her to carry the whole relationship, let alone the conversation.

"I never thought I'd hear myself saying this about someplace so far north, but this is a truly beautiful place. And Amber Cove Inn itself sure is interesting."

"What's interesting about it? The place or the people?"

"Both."

"Which Insiders are here right now? This is my first dance of the summer. And my last, unless you're planning to stay around."

Blanche ignored his last comment. "Let me see, there's Mattie Harris, Veronica and Martin Tatterson, Hank and Carol and the Crowleys, of course."

"That's everyone but the Carsons, who I hear are selling out, and Al J." Stu said. "You hear about his wife, Faith?"

Blanche nodded and they danced in silence for a few moments, as though they'd both forgotten what they were talking about, or agreed it wasn't what they said that mattered. Stu held her closer than Hank had. She was aware of every point of contact between them. She looked around for a distraction. There was Mattie coming up the terrace stairs. Arthur Hill rushed down to offer her his arm. He managed to turn an act of courteousness into bowing and scraping. Mattie pushed Arthur's offered arm away and handed him her walking stick. She used the wooden bannister. When she reached the terrace, she thrust out her hand for her walking stick. Blanche couldn't tell whether Mattie thanked Arthur, but she didn't look at him or join him at his table, as he gestured her to do. Blanche smiled to herself. Mattie was not likely ever to be mistaken for a nice little old lady. She gave Blanche and Stu an imperious nod as she passed the dancing couple on her way to the bar.

"Is it time to start talking about that third and fourth dance?" Stu asked her.

There was something about his slow speech and low-keyed flirting that reminded her of home.

"Where you from? Your people, I mean."

She was surprised to learn his folks had been right there, in the village of Amber Cove, for generations. She still thought of up-south blacks as having all been born in and around the big cities. She rarely met a northern black with a northern small town background.

"What was it like?" she wanted to know.

He stood up straight and stared toward the sea. "I spent my summers at Amber Cove Inn. My dad was the pharmacist in the village. So was my granddad. The first black pharmacist in the state, if not the country. I played with most of the people here, or their children."

Blanche told him about her kids staying with the Crowleys. She didn't mention how long she, herself, would be around, but she didn't have to.

"Oh, yes, I remember now. They mentioned you were coming. Ten days? Is that how long Dave said he and Chrissy would be out on the boat?" Stu was really grinning now. "Lucky me!" He swung them around full circle as the song came to a close.

Blanche felt like she was in a car with a slightly drunken driver going a little too fast down a steep hill.

"Would you like to go back inside, or . . . ?"

"I think I'll take a walk."

"May I come along?"

"I don't think so. Maybe I'll come back later."

"Maybe?!" He sounded deeply disappointed.

Blanche waved and walked quickly away before he could protest further. She couldn't avoid the fact that she was on the run. She'd suddenly felt as though Stu had put her in a headlock. Why didn't she just tell him to back off, not to hold her as though he knew her body, not look at her as though she were his favorite dessert? She wasn't totally unaccustomed to being hit on. She knew she was attractive to the kind of black men whose African memory was strong enough for them to associate a big butt black black woman with abundance and a smooth comfortable ride, men who liked women who ate hearty and laughed out loud. Mostly they were men who worked with their hands at jobs not designed to be enjoyed. So they let their cars and clothes and personal styles describe who they were instead of their job in the sanitation department, or as a bag handler at the airport, or hotel doorman. They put their passion in their love affairs and their favorite sports teams instead of working for a promotion or to expand their stock portfolio. Stu wasn't that kind of man. He didn't act like one and he certainly didn't live like one. He was a member of one of those First Black Families. He probably went to private schools and had never seen a cockroach— unless he went south during the civil rights movement. And then there were his looks. He wouldn't be the first light-skinned man who'd thought her blackness meant an automatic trip to paradise in gratitude for his willingness to screw someone as black as her, was how she thought the reasoning went. If Stu was among those men, he hadn't showed his hand yet and she would cut it off at the shoulder the minute he did. No, it wasn't who or what Stu was that really concerned her. She didn't like leading with her loins. Or rather, she liked the feeling of doing it without going too far. There for a minute, she hadn't been sure there was such a thing as too far where this man was concerned. But even while her nipples continued to tingle at the thought of him, there was something about him, beyond sex appeal and charm that she couldn't identify; something she felt he wanted from her besides the obvious. She didn't know what it was, so she couldn't say whether it was good or bad. She just knew it was there, like a door that needed opening before she could go much further. Maybe that was what had her on the run. Maybe it had nothing to do with Leo.

She walked slowly along the path. The night was cool and indigo. Mother Water was still flashing her silver and the nearly full moon created shadows like black holes beneath the trees. She heaved a large sigh. It had been a long time since anyone but Leo had so totally appealed to her sexually. She thought back to the last time she'd been so physically attracted to another man and acknowledged that every time she'd left her head in her diaphragm pouch, she'd lived to regret it. Ah well. This time at least she wouldn't have to regret having had sex. She could relax and play all the boy/girl games she wanted. Instead of heading directly toward the dance, she walked across the lawn to a spot where she could see people dancing and talking on the terrace.

The hot couple and the jogging couple were on the dance floor, as well as other people she'd never seen before. Stu was talking to the young man she'd seen drinking beer in the bar. She listened to the Lawrence Welk sound-alike music and watched the dancers moving beneath the colored lights. They reminded her of pastel colors. Beautiful, and serene, but with none of the fire of the red-and-purple-loving black people she knew. There was nothing in the way these people moved on the dance floor that said their people invented rhythm. There was no swing in their walk, none of the shoulder, hip or hand language that spoke volumes among black people. Was having your juices watered the price of living and working outside the black community, as she was sure most of these folks did? Their teeth were all wrong, too—too straight, too white, too real. There were no bad feet among them. No runover shoes, no small runs on the inside of the leg of the pantyhose, no marriage of color and style for the sheer purpose of expressing personality. No hint of molasses in their voices. While the food here was excellent, she hadn't seen any collards, cornbread, sweet potatoes, fried chicken, grits or any other staples of the black diet as she knew it. As far as she could see, the things, beside color, that made a person black were either missing or mere ghosts of their former selves. It was sad. Still, for all that, there was an air of gaiety about the dance, almost of relief. She remembered what Mattie had said about this being the first post-Faith dance. Suddenly, she'd had all of Amber Cove she could handle. It had been a long day and she needed to rise very early. Mother Water was expecting her.

Chapter Four

Blanche pressed the lever on her alarm just before it was to ring at four A.M., rose, showered, washed her hair with African Formula Genuine Black Shampoo And Conditioner and dressed in a loose white blouse and skirt. She gathered the small bundle from Madame Rosa and her flashlight, grabbed a towel, and left her room for the beach. The chill grass startled her feet. She didn't know if the shivers that ran up and down her back and arms were caused by cold or excitement. She knew people who would think she'd lost her mind if they saw her out, "playing around with them roots and such," as her mother had said when she'd seen Blanche's ancestor altar.

Blanche had once read a book that talked about black people as spiritual people, and white people as material people. She'd thought this was a put-down—a way of saying black people didn't have enough contact with reality. At the same time, she'd thought the main reason black women in their thirties and forties threw themselves into the church was because they were lonely; their husbands were running around on them, or they were looking for husbands. Her own needs had proved her wrong. She now understood that her urge to hug trees, talk to the ocean and lean on the dark as though it were a mother's welcoming arms came from the same place as other women's need for church and god. Now that she was aware of it, she could see the ways black people accepted spirituality as normal. It was as much a part of her African heritage as the heavy dose of melanin in her body. Her mother claimed to be shocked by Blanche's "praying before idols." But she'd sent Blanche faded and cracked photos of aunts long dead, and a rock shaped like a big-hipped woman. She'd also sent a bit of Grandmama Robinson's crochet work and called to say she thought it might make a nice altar cloth. It was in her mother's blood, just as it was in her own.

The older she got, the stronger her need to be connected to something that was larger than the world as she knew it. By the time she'd reached Boston, it was like an extra presence in her house, whispering to her about candles and incense and dancing beneath the full moon. She'd always practiced a kind of haphazard spirituality—having her cards read regularly and an occasional bone casting by a Yoruba priestess. She'd avoided the Christian church all of her life. As a child, being in church had always made her dizzy. As she grew older and learned more about the world and her place in it, she became convinced her problem with Christianity was due to its being the religion of the people who had enslaved her ancestors. How could the religion pressed on her people as a pacifier be the best pathway to her spiritual self? She couldn't separate Christianity from the memory of the famous picture of slaves laid out like sardines in the bottom of a ship, or the iron slave necklace she'd seen in a museum in Richmond. After she'd watched Ali Mazuri's public television series on Africa, she'd felt the same about Islam. But she also needed something beside the day-to-day. She'd considered finding the Yoruba house in Boston. But she could think of no reason why the Yoruba religion would be any less male run, with all the crap that went with that.

One day she saw a newspaper article about people who'd founded so-called churches as tax shelters. It occurred to her that she could design her own religion, too. She already knew who and what to worship. Instead of looking for a place to worship, she'd built one. She turned her tendency to talk to her dead grandmothers into ancestor worship. She began collecting pictures of all her dead relatives and built an altar for them—and up-ended wooden crate she sanded and shellacked and covered with Grandmama Robinson's crochet work. She bought candles and flowers for her altar. Her hippy-woman rock from Mama, the rock from Africa and the one from Australia, given to her by a geologist ex-employer, also went on the altar. Every morning, she lit the candles and incense and talked to her ancestors about her problems and dreams, her wishes for her children, her hopes. She accepted as correct her childhood perception that she was somehow connected to the tree she climbed, the water she swam in and the air that filled her lungs. She routinely called on all the forces in the universe for power. Since she'd begun her religious practice, she felt more firmly rooted in, not on, the ground, as though she had been joined with everything that sprang from it and the sea and air that made it possible. It seemed extra right that Madame Rosa had sent her here to find the answer to her dream. The sea was the place where she found the peace and cleansing her friends said they found in church or the mosque. Whenever her life got out of hand, she headed for the sea.

Now she stood open mouthed and lost in the wonder of the sky. The stars seemed to flare up, as if to challenge the returning sun. She lighted her way past the boulders where she'd sat the day before and walked until the beach curved and the Inn disappeared behind her. The sky was beginning to lighten. When she reached a spot that felt right, she waited for the first sight of the sun. When the sun began to show, she turned her back to the ocean and walked into it. She held the small packet from Madame Rosa over her heart in both hands. Every muscle in her body clenched from the shock of the cold

water. She fought to control the clatter of her teeth. Her wet
skirt held her calves captive. As sunlight touched the beach,
Blanche repeated what she'd told Madame Rosa about her
dream, the hollow feeling when she waked, the grief, but
never any memory of what happened in the dream. She asked
what the dream meant, as well as for the ability to remember
it after she'd waked. She asked for guidance in this problem
with her kids putting on airs and taking on attitudes that she
knew were dangerous. She asked for deliverance from the
memory of Leo and for a long, long life for Mama. When
she'd asked her last question and unloaded her last worry, she
pressed the packet to her chest and held it there then moved
it to the top of her head. She poured all of her worries and
concerns into the packet, just as Madame Rosa had in-
structed. When she was done, she threw it as far from shore
as she could. She stepped quickly out of the water and dried
her freezing feet. She wished she'd remembered to bring a
pair of socks. She slipped on her sandals and left her flashlight and towel on a rock while she walked farther along the
beach. She could feel her mind unclench. She walked until
that was all she was doing—walking, looking at the sea and
birds, listening to the waves and walking. When the beach
abruptly ended in a high bluff, she turned around and walked
slowly back the way she'd come, feeling more relaxed than she
had in weeks. Her only desire was to take a long, hot shower
followed by a long, sweet, dreamless nap. She picked up her
towel and flashlight on the way to her room.

  She was stepping into an after-nap shower when the phone
rang.

  "Hi. It's Stu."

  "Hey."

  "I'm sorry you couldn't make it back to the dance last
night. I missed you."

  Blanche had nothing to say to that.

  "What are you up to, today?" Stu asked. "I'd love to see
you."

  "Christine and David will be back today." Blanche told

him. "I'll probably spend the day with my kids. And I want to give Deirdre and Casey some time to get used to me. What about Tuesday?"

"OK, if you insist."

As she turned from the phone a picture of Leo's sleek blackness formed in her mind and made her stomach lurch. Did he miss her at all? She shook her head vigorously and decided to wash her hair. She'd have liked to talk to Ardell about the dance, but this time of day on Sunday she was at her weekend job at the nursing home where she was only allowed three minutes for personal phone calls and only one call a day. So Blanche washed her hair.

Afterwards, she wiped the condensation from the medicine cabinet mirror and stood naked before it, oiling, then cornrowing her damp hair, enjoying its soft, wooly texture. There was a hint of rusty brown in its blackness and more than a handful of gray. She moved her fingers quickly down the parted section. She thought about Veronica Tatterson and her hair products and marvelled that something that felt so good could be such a matter of shame and distress to so many people. Most of the black women she knew, especially the younger ones, could hardly stand the idea of their hair in its natural state. She shook her head. Us and our hair, she mumbled as she smeared lotion over her ample thighs and buttocks, it's as deep as our color stuff. Her stomach reminded her that she hadn't had any breakfast. She dressed in slacks and a shirt, folded her Panama hat—left to her along with five hundred dollars in the will of Mr. Rosenberg, an old employer, because she'd often admired it—and stuffed it in her oversized shirt pocket.

Despite the urging of her stomach, she naturally headed toward the sea once again, freeing her mind from thought with each step. By the time she'd removed her sandals, her full attention was on what lay before her. She closed her eyes, turned her back to the sea and stepped into the icy water. Cold rocked through her but she smiled as she turned to face the ocean. She opened her eyes. "Good day, Mother," she whispered. She let the sight and feel of the water flow through her again. She rested there for a moment.

The children will be back today was the first thought that floated into her mind. It pleased and soothed her even more. She stepped back from the sea and wiped at the water on her feet and ankles. They would be ashy before she finished eating. She saw herself hurrying back to her room to slather lotion on her feet as though dry skin were a cause for shame. She put on her sandals and headed for the terrace. Anyone, including herself, who was offended by her damp and soon-to-be-ashy feet, didn't have to look at them.

Brunch was being served buffet style on the terrace. Mattie waved to her from an umbrella-topped table.

"Good morning, Blanche. Sit down and I'll get someone to fetch you some vittles."

Blanche smiled. And you'll tell me what to eat, too, if I let you, she said to herself. "Be right back." Blanche headed for the buffet table. She could feel Mattie's eyes on her. Just like Mama, Blanche thought. And like Mama, it was good for Mattie to occasionally have her orders at least altered if not disobeyed. Of course, Mattie's need to give orders was no stronger than Blanche's need to alter all orders whenever possible. Like two sides of a coin, she thought.

As at dinner, Blanche was pleased by both the array and presentation of the food, although she'd have preferred grits and biscuits to croissants and eggs Benedict. She settled on a fruit cup to go with her OJ and coffee, to start and returned to her table.

"I saw you dancing with young Stu," Mattie said.

Blanche smiled at the young part. Of course, when you were Mattie's age, who wasn't?

"Strange boy. I wonder what made him come back here? His family never expected he would, I'm sure."

"Were his parents friend of yours?"

"Friends?" Mattie seemed to consider for a moment. "No. His mother was a shy woman. Weak. A recluse for much of her life." Mattie made shy and weak sound like heroin addiction and child molestation.

"And his father?"

"Rudolph? A fine man. Kind, considerate gentlemanly. First rate mind."

"Any brothers or sisters?"

Mattie shook her head.

Blanche sensed something more about Stu's family, but Mattie didn't say it. They were both distracted by the arrival of the woman who'd talked bad about Faith in the bar last night. This morning, she wore a purple and white caftan with matching purple mules. Her companion was equally relaxed in a forest green sweat suit and loafers.

"Excuse me," Blanche told Mattie and went to stand in the buffet line behind the woman in the purple caftan. Blanche jostled the woman's arm. The woman looked sharply over her shoulder, as though expecting a rear end attack. Blanche grinned and held out her hand.

"Hey, I'm Blanche White. How you doin'?"

The woman look relieved and took her hand. "Linda Isaacs. This is my husband, Gabriel."

Blanche shook hands with him, too. "I saw you folks in the bar yesterday. Before dinner," Blanche told her, deciding to get right to the point. As she expected, Linda was eager to talk.

"Aren't they something?" Linda jerked her head toward the gathered Insiders. "As hincty a bunch of Talented Tenths as you'd ever want to see."

Blanche laughed. "It's been a long time since I heard that old DuBois's thing about the light-brights being the natural leaders of their darker brethren."

Linda piled her plate high with shirred eggs and Canadian bacon, finger-sized smoked sausages, a bagel and fried tomatoes. "And ain't these just the people he had in mind to run black America and teach morals to all the poor really dark darkies? I *know* these Negroes think they're the chosen ones!

And to think, I'm the one who wanted to come to this damned place! You're the first person we've met since we've been here! Those others hardly speak." She gave Blanche a bold look. "I don't mean no offense, but quite frankly, honey, I'm surprised they let you in."

"They didn't know I was coming," Blanche offered her palm with the comment. Linda slapped it and they both laughed.

"They weren't exactly expecting you, either, I bet," Blanche added.

"You heard, huh?"

Blanche nodded in the affirmative.

"Yeah girl, that woman talked about my clothes like I was dressed in rags. If it hadn't been for Gabriel, she'd a died with a black eye. None of them others said a word, but I saw their faces. I'm glad today is our last day in this place!"

They talked a few minutes more, long enough for Blanche to learn they made their money from their limousine service, clothes cleaning business and government-subsidized apartments. She got the feeling that Linda was the one with the business brains and Gabriel the one who could charm the workers into working. They ended their little chat in agreement that Amber Cove Inn could be a really great place with some changes in the food and clientele. Linda announced that her eggs had gone cold and replenished them. Blanche was sorry they were leaving.

Mattie was spreading orange marmalade on half a slice of dry toast with an air of indifference that Blanche decided not to break, unless Mattie admitted she was curious about Linda and Gabriel. Mattie held out for half a minute more.

"All right, Blanche, you win. Let's have it."

Blanche laughed and told Mattie almost word for word what she and Linda had said.

At the end of her retelling, the young man she'd seen drinking alone in the bar yesterday escorted a young woman to the table where Martin and Veronica were sitting. The young man had Martin's forehead and the same long neck and sandy hair as Veronica Tatterson. But it was the woman he was introducing to them who held Blanche's attention. Her face was the twin of the face on a bronze head of an African woman Blanche had seen in the Afro-American History Museum. This woman was deep black with a rosy luminescence that didn't look like makeup. Even from a distance, Blanche could see that her eyes were meant to break hearts. Her face could have been the model for a profile on an African coin. Her full features were perfectly balanced in a mobile, expressive face. She was a big woman, too, not fat, but muscular and an inch or two taller than the young man. Dreadlocks hung to her shoulders. She was seated now, motionless, seemingly aloof. All the young man's attention was focussed on her. The Girlfriend Meets The Parents, Act One, Blanche thought. She watched the introductions and Martin's attempt to start a conversation that didn't go on for long. Only the young man seemed to be finding anything enjoyable in the event, and only when he was looking at the young woman.

Mattie's eyes followed Blanche's gaze. "Isn't she remarkable? Tina the Magnificent. The younger man is her beau. Durant Tatterson, Martin and Veronica's only son."

"Tina the Magnificent is the perfect name for her. But his parents don't look impressed."

Mattie chuckled. "Oh they're impressed, all right. They're in shock." Mattie gave Blanche a sidelong glance. "You can guess why."

Blanche didn't need to guess. Poor child, she thought. She wondered how soon after the first baby was born of the rape of a black woman by a white man did some slaver decide that light-skinned slaves were smarter and better by virtue of white blood? And how long after that had some black people decided to take advantage of that myth?

Mattie dabbed at her mouth with her napkin. "Well, as interesting as this little drama may be, I promised my agent a phone chat about my next book before she meets with the publisher tomorrow. My phone is likely ringing away right now."

Mattie had hardly left before Martin and his wife finished their meal, rose and left Tina and her young man at the table. The young man looked after them, then at Tina, then at his parents again. He said something to Tina and hurried after his parents. Tina watched him for a moment, then rose and headed for the breakfast buffet. She put some things on a tray and looked around as though she needed a seat, other than at the Tatterson table. Without thinking about it, Blanche beckoned to her and pushed Mattie's plate to the side. "No one's sitting here," she said.

"Thanks." Tina held a tray with two peaches, an orange and a glass of iced tea.

"I'm Blanche White."

"Tina Jackson." She smiled a tight little lips-only smile and sat down. She picked up her orange.

"What happened to your friend?"

Tina shrugged and tore the orange apart as though she hated it. Blanche watched and waited.

"He told me his parents need time to get used to me, like I'm a freak or something!" The words exploded out of her in a voice just below a shout. She noticed people looking in their direction and lowered her voice. "I wouldn't have come if he'd told me they were here. I don't know why I agreed to come here anyway! Everyone knows about the light-bright preference at this place. They only want you if you're . . ." She blinked back tears.

Blanche reached over and grasped Tina's wrist. She gave it a strong squeeze and let it go. "It don't have nothing to do with you honey, they don't even know you. Don't take it personally."

Blanche watched Tina consider this advice.

"Really, it ain't about us," she told the young woman. She thought about Veronica and her hair products. She was tempted to tell Tin about the incident, but it was only adding kerosene to a fire ready to rage out of control. "It's about them," Blanche added. "They hate themselves more than they hate us, I think."

Tina tore her orange into sections. "Yeah. I know. But it makes me so mad! I just wanted to grab them by the throat and squeeze."

"And Mattie thinks there's something wrong with young black women today!" Blanche laughed.

Tina's face lit up. "That really was her? I thought it was, but I didn't want to stare. When I first saw her, I wanted to just walk right up and hug her! I mean, she's like a living treasure, like a walking shrine! Her book really changed my life."

"In what way?"

"Well, I guess I really hadn't thought about what kind of person, not woman, but person, I wanted to be until I read her book. She made me see that a lot of what we're told makes a good woman is not what makes you a good person. You know what I mean?"

Blanche nodded. "Yeah, I know, like be quiet and sweet and don't talk back. I wish Mattie's book had been around when I was your age!" Blanche finished her tea. "I promise I'll introduce you, but you've got to promise me you won't crush the woman to death."

Durant Tatterson climbed the steps from the grounds and looked around until he spotted Tina.

"Have you met Blanche White?" Tina asked him when he approached. Her voice was high and tight.

"Pleased to meet you." Durant shook Blanche's hand and nodded before turning to Tina.

He had an average build, slim and not too tall; a nice face, all the features in balance, nothing stood out. Harmless as chocolate milk, she thought. At Tina's age she'd liked the boys her mama warned her against—the ones who looked at you like they knew what you dreamed last night.

"Tina, could we talk, please?" Durant asked.

"No." Tina abandoned her orange, and bit down hard into a peach. She stared straight ahead.

Blanche was suddenly absorbed in the last bit of toast on her plate. She willed Durant to sit down in the empty chair across from her and pretend she didn't exist.

"We have to talk, Tina. It doesn't make any sense to . . ."

"Nothing about this makes any sense, Durant! You never should have tricked me into meeting them. You never . . ."

"It was the only way! You're as bad as they are!"

"Don't put me in the same category as your color-struck parents."

Durant groaned and sank into the chair across from Blanche. Blanche knew she should leave but had no intention of doing so.

"I'm sorry, Durant. It's not your fault your parents don't like dark-skinned people. But none of this would have happened if you'd been honest with me. I'm leaving tomorrow morning and that's that." Tina rose, grabbed her remaining peach and ran across the terrace.

Durant's polite, "Excuse me, please," and his, "It was very nice to have met you," directed at Blanche, were nearly swallowed as he pushed his chair back and ran after Tina. She headed across the lawn toward the beach. Durant ran down the terrace steps. When he reached the grounds, he was intercepted by his father. He placed his hand on Durant's shoulder and spoke to him. Durant shook off his father's hand. As Durant turned away, his father reached out with a gesture that reminded Blanche of a mother trying to stop a toddler from falling. Durant looked at his father, but kept walking toward Tina. Martin slowly dropped his arm. His face was naked with a pain half the parents in the world knew well. It told her more about the man than anything he was ever likely to say. Only the cause of his particular parental pain kept Blanche for feeling some sympathy for him. Martin watched his son for a few moments.

Blanche thought Durant would be very lucky to keep her and wondered if it would be as lucky for Tina.

"Mama Blanche! Mama Blanche!" Malik came barreling up the stairs from the lawn. Even though she'd felt him running toward her before she saw him, he nearly knocked her off her chair, his strong, young arms hugging her hard.

"Did you miss me, Mama Blanche? Did you?"

"You know I did, sweetie." She held her other arm out to Taifa whose lips were trying to smile while a frown was forming on her forehead. Blanche wasn't surprised. Half the time Taifa acted as though Blanche could do no wrong. The other half the time she treated Blanche with a disdain that bordered on pity and made Blanche's head throb. Taifa was at an age when it was normal to want some distance between herself and her parent. What worried Blanche was the basis for that distance. That's where she thought the school came in. Instead of Taifa dismissing her for being old fashioned and not hip enough or whatever the new word was, Blanche felt Taifa looking down her nose at Blanche's world and therefore at Blanche.

"What's the matter, girlfriend?" she asked the child. They were on their way to the Crowleys' cabin so Blanche could pay her respects. Malik had run on ahead.

"You mad about something?"

"Nothing's wrong, Mama Blanche. I'm not mad about anything. Honest." Taifa stopped to scratch her ankle.

Blanche gave the girl a long, level look. Labor pains and breast milk. If she'd done twenty-four hours of the former and provided the latter, would Taifa be less likely to lie to her? She had only to remember her own girlhood and the hell she'd made of her mother's life to know the answer. Under Blanche's unwavering glance, Taifa developed a serious interest in the scenery. "It's pretty here, don't you think?"

"It sure is. It's a great place to think. I'm glad I came up a day early. I found a perfect place to do some ritual cleansing, too."

Taifa didn't respond. They'd already had many lengthy conversations on the issue of Blanche's unorthodox spiritual practices. The major problem, as far as Blanche could figure it out, was that the child was afraid her friends would think it weird.

"Time to think about what?" Taifa asked.

The question made Blanche stop and take a serious look at Taifa's tall, leggy body, with its just-budding breasts. The girl's big, dark eyes didn't waver from Blanche's face. Blanche approved. The girl was no wimp. She whined sometimes, but she was a scrapper, like all the women in the family.

"Oh, what's going on in my life, what's going on in your life, what I need to do to grow up to be the woman I want to be and to help you and Malik be the best people you can."

Taifa gave her a puzzled look. "But you are grown up!"

"Only in a manner of speaking. I don't think any of us is ever all grown up. No matter how old we get, life's always got a lesson for you. Most likely one you've learned ten times before," she chuckled. "That's all growing up means, you know, acting like you know what you've learned."

Taifa didn't seem all that enthusiastic about Blanche's definition of adulthood. She brightened as she provided her own: "And making lots of money, and having your own apartment and a nice car and going on vacations and to parties and stuff, and having boyfriends and maybe a baby. That's part of being grown up, too, isn't it?"

Blanche could feel Taifa champing at the bit to get to her tomorrows. She wished she could convince the child to take her time. She noticed that marriage wasn't included in Taifa's litany of adulthood markers. She wondered how much her own suspicion of the institution had to do with that. Probably not a lot. Given the items Taifa had included, there was no reason for Blanche to believe she'd had any influence on the girl's fantasy future whatsoever.

"I'm glad to see you, Mama Blanche. I really am." Taifa's eyes and voice were anxious for Blanche to believe her.

Blanche touched the child's shoulder. "Likewise, honey, likewise."

Taifa took Blanche's hand. They walked the rest of the way in silence.

"Blanche! Glad you could come! Good to see you!" David Crowley's round, smooth-cheeked face beamed at her. He gave her a one-armed hug and a peck on the cheek. His usual high-yellow coloring had been bronzed by the sun.

Christine Crowley came out onto the porch. "How are you?" The two women hugged. Blanche was once again struck by how much Christine and David looked alike—same coloring, same fresh, round faces.

"Arthur left us a strange note. Not very informative. Just that Faith Brown who has a place here had had a fatal accident. Have you heard anything?"

Blanche told them what she'd heard. Neither Christine nor David spoke. Blanche wondered if they, like Hank and Carol, had reason to be glad Faith was dead.

"You're not the only ones who didn't like her," Blanche reminded them.

Christine laughed an embarrassed laugh. "It's true. We don't know how to respond to the death of people we're supposed to like. You'd think as doctors we'd have a ready-made response to death."

"What do you mean, 'supposed to like?' "

"Oh, you know, Blanche. Someone you grew up around, who attended the same weddings and dinner parties. Someone who's in your set, even though you might wish otherwise."

It was the third time someone had used the word "set" in trying to explain the relationships among people here. It was a word Blanche associated with exclusive clubs and people who put on airs.

"The irony of it is that it couldn't have happened if she hadn't refused to rewire when everyone else did," David said. "Well, at least we should show some sympathy for poor Al J.," he added.

The three of them exchanged glances, then burst out laughing.

"Maybe he loved her." Blanche suggested.

"Well, he'd have had to, wouldn't he?" Christine countered.

Blanche and Christine laughed.

"He once told me he was addicted to her." David gave Christine a look so deep and intimate, Blanche looked away.

Christine ignored David's remark. "Taifa and Malik haven't been a bit of trouble," she said. "I wish Casey and Deirdre were so well behaved," she added.

Blanche didn't think she'd ever heard Christine or David refer to one of their children as "my child." Blanche took it as a sign of the high quality of their shared parenting.

"Hey, you two!" Blanche turned to Deirdre and Casey Crowley. They both had their parents' coloring and round-faced cuteness, as well as Christine's delicate hands. They were a good match for Taifa and Malik. Casey added some spice to Malik's good-boyness. Deirdre was more serious about her schoolwork than Taifa, but Taifa was competitive enough to try to keep up with her friend. Casey and Deirdre smacked loud kisses on Blanche's cheeks before they ran off with Taifa and Malik toward the sparsely wooded area beyond the cottage.

The adults settled on the porch around a drinks caddy. David fixed Blanche's gin and tonic as though he did this every day. It was flattering to be remembered. As usual, Blanche was aware of the everydayness of the vibes she got from them. Somehow Christine and David managed to be just folks, even though she knew they both came from money. That dose of arrogance that so often went with privilege, and was almost a must for doctors, seemed to be missing in them. They brought their kids to the Kwanzaa celebrations in Roxbury—Boston's major black community and Blanche's current community as well. They both gave time to the community health clinics and exercised at the Roxbury YMCA instead of some posh health club. Still, she would not likely be on friend terms with a pair of doctors if their kids didn't go to the same school.

David wanted to know how she was adjusting to Boston and agreed when she told him it was likely the most racist city in which she'd ever lived. Christine questioned her about who she was working for now and how she was being treated which segued into Christine's complaints about the arrogance of the medical director of pediatrics at Boston General Hospital. Listening to Christine and David talk about the need for the residents and interns to join the union, they could have been a waitress and a truck driver or a schoolteacher and a postal worker or any other combination of competent hard-working colored folk who believed in the race and felt some responsibility to move it, and therefore themselves, forward. She wondered what their mamas and daddies had taught them about being a well-off black person in a world of poor blacks that made it possible for them to remain connected in a way she doubted any of the other Insiders were. The three of them talked about the children, the sea, the weather and the state of the economy. They agreed the so-called UN peace mission in Somalia was creating more problems than it solved; shook their heads at the thought of U.S. troops on African soil; and worried about what the New World Order was going to mean to black and brown people around the world. All of which led them to appreciating how fortunate they were to be in this beautiful place for a little while. In the small silence that followed, Blanche was aware of holding two conversations: David and Christine were both talking to her, but had hardly said a word to each other. She looked at them over the top of her glass. What was up?

"Who've you met?" Christine fished an ice cube from her glass and chewed it with perfect teeth.

Blanche began with Mattie Harris.

"She's wonderful, isn't she? She's exactly what I'd like to be when I'm an eighty-year-old matriarch!" Christine's voice had the same hint of reverence Blanche had heard in Glenda's and Tina's voices.

"Do you know her well?"

"Not really. My parents gave a lot of cocktail parties and clambakes for the Amber Cove crowd. Mattie came to many of them, and, of course, we visited. I remember Mattie as always very still, like she was waiting for something. I was always sneaking peeks at her. I was fascinated by that stillness.

A part of me probably hoped to catch her fidgeting or scratching or something. I was that kind of kid."

"Yeah," David added. "Mattie was cool. You know, kind of with us but not of us? I once heard my mother say that Mattie put on a lot of airs for an ugly shapeless girl whose only accomplishment was hooking Carlton Syms." David shook his head, "Poor mama, she really got it wrong that time!"

"You mean because of her books?"

"Not just her books, Blanche." Christine's eyes gleamed with glee. "Some of Carlton Syms's most important and celebrated essays, both on education and social justice, are actually based on Mattie's work. That's what it says in a new book out about Mattie's influence on the feminist movement." Christine gave Blanche that especially joyous, triumphant and knowing look women exchange when one of their sisters beats the boys at one of their games.

"If you've met Mattie, then you must have met Carol and Hank," David said.

"I liked Carol." Christine poured more seltzer in her glass. "She's so real. She was probably one of those kids who told the other kids there's no Santa Claus and that our parents still like having sex, even though it had already served its ultimate purpose of producing us."

"She used to be a dancer on the West Coast, you know." David was munching nuts between words. "Seattle, wasn't it, Chrissy? Had an auto accident that ended her career. I think that's why she came east and opened the dance school. You know the one I mean. In Brookline. Deirdre and Casey take lessons there."

Blanche knew about the school. She and Taifa had had a number of go-rounds on the subject of why Taifa couldn't take lessons there instead of at the Dance Institute of Roxbury. Taifa said Blanche was too mean to send her. Blanche kept trying to explain to Taifa about the differences including, but not exclusively, cost. She was more and more concerned by Taifa's refusal or inability to understand.

"What about Hank?" Blanche looked from Christine to David.

"Hank's OK," David told her in the uninformative, slightly defensive tone that black men use to protect a brother from scrutiny, especially one they, themselves, teased or put down in some way. Blanche and Christine smiled at each other.

Blanche felt no temptation to tell them about the conversation she'd overheard between Carol and Hank.

"Hank's a watcher, like you," Christine smiled affectionately at Blanche. "But he doesn't just see everything, he feels it, too. A dangerous way to live."

"He seemed kinda far away, I thought."

"Ummhum, I know what you mean. I've felt that from him sometimes too. I wonder if that's his way of trying to protect himself. He's like a person with no emotional immune system, you know what I mean?"

Blanche nodded. "Thin-skinned," she said.

"That's right. I know Carol's been worried. There was a big mess about his last promotion. The usual situation: The white males own the place and are determined to keep it that way. They used the usual argument, accused him of only being considered for a promotion because the University needs to fill its affirmative action quota. Sure it's tired," she said in response to Blanche's expression. "But it still works on some of us, although it's hard to understand why. Especially in Hank's case. He graduated first in his class in every school he ever attended. People who know say his research and his teaching are both top-notch. Still, he was always kind of uncertain and shy and . . . Once he tried to . . . I know Carol's been worried about him being so depressed by all this. He was in a very bad way for awhile."

Now Blanche knew what Carol meant about the white boys having Hank on the run, and why Carol's body language had disagreed with Mattie's insistence that Hank was fine. She also understood what Hank meant about his coat being too big. Poor man. To let yourself be jerked around when you, yourself, were Dr. Big Dome was too sad. She thought about what Mattie had said about males and romanticism and wondered how many black women professors were out there falling for that bullshit. By the time a sister got that far, it ought to be pretty hard to convince her she wasn't worthy of the prize.

"Hank's OK," David announced. "He just needs some toughening up."

"Have you met the Tattersons yet?" Christine wanted to know.

"Not exactly, met," Blanche told her, "But we have come to each others' attention. And I saw them meeting the girl-friend."

"I just bet you came to their attention," David hooted. "Martin and Veronica are a couple of throwbacks."

"I Just wish they were that rare," Blanche told him. "But it seems to me I been running into one version or another of Veronica and Martin all of my life."

David shook his head. "I guess I just want to believe most of us have gotten over color prejudice."

Blanche laughed. "Not as long as blue-eyed blondes are the flavor of the month. Ain't like we're in this alone."

"That's true enough," he agreed. "Chrissy, remember Monica Shapiro, in med school? She used to moan about her mother always being after her to get a blue-eyed, blond doctor boyfriend?"

Christine turned to Blanche. "She found one, too. They got married. After about five years, she got tired of the beatings and left him." Christine extended her palm to Blanche who slapped it and laughed.

"Meet any Outsiders?"

Blanche told them about Linda and Gabriel.

"Oh yes, Faith's victim. We were there the night Faith was so awful." She shook her head in dismay. "I never understood the woman, I must admit. She seemed mean for the hell of it, as opposed to because of something that might have happened to her."

"Who else have you met," David asked.

"Stu."

David sat forward in his chair. "And?"

"And nothing," Blanche told him. We met. We danced."
She shrugged without mentioning Tuesday.

For one of the few times since she'd been there, Christine
and David shot each other a look.

"I think he's fine." Christine said. "I always did." She gave
Blanche a speculative look. "And one of the few single black
men around here."

"That must make the local ladies happy," Blanche decided
to end the conversation before it went any further.

She set her empty glass on the caddy and rose. "I didn't
come to stay. I only wanted to holler at you. I think I'll walk
the monkeys into the village. You two could probably use
some child-free hours." Or maybe not, she thought in response the look that passed between them.

The children were playing tag ball on the lawn. The girls
were the quickest—ducking and twisting, leaping just in time
to avoid being hit by the ball. In a year or so, they'd disdain
such a game with their little brothers. Now they all shrieked
for the joy of making sound. They could have been cousins,
they were so close in looks and color—reddish with sandy hair
and light brown eyes. In Taifa's and Malik's case, inherited
from their Geechee father. The ball caught Casey on the
ankle. He picked it up and threw it toward Malik.

"Mama Blanche!" Malik kicked the ball back to Casey and
ran toward her. Casey was close behind him. Blanche walked
out to meet him and, despite her better judgment, gave him
a smacking wet kiss on the cheek, which he accepted with an
"Ah, Mama." He smelled of sweat and milk and boy.

"Oh, isn't he the sweetest baby," Casey teased. Malik
pounced on him.

The girls strolled toward Blanche with more decorum.

"Hello my beauties."

They looked at each other and grinned.

"What happened to Mrs. Brown?" Taifa wanted to know.
Deirdre nudged her in the ribs and gave her a nervous look.

"She died."

"From what?" Taifa asked.

Blanche was glad Taifa knew she'd get nowhere with her by beating around the bush. "She was in the bathtub. Her radio fell in the tub and she was electrocuted."

For a few moments, the children were silent. Blanche steeled herself for questions about death.

Deirdre turned to Taifa. "Water conducts electricity."

Taifa nodded in agreement. "Just like science class." They looked at each other as though Faith's death proved that their teachers really knew what they were talking about.

"Are we going to the funeral?" Malik wanted to know.

Blanche shook her head in the negative and remembered what it felt like to be old enough to know that everyone must die, yet young enough to expect to live forever. They likely thought anyone Faith's age was dead even if she was breathing.

"She told us she was going to bake something special for us today," Malik said.

"Faith?"

"She gave us cookies," Casey added.

"She made them for us," Malik told her. "She said she always wanted two little boys like us."

Taifa poked Deirdre with her elbow. "She never gave us anything, did she Dee?"

Deirdre shook her head vehemently. "She didn't even talk to us. I don't think she liked girls. Some people are like that."

The children all nodded as though they knew exactly why this was—doing that trick of suddenly dropping their childness to become not adults, but their core selves, the persons they were now and would always be, no matter how long they lived.

Deirdre sighed. "Well, at least she didn't have any little boys who wouldn't have a mother now."

Reassured by this knowledge, they abandoned their ball and raced down the beach past people lounging on the lawn, past the tennis courts, beyond the Inn and on toward the

small village. Casey's shrill, "I won! I won!" was quickly followed by a chorus of "No you didn't!" Their voices flew by her
on the back of the wind. Blanche turned her face up to the
sun. Lord! That felt good. She could feel the heat penetrating
to her marrow. Oh yes, this was just what she needed. No
sirens or car radios, no belching busses, no superfast city
pace. The clear air, the deep green pines and blue, blue sea
came together in a scene so perfect there were no words for
it. She nearly skipped the rest of the way to the village.

The boys tugged her toward the crafts shop, the girls toward the ice cream parlor. Blanche dug in her pockets and
gave them all some spending money, then decided to follow
the girls into the ice cream parlor.

She had to be quick not to be caught with her mouth
hanging open. She remembered that Stu's dad had been the
pharmacist here, but she'd somehow got the impression that
although Stu was from here, he was presently a guest at the
Inn. Now she waved to him as though she'd expected to see
him here—behind a soda fountain, wearing a white apron
and one of those submarine-shaped hats. She was glad he was
a man who worked with his hands. The two girls preceded her
to the counter.

Was it having a little money, being in town or perhaps the
looks of the man behind the soda fountain tipping his hat to
them that caused two perfectly normal loud and raucous little
girls, to become silly little prissies? Granted, Stu had the kind
of looks that could make lots of girls of all ages stand up
straight. But she had a feeling these two were at the practice-
your-fem-skills stage where they'd do their number for any
man who tipped his hat and acted like he thought they were
cute. Taifa and Deirdre minced down the wide aisle to the
old-fashioned hardwood soda fountain counter and arranged
themselves on stools near the middle.

Stu tipped his white cook's hat even further. "Bon jour,
mademoiselles. How may I serve you?" His phony French
accent was accompanied by a wide smile. The two girls put
their heads together, covered their mouths with their hands

and giggled. Stu drew Blanche into the game with a wink. Blanche took a seat two down from the girls. She watched Stu tease and flatter them into repeated fits of giggles and coyly lowered lashes. Every once in awhile they'd cut her a see-how-well-we're-handling-him look.

Where do we learn that shit? she wondered. She'd practiced the same moves when she was their age. Did it come with mother's milk, this reflex to play to the guys? To massage their little egos to over-size? She'd seen girls hardly able to walk bring grown men to their knees with a well-placed "Da-da." It'll only bring trouble she silently yelled at the girls. No need to say it aloud. They wouldn't understand. Not yet. Not until it was too late. Would they wonder why no one had told them? Or why they hadn't listened? She hoped so. She hoped they'd be recruited by a bunch of nine-to-twelve-year-old black girl revolutionaries.

Stu sliced bananas with a speed and flare that earned "ahs" from the girls, dipped ice cream and swirled whipped cream, all the while keeping up a playful banter. He was very good with his hands and with little girls. His full lips were so finely defined they seemed to be outlined. He looked up, caught her watching him and gave her a sweet smile. Blanche caught herself sitting up a little straighter and sucking in her stomach. No wonder she didn't want to tell the girls what to do.

"Voilà! Mademoiselle Deirdre." He placed her concoction in front of her. "And your friend, she is?" Deirdre told him. "Et voilà! ma petite Taifa."

The girls dove in. Stu came to stand before Blanche.

"And what can I get for you, Ma'am?" No phony French accent now, only those honied tones that made her want to squirm. She asked him for a glass of iced tea. While his back was turned, she ordered herself to be cool. He set a tall beaded glass of dark tea with a slice of lemon and a sprig of mint floating on top in front of her.

"Stu, I didn't realize you . . ."

"That's the first time you've said my name," he interrupted. "Say it again."

"Not while you're working. I wouldn't want you to swoon on the job."

Stu leaned on the counter. "I loved dancing with you."

They were both suddenly aware that the girls had gone completely silent. They seemed to be deep in the banana splits, but Blanche knew better. She leaned back from the counter.

Stu began wiping the space in front of her. "So, Dave and Chrissy are back," he said, nodding in Deirdre's direction. "We go back a long way, you know."

Something about the way he said it made Blanche think he was offering David and Christine as references.

"I first saw you when you were in your mother's arms," he told Deirdre. "Casey, too." He turned his gaze back to Blanche. "I was amazed to see how they'd grown! I only came back to take over my Dad's business last fall." He chuckled. "Boy! We were devils, wild devils." He looked quite pleased about it.

Deirdre's eyes lit up. "What kinds of devil things did you do?"

"I remember the time we stole old man Roscoe's dinghy." He pointed at Deirdre. "It was your mother's idea. She was Chrissy Fields, then, of course."

"What happened? Did my parents get in trouble?" Deirdre's voice was sharp with the possibility of some leveling information from her parents' childhood.

He wiped the already clean counter. "Old man Roscoe wasn't a bad sort. He didn't tell our parents we were responsible for the hole in the dinghy, but he did make us repair it. Our parents thought it was so nice that we were voluntarily helping the old man." They all laughed. The girls began whispering between themselves.

"I had a great time last night." His voice reached out and caressed her cheek. Out of the corner of her eye, Blanche saw Deirdre and Taifa exchange knowing glances.

She realized that she'd already decided to like this man, even though she was generally extra suspicious of good-looking men. And it wasn't just horniness, or Leo. Niceness seemed to float from him like waves of cologne.

Malik and Casey tumbled through the door. "Can we have ice cream, too?" Blanche got them cones to go.

"By the way, the name's Robert Stuart. Friends call me Stu," he told Malik and Taifa.

"Her name's Blanche," Taifa offered without being asked. "And he's Malik."

Stu shook Malik's hand. "Pleased to meet you." He turned to Blanche. "See you." He refused to take her money. The girls were hardly outside before they began teasing Blanche about her new boyfriend.

"She doesn't even know that guy, you dopes!" Malik shouted. He and Casey chased the shrieking girls toward the Inn.

The sun seemed hotter. Blanche unfolded her Panama and put it on. Taifa skipped back to walk beside Blanche. "Mama Blanche, can I borrow your hat?"

Blanche shook her head in the negative. "Unh-unh. I told you to pack your visor, but you wouldn't. You said you didn't need one."

"Please, Mama Blanche!"

"No. You can walk under the trees a little further on."

"Please," Taifa wheedled. "It can't help *you!*"

Blanche slowed almost to a stop. "What do you mean?" she asked. Her voice was quiet, cautious.

Taifa hesitated, squirmed, twisted her fingers and then her hair. When it was clear Blanche wasn't going to let the issue pass, the child sighed with impatience.

"Well, you're already dark. It doesn't matter if you stay out in the sun."

Blanche's first impulse was to look up and around. The impulse hurt her. As a child her first response had always been to look around to see who had witnessed her being called names that said black was ugly. The Tar Baby and midnight monkey taunts, were easier to fight when there were no bystanders to hear and stare and jeer. She couldn't look at

Taifa. Tears stirred behind her eyes. She fiddled with the brim of her hat, hiding behind her upraised arm, blinking and willing her tears away.

When she was ready, Blanche reached out and took Taifa's arm. She pulled the child to her side. She wanted them to be touching. She wanted her warm, familiar hands stroking Taifa, reminding her of the love that lay within that touch, even through the hard parts.

"How come you're so worried about getting darker?" Blanche was careful not to stiffen her spine or tighten her grip on Taifa's arm.

Despite her attempt to be nonchalant, Taifa was suddenly still in the way of a rabbit caught in the beam of a flashlight. Blanche could feel her trying to figure out what she'd done wrong. Blanche wished she could help her, make it easier for her. Blanche waited a bit longer then gave Taifa a little tickle. "Hey! Wake up! I'm talking to you!"

Taifa sighed. "Well, you know, Mama Blanche, if you have dark skin, people laugh at you and say you smell bad and nobody wants to be your friend." She spoke all in a rush and in a tone that implied she was only repeating what everyone knew.

"Sometimes it's hard being dark-skinned, just like it's sometimes hard to be any shade of brown or yellow. But it's not awful. We're just as cute and wonderful as anyone else."

Taifa gnawed her bottom lip. "I didn't mean to hurt your feelings."

"I know you didn't, honey." Blanche wondered who the tortured child could be. She thought she'd met all the black children at Taifa's school and definitely knew all the little girls in her neighborhood. There were none dark enough for this treatment, but then she wasn't the one who said how dark was too dark. "Do you know someone like that? Someone people make fun of 'cause she's dark-skinned?"

Taifa's head bobbed up and down. "Mariette. She came to our school after Christmas. She's gone now, though."

"Gone where?"

Taifa shrugged again. "Her parents put her in another school."

"Did you think she smelled bad?"

Once again, Taifa shrugged her no comment then began to squirm. Blanche lifted her arm from around Taifa's shoulders.

"Did you think she was ugly or stupid?"

Once again Taifa lowered her head.

"What did Deirdre think?"

Taifa relaxed a little. "Deirdre said it was stupid to pick on her; that we all have African blood and should stick together."

Blanche chided herself for not having tackled this subject a lot sooner, as Christine and David obviously had.

"The only bad part of being dark-skinned is how people treat you. Dark-skinned people look like the first Africans who were brought to America, and probably like the first people in the world. I'm proud of that. But lots of people ain't proud. Some want to forget we ever had anything to do with being pure black, or Africa. Even for whites, hating dark skin is like hating your mama, since all human beings came from Africa." She wanted to go on, but she knew she'd said enough, for now. This was only the beginning.

Chapter Five

❧

By dinnertime, Taifa and Malik had all but forgotten they'd been separated from Blanche for weeks. She was there now, accessible whenever they felt like leaning against her arm, letting her take much of the weight of their sweaty bodies, or demanding to be fed, listened to, taken seriously, humored or hugged. Blanche and Taifa's color conversation still stood between them as real as another person, but Blanche could reach around it, although not easily. Taifa seemed wary, as though she suspected a trap.

The Inn provided a children's table, which freed parents for more adult conversation. Mattie, Carol and Hank were already at table when Blanche and the Crowleys arrived, as were the Tattersons, but not Durant or Tina. In the Outsider section there were a number of people Blanche had never seen before. Couples. New arrivals, she assumed. Mostly about her age and older, all with that look of ease Blanche associated with the unquestioned assumption of their own high personal worth based on money, particularly family money. She had never seen anything like the relaxed, social manners of the wealthy in any other community she'd been in or lived in.

"I had that awful twenty-four-hour stomach flu three times last winter. You'd think being a doctor would win me an exemption." David filled Blanche's wine glass.

"But while I couldn't seem to do much for myself, I did have a doctor. A wonderfully kind and caring one, too." He reached across the table and squeezed Christine's hand. He tried to smile into her eyes, but Christine lowered her head.

"She even blew up one of the air mattresses and made up a bed for me on the bathroom floor, so I wouldn't have to try to crawl to bed after each bout, didn't you, Sweetie?"

Christine's lips formed a remnant of a smile.

"Now is that true devotion or what?" David beamed. Christine watched him fill her wine glass, then his own. Blanche could feel his attempt to woo Christine, like a toddler trying to budge a mule.

When the Crowleys had first invited Taifa and Malik to summer with them and their kids, Blanche hadn't been able to imagine why the overworked parents of two would want to take on two more kids—despite their explanation that there wouldn't be any other children at Amber Cove this summer for Casey and Deirdre to play with. Seeing them together she recognized another possible reason: Nothing like a houseful of children to keep from having to talk to each other. Were they simply tired of each other? How did you keep a relationship alive with a person you'd lived with for ten or twenty years? Some people, like Aunt Mae and Uncle Charlie, seemed to move close enough to become a whole that was different from each of them but didn't take anything away from either of them. Other couples, like Iris and Carl Johnson, who'd owned and lived on the top floor of the building where she'd lived in Brooklyn, seemed to have pulled so far away from each other their relationship was a crater dug with nasty words and filled with possessions they owned jointly and which neither would give up. Other couples she knew seemed to continue to like each other and respect each other, but bored each other to death, or only got along when they were apart. She looked from David to Christine. David was staring into his wine. Christine's elbows were on the table. Her small sharp chin rested on her folded hands as she stared out to sea.

Lord! She wished warring couples would stay away from people. She hoped their boat trip helped. In the meantime, she had something she wanted to talk about.

"Did either of you ever meet or hear about a little girl at Wilford Academy named Mariette."

"Black?" David asked.

"Definitely."

Christine lay down her fork. "Oh-oh. That sounds ominous."

"It is." Blanche told her what little Taifa had told her about Mariette.

"Damn! This is the first we've heard about this. I hope those whitefolks didn't try to handle this on their own." David said.

Christine leaned across the table toward him. "David, you're president of the parents' association. Why don't you give the head master a call?"

David nodded. "I will, I will." He spoke again, quickly, as though afraid of losing Christine's attention. "Remember our first dance here, Chrissy? You had on that wonderful blue dress, the off-the-shoulder one, remember?"

Christine smiled wanly, but she didn't answer. The food on her plate suddenly needed all of her attention. Blanche wished she were alone in her room with her book and a nice piece of fruit instead of stuck in the middle of love going loopy. They ate the rest of their dinner rather quickly and quietly. The children were still making chocolate sauce swirls in their ice cream and David and Blanche were still drinking their coffee when Christine suddenly rose.

"Excuse me, please. I need a walk." She looked taut as a bow. She dropped her napkin on the table and walked out on the terrace and down the stairs.

"Honey, don't you think you need a sweater?" David called after her. He watched for as far as his neck would let him, then turned back to Blanche. Damn Christine for leaving her in the middle of this shit!

David ran his hand down his face and groaned. "Sorry Blanche, but as you see . . . I've tried. She . . . Maybe you could talk to her. She respects you. She . . ."

"May I join you?"

Blanche wanted to jump up and kiss Mattie.

"Carol and Hank are having a very boring discussion about tennis. I thought I'd table hop. Do you mind?"

David stood, pulled out a chair for Mattie and reordered his face. Blanche pushed Christine's coffee cup aside. He asked Mattie if she'd like anything and went off to fetch her a rum from the bar.

"You looked like you needed rescuing."

Blanche was surprised. It hadn't occurred to her that Mattie had realized she was in a jam with David.

"It's not exactly common knowledge, but it's been pretty obvious to some of us that Christine is no longer interested in David." She gave Blanche a level look.

David returned with Mattie's drink. He set it carefully down before her. He didn't sit down.

"I think I'll head back to the cottage, get the kids settled down."

Blanche told him she'd be along later. She turned to find Mattie watching her.

"Do you think we get what we deserve?" There was a serious note in Mattie's voice to which Blanche responded in kind.

"More likely we get what we put out there, what we give, I mean. That's what I was raised to believe and I still do, I guess. No. I don't guess. I know."

A cloud passed across Mattie's eyes. "I'm not sure I want you to be right. Don't you have regrets? Anything you hope you don't have to pay for?

"Sure. Don't we all? I just ain't got a lot of hope that I'll get away with anything. I sure don't feel like I have."

"No." Mattie picked up her parked walking stick. "Perhaps you'd care to join me in a constitutional?"

The two of them walked slowly down the terrace stairs. They could see Durant and Tina standing on the beach. Tina's gestures looked like a fight in progress.

"Looks like fireworks." Mattie took Blanche's arm and turned her away, along the path that eventually led to the village.

"I'm surprised you didn't want to stay and watch," Blanche teased her.

"Almost anything is more interesting than young love. Or young anything. The longer I live, the more boring youth becomes. So redundant. Each generation rediscovers the wheel of rebellion, the wheel of love, and so forth and so on. We hardly know which end is up until we're in our thirties. Sometimes I think we all ought to be locked away with books and music until we reach thirty-five, Do you agree.?"

"But, if we don't get to make those two trillion and ten mistakes we have to make before we're thirty-five, what in the world can we do with thirty-five?"

Mattie nodded. "Good point." She walked a bit before she spoke again. "Do you think the marriage will fail?"

Blanche knew who Mattie was talking about, but she didn't want to use Christine's and David's marital problems for conversational ping pong.

"I heard about the article about you and your husband's work," she said.

Mattie leaned on her walking stick. Her eyes were on the sea. "Ah yes." She slowed her steps even more. "I once felt Carlton had made me as much, if not more, than my parents did. They brought me into in the world. He made it possible for me to take advantage of what this wonderful world has to offer in the way of travel and beauty and comfort. I didn't begin painting until Carlton took me to France, you know."

Mattie laughed then fell back into seriousness. "The human mind is so amazing! I read all of Carlton's work. I proofread his galleys and read the drafts. I remember our conversations. Even today, I recall my contribution to those conversations and the way Carlton always took notes and read everything I ever wrote. I can still see the amazed grin that often spread across his face while I rambled. He was always complimenting me for being able to go right to the heart of things. Yet when he was alive, I never thought of his work as being dependent on mine, or of the acclaim he got as being rightly mine." She frowned, shook her head and turned to look at Blanche. "Isn't that amazing?"

Blanche was sure this wasn't the first time Mattie had asked that question.

"Maybe somewhere in the back of my mind I knew, but wouldn't let myself know because I wouldn't have been able to handle it. What would I have done? Confronted the man who had given me a life of privilege and freedom and accuse him of exploiting me, of stealing my ideas?"

Blanche knew the question wasn't meant to be answered, but that didn't stop her. "Yes," she said. "That's exactly what you ought to have done. And you probably would have, if you could have."

Mattie thought for a second. "Maybe I wanted to pay him back for all that he'd done for me."

"Or maybe you were so pissed off you knew you would have had to strike out on your own and try to make it alone, like the rest of 'our sort.' Not a pretty prospect when you're in the catbird seat."

Mattie was startled, then chuckled. "You know Blanche, you have all the makings of a first-class bitch."

Blanche gave her a shocked look. "Why I sincerely hope so!"

The both laughed.

Blanche walked Mattie to her cottage, then headed back toward her own room at the Inn. She had a date with Christine for a tour of where everything was to be found in the cottage, but she didn't want to get there before Christine came back. She walked across the lawn, cool grass tickling the sides of her feet. With the help of the high, bright moon, a tall, wide tree cast a shadow like a black lace-edged fan across the lawn. Blanche peered into the darkness, looking for the presence that she sensed there. It was Tina, sitting on a stone bench at the base of the tree, her legs drawn under her.

"Hi, Blanche." Tina put her legs down and scooted over in a way that invited Blanche to join her.

Blanche could almost smell Tina's longing to talk, and she was pretty sure who Tina wanted to talk about. But Blanche wanted to know who she was talking to first.

"Where you from, Tina?"

"North Philly. In the projects," she said with enough challenge to identify her neighborhood as having a bad rep.

"I'm from Farleigh, North Carolina," Blanche told her. She nudged Tina with gentle questions until they were casting pieces of their past into the night like lights strung together to illuminate them for each other, lights composed of the pros and cons of growing up in a northern city and a southern town—up south versus down south, they agreed; sisters—they each had one (although Blanche's sister had died), and Tina had a younger brother besides; parents—their mothers were strong women and their fathers were gone—one missing, the other dead; grandparents—neither expected she'd ever get over the loss of them.

They talked long enough for it to become clear that the differences in their age, education, relationship status, geography, and so forth were small compared to the fact that Blanche knew without explanation what Tina meant when she said she'd felt so invisible her first year at Brown University that she'd sometimes pinched herself to make sure she was still in the physical world; and that Tina nodded her understanding when Blanche told her that while she loved her children beyond measure, mothering did not come naturally to her.

Heart talk, Blanche thought. Her term for the way women gave each other bits of lives and history as a way of declaring their good intentions toward each other. Why would you mess with someone who knows your business? She remembered what Madame Rosa had said about making connections here. She'd been thinking about connections with the sea and the trees, not people. But now she was sure Tina was one of the connections Madame Rosa meant for her to make here.

She and Tina went on to agree that black folks were still getting the shitty end of the American stick, even among the middle class; that they liked their work—Tina loved watching people learn while Blanche liked being able to choose who she worked for and when. They gave each other five when Blanche said "God Bless that Child That's Got His Own," was her personal anthem.

"My mother says I'm too hard on Durant about his being dependent on his parents," Tina said, which finally wound them back to where Tina had wanted to go in the beginning, but now with much more investment on Blanche's part.

"Mom really likes Durant. She's never come right out and said, but I know she thinks I'm going to screw up the relationship. She's always telling me to try to understand him better."

Blanche thought understanding herself was a better use of any young woman's time.

"What exactly is it that you ain't supposed to understand?"

"Oh, why he let's his parents pay his rent and give him credit cards and a car. My Mom says people whose parents have a lot of money live like that. I say it gives his parents a way to pull Durant's strings."

Blanche liked this young woman more and more.

"I've never met anyone as sweet as Durant. But sometimes he just doesn't get it."

Blanche smiled to be reminded of when she'd been young enough to think her few moments of experience with men meant she knew something about any one of them.

"Is that his specialty, bein' sweet?"

Tina's face went blank.

"You know, his specialty," Blanche repeated. "Like the way he kisses, or his jokes, or his sweetness. The thing that makes you press your knees together and give a little moan." Blanche demonstrated what she meant.

Shock flashed across Tina's face but was quickly replaced by delight. Blanche settled in to learn more than she wanted to know about Tina's heartthrob. Tina talked and giggled and sighed her way through how she met Durant at Brown, where they'd both gone to school—she from her inner city high school on a partial scholarship and education loans, and he following in his Dad's footsteps. They'd decided to live together when they graduated last year, although Durant would have preferred marriage. Tina wasn't sure. Now she was teaching English As a Second Language in Boston, while he was a biochemistry graduate student at Harvard. When Tina was done, Blanche still didn't know what it was Tina saw in Durant. She wondered if Tina knew.

"So, that's our story," Tina concluded. "I was just soaking up the last of this gorgeous place before I'm run out of town. No. That's not fair. Nobody's making me leave. I just wish . . ."

"What?"

"Well, it pisses me off that I have to leave here." She looked toward the ocean. "This is the most beautiful place I've ever seen!" She turned to look at Blanche. "Did you hear about the woman who died here last week?" Blanche just nodded.

"It really made me think," Tina said. "In a way, her dying makes me want to stay here even more. She wasn't sick or anything. You never know what could happen. This could be the last time I ever see the ocean."

"Then why leave?"

"Money. The usual reason. Durant didn't tell me his parents were going to be here. I thought we'd be staying at their cottage for the week. But the minute they showed up, I moved into the Inn. I can't afford even in their dinkiest room after tonight."

"And you won't let Durant help you, right?"

"How'd you know?"

"Because I wouldn't either." Blanche was glad Tina could still smile.

"It's too bad you've got to leave." They sat in silence a few moments. The sighing of the breeze in the trees mingled with the shushing sea in an embroidery of sound that was nearly visible in the air. Blanche thought about Veronica. Even if

Durant left with Tina, the girl would feel run off. Of course, a little bit more of Durant's mother might convince Tina she needed a new boyfriend. And then there was Taifa. Tina was bright, well-spoken, independent, fiery, seemed to believe in something more than making money, and she was dark-skinned. She didn't really know the young woman, but still . . . "Wait here 'til I come back, will you?" Blanche hurried off to her room.

"Great!" David said when Blanche got him on the phone. "The sofa opens. She can take care of these wild monkeys and you can get some real vacation."

Blanche went back to Tina. "Come stay with me! I'm moving into the Crowleys' cottage tomorrow when they take off. It'll just be me and the children. There's a sofabed in the living room."

"Really? Could I?" Tina sat up. "I can watch the kids, and I'm a good cook! And I've got references, too. You can call the English As a Second Language Institute where I work, or Dr. Lawrence at Brown, I took care of her kids for a summer."

She said she'd take her things to the cottage in the morning and ran off—to find Durant, Blanche guessed. And they say black people don't stick together, she laughed.

When she finally got to the Crowley cottage, she stood outside looking in at the children playing Monopoly on the floor at David's feet. Malik had lost his money first and was nodding sleepily on the side. Blanche was taken by how much all four children looked alike—round-faced, with light brown eyes, and lean, red-tan bodies bronzed by the sun. They had a poise and confidence and ease in their surroundings that Blanche was sure her two hadn't learned from her. When did they reach the age where they had more in common with other people and places than they had with her and the place she occupied? Only natural, she told herself, but it didn't feel like it.

She went in and got Malik up and into bed and kissed him and Taifa good night. Christine walked Blanche through the cottage, showing her where to find everything.

"Did I tell you the Inn sends someone on Tuesdays and Fridays to keep the mess under control?" Christine gave Blanche a concerned look. "Is that OK?"

Blanche smiled and nodded. She appreciated Christine's concern. The maid with a maid was not your usual situation. She was also pleased Christine didn't assume she'd do the work herself. They continued their tour.

The Crowley's cottage was the kind of place in which Blanche was accustomed to working: Lots of expensive, bare wood, an air of being used but without the shabbiness she often found among the very wealthiest of white people. Elegantly framed originals on the wall, kitchen equipped with bread-maker and a cappuccino/espresso machine. Everything had the over-clean glow that said outside help.

Finally, Christine showed her into the master bedroom, closed the door and sat on the bed. Blanche went to stand by the window and looked out at the lawn and the sea in the distance. She was waiting for Christine to get it together to tell her what she suspected she already knew.

"Blanche, there's something . . . I want . . ." Blanche turned and looked at her.

"You know already, don't you?"

Blanche didn't say anything.

"David's two years younger than me, you know."

Blanche nodded. She knew what Christine meant. She'd learned early that males of the same age as she were really younger.

"We've known each other forever. Our mothers were best friends. Our fathers played golf together every Saturday. It's like being married to your brother, or yourself. Sometimes I wake up in the middle of the night struggling for air. Most of the time, I feel like a fuel pump with five outlets, one for my aging mother; one for my patients; one for David; and one for each of the children. And all of them are in constant use, draining me of every thought, every dream, every drop of energy, every . . . Nobody gives me . . ."

"What now?"

Christine laughed. "You certainly go right to the heart of the hard part. I don't know. I only know that I can't go on like this."

"Have you talked to David?"

Christine nodded again. "He's so confused! What else? He could understand another man. He can't imagine why I would want to be alone, away from him, from the children."

"Are you planning to leave?"

Christine jumped up from the bed and paced the floor. "I don't know, Blanche. I love David and the children. I'm proud of the way we're raising them. But I need some air, or I'll suffocate!"

"Then why are you going off with David on the boat?" Blanche wanted to know.

"I thought it would give us a chance to really talk. A chance to make him see that things aren't . . ." She gave Blanche a bleak look. "Anyway, we seem to be at our best when we're on the water."

"Don't look so down, honey. You and David have figured out how to raise two great kids and you still at least like each other. You can work something out." Blanche wondered what it felt like to have to negotiate your freedom with a man, as though you weren't in full ownership of yourself. She silently wished Christine luck.

Blanche was in a hurry to get back to her room. Ardell would be home now. Showered, had her dinner, laying back in that beat up old lumpy armchair she refused to part with. Blanche was so eager, she could hardly dial the phone. Ardell answered as if she'd been waiting for Blanche's call.

"Hey, girlfriend. Whatsup?"

Blanche laughed. "Everything but the ground and I ain't sure of that."

They postponed the niceties and went right to Blanche's report, including her arrival at Amber Cove; Arthur Hill; the Outsiders and the Insiders; Mattie, Hank and Carol; Tina, Durant and his family, and Faith's fatal accident. She took a deep breath and added what David had said about Faith's wiring and what the boys said about homemade cookies.

"In other words, if she hadn't been so cheap, she'd still be alive. Too bad she couldn't figure out how to spread those cookies around a little more," Blanche said.

"Damn, girl! You ain't been there but two days. You'll really need a vacation when you get home. Whatsup with the kids? You didn't mention them."

Blanche hesitated half a second. "They're having a great time.

"Hummm. So what's wrong?" There was no doubt in Ardell's voice.

Blanche heaved a huge sigh. "Oh Ardell, Taifa's going through a color thing." Blanche told her about the conversation with Taifa.

"Oh baby, I'm so sorry. I really am. But you know you have to expect things like that with our kids. They ain't stupid. They see what happens on the street. They watch TV and hear grown-ups talk. They see who gets treated which way and why. It's a wonder we ain't all color-struck."

Ardell's tone called forth the image of a black person struck by blinding white lightning that made them hate their own color. It was an image from when her mother had first tried to explain to little Blanche why so many children she thought looked like her called her names.

"Yeah, I guess you're right, Ardell. But it sure hurt, girl. Here I am, black as the ace of spades and my child, my child! tells me she can't even bear to get a little sun on her narrow behind for fear of being dissed. Now what the hell am I supposed to do with that, Ardell?" Blanche's throat tightened as she spoke.

"I don't know how you gonna deal with it, Blanche. But I know you can, 'cause you got to." She was quiet then, waiting for Blanche's tears to subside.

"Well all the news from here ain't depressing. I met a man."

"Ooh-wee! Start at the beginning and don't leave out any of the juicy parts!"

Blanche told Ardell how she met Stu, about the dance and her plan to meet him later.

"You don't sound all that enthused."

"It ain't me. It's him. I like him, even if he is a bit too fine for my taste. But I can't figure him out."

"You sayin' you can't think of no reason why he wants to be around you? That what you saying?"

Blanche thought for a moment, then: "It's like when you get one of them postcards saying you won an all-expense-paid trip to Hawaii. It sure sounds good, but you can't quite believe somebody out there is giving you a free trip for nothing. So, you ask yourself, what's the catch? The trip still looks good. Postcard got a color picture of the beach and palm trees and a fabulous hotel, but you still know there's a catch and you got to figure out what it is before you start packing to go nowhere, or to take a trip you can't afford. See what I mean?"

"Hummm, well, I guess you got a point. But you know I had to ask. You up there going though funny shit with your child and living among them Caucasian-ettes, I thought I better check to make sure it wasn't making you think like a fool."

Still, Blanche took Ardell's comment as a warning. She was not made of steel. The subtle and not so subtle snubs from the jogging couple and Arthur Hill, the way the guests had looked at her when she first entered the dining room had a much better chance of poisoning her because of Taifa. The hole of self-hatred she'd climbed out of as a young woman was still gaping wide and deep. Just because she wasn't teetering on the edge anymore didn't mean she couldn't be lured back. For the third time since she'd arrived, she warned herself to have a care.

"Relax, honey," she told Ardell. "I really am OK. This mess with Taifa did throw me, but you're right. It's to be expected in this world and especially going to the kind of school where most of the black kids are likely to be light-skinned.

"And trust me, my thing about Stu is really about him. You know men his complexion, especially those from proper Negro families, ain't usually got enough soul to be moved by my fine black frame—unless they're looking for an easy lay. We'll see if he's for real when I tell him how I make my living."

"You sound like you want him to step wrong, maybe you're just prejudiced against the man. But I guess you know what you're talking about when it comes to there maybe being a catch. Remember Harvey? That's what you said about him, too."

Blanche and Ardell cracked up over the memory: Two years ago, Ardell had gone out with Harvey five or six times. Each time, Ardell had put her best foot so far forward she'd developed a blister. "Something funny about him," Blanche kept saying. Harvey continued to call but remained lukewarm. The cooler he was, the more Ardell had wanted him, despite Blanche's advice to go slow. Then one weekend Ardelle ran into Harvey in Atlanta. He'd been dressed in a black lace dress with red accessories. He'd announced that he was a non-gay cross-dresser who admired Ardell's taste in clothes. When Ardell told him she wanted to think about what this meant to their budding relationship, he'd added that if she decided not to date him anymore, he hoped they could go shopping together sometime. Ardell had told Blanche that while she wished to be big enough to handle it, she wasn't.

They laughed and talked until Blanche was caught up with the antics of Ardell's grown son, Maurice—a studio back-up singer in Atlanta; the latest outrage from Ardell's supervisor at the electrical parts factory—her regular daytime job; Ardell's latest encounter with Blanche's sharp-tongued mother; and the news about Shirley's pregnancy, Velma's divorce; and Miz Carter, whose duties as church organist had apparently been broadened to include certain private services for Rev. Brown.

When she got off the phone, Blanche felt even further removed from the world of Amber Cove. Here, Rev's antics would likely be condemned because it made the churchgoers look bad to whitefolks. The hoots of laughter accompanied by slapped palms that this gossip would generate over tonk games in her hometown neighborhood would be missing here, too. Did Stu even know what tonk was? Could he tell the difference between Howlin' Wolf and B. B. King? What would he think of her mama's rickety little tar paper house in Farleigh, NC? And why did she care? They'd only been together twice. While she could still feel the heat of his body against her as they danced, she wasn't stupid. She knew that was a poor measure of anything but the desire to be doing that thang. Still, she did like what she'd seen of the basic him. As for the catch, it would keep until tomorrow.

Chapter Six

 ⌒

The phone woke her.

"Get up, sleepy head! We're off to the briny deep!" David sounded eager to be gone.

Tina already had the kids well in hand when Blanche arrived. Christine and David wore matching shorts and caps with CAPTAIN printed on them.

"Two captains?" Blanche asked.

"That's right." David lay his arm along Christine's shoulders. "Behind every great Captain is a woman who thinks she's Captain. I thought I'd play along with the fantasy and let her wear the hat."

Christine poked him in his ribs. "He gets like this if I don't give him close supervision. He'll know his place when I bring him back to land."

Blanche looked from one to the other, trying to gauge how much of this cute couple routine was for real. Had they come to some understanding in the night? Neither of them seemed tense, neither of their smiles had any rigor mortis in it.

"Come on, woman!" David grabbed Christine's hand,

dragging her toward the front door. Casey and Deirdre flung themselves at Christine who hugged them, straightened Casey's shirt, brushed back Deirdre's hair, all the while asking them to behave, to take care of each other and not give Blanche and Tina the blues. Casey and Deirdre shifted over to David, and Taifa and Malik moved in on Christine for a less intense kiss and hug good-bye, which David repeated.

After they'd all waved David and Christine off, the girls grabbed Tina by both hands and dragged her down the beach whispering and giggling as they went. The boys announced they were going to build a stone fort on the beach. Blanche walked slowly back to the Crowleys' cottage. The world seemed freshly washed and sparkling, even at noon. She listened to the silences in between the waves. She hadn't heard a plane since she'd arrived. She made fresh coffee and took it and her Octavia Butler book out to the front porch. For the first time since she'd arrived at Amber Cove, her mind fell into the well-worn groove of feeding and planning to feed. They'd have a cold cuts, fruit and salad kind of lunch instead of going to the Big House to eat. Deirdre and Casey needed some close time to get used to her.

She'd only been reading for a few minutes when she heard Taifa's voice. She looked up to see Taifa and Deirdre running toward her. This was not a race, or running and shouting for the hell of it, or we-gotta-pee kind of running, either. Blanche laid her book aside and hurried toward them. They were both too breathless to speak. But they weren't bleeding. Blanche looked down the beach in the opposite direction from which they'd come. She could see Malik and Casey intently piling rocks. She looked in the direction from which the girls had come. "Where's Tina?"

They pointed down the beach.

"She sent us, Mama Blanche."

"Clothes," Deirdre panted. "On the beach."

"She said to bring you," Taifa added.

Deirdre bobbed her head up and down in agreement. Both girls' eyes seemed unusually wide. Blanche fastened her sandals and hurried after them. As they drew closer to where Tina was waiting, the girls fell back to walk at Blanche's side, each of them took one of her hands.

The clothes were very neatly folded: a pair of well-worn gray cord slacks and a white polo shirt on top of a pair of leather sandals. The corner of something that could be a pair of jockey shorts stuck out from between the trousers and the shirt, like meat in a sandwich. The clothes were topped by an envelope held in place by a wallet. The bundle had been there long enough to acquire a thin shell of fine, sandy grit. Tina stood nearby staring down at the pile. Blanche sent the girls back down the beach and told them to stay with the boys at the fort.

Blanche glanced at Tina, then stepped to the clothes. She reached out her hand to lift the wallet and look inside, but she didn't need to: She recognized the sandals. She flipped the wallet open anyway, just to make sure. It was not a thing to make a mistake about. She looked down at the name on the driver's license in the wallet and quickly up at Tina.

"Honey, go find Carol Garrett. Tell her to come here right away, will you? Then go ask Mattie to please come to Carol and Hank's cottage, that it's urgent." She reached out and took Tina's arm. "You OK?"

Tina took a deep breath, and nodded.

"If either of them asks you whatsup, tell them you don't know. Then stay with the kids, will you? Thanks, honey."

The envelope beneath the wallet had "Carol Garrett" written on the front. Blanche put the wallet back and waited in the bright white sunlight for Carol to come and have her life ripped wide open. The sea was calm, as though the early morning human sacrifice had eased some of its restlessness.

Blanche stood watch over the clothes, remembering the haint she'd seen in Hank's eyes. Had he been planning this the night they talked? Was he planning then to shed that too big coat? What had made life so unlivable for him? She'd had times when she'd felt it would be a relief to get run over by a truck, but it had never occurred to her to jump in front of one. When had she begun to understand that her pain was at least changing, if not healing, almost as she felt it? "Almost everything can be waited out," she'd once been told by a man who'd spent thirty years in prison for a crime he didn't commit. What was it that Hank couldn't wait out? Or didn't know he could wait out? She turned her head and watched Carol hurrying toward her. Blanche steeled herself for what she was about to face. She wished she'd thought to send Tina to get Arthur Hill and let him handle this. She went to meet Carol.

"What is it, Blanche?" She looked down the beach. "I thought Hank might be here. Have you seen him? I haven't seen him all morning. He went out before I got up. I'd just come from checking to see if he was at the Big House when Tina showed up." She sounded slightly irritated about having to delay her search for Hank for whatever was bugging Blanche.

Dear Ancestors! Why me? Blanche stood directly in front of Carol, blocking her view of the clothes and making it impossible for Carol to keep walking. Blanche reached out and took her hand.

"The kids found some clothes and things folded on the beach. They're Hank's. There's a note." Blanche stepped aside.

Carol walked toward the clothes as though the ground between her and the neat stack were mined. Blanche had to fight the urge to grab her and hug her, stop her from learning what she already knew.

Carol stared down at the things on the beach for a long time before she stooped down and slipped the envelope out from under the wallet. She turned the envelope over and over before opening it. Her head was bowed so Blanche couldn't see her face clearly. She took a deep breath and quickly ripped open the envelope. She let it flutter to the ground while she unfolded the single sheet inside. When she raised her head she looked dazed and flushed and swollen, as though her face had been slapped repeatedly. She let the note slip from her fingers and knelt beside her husband's clothes. She ran her hand across the wallet and folded pants. The tenderness in her movements brought tears to Blanche's eyes. Carol's body began to jerk in seizure-like spasms. Sobs like dry heaves racked her body. Her outstretched hands trembled as she lifted the wallet and held it to her chest. Her eyes were all tears now. She reached out her left hand for the folded shirt and held it to her face. A high-pitched keen began from behind it. As Blanche knelt beside her, Carol pitched forward so that her forehead lay cradled on Hank's trousers and sandals. She began banging her head up and down, up and down.

"No, no, no, no, no, no, no, no," she chanted without seeming to take a breath. Blanche tried to pull her upright but Carol resisted.

"I thought you might need some help." Tina reached down and grasped Carol's shoulders.

Blanche scooped up Hank's note and slipped it into her pocket. She and Tina half-carried/half-walked the now silent and nearly limp Carol back to her cottage.

Mattie was waiting on Carol's porch. "What's happened, what is it?" She attempted to follow Blanche, Tina and Carol into the cottage. Carol didn't seem to notice her presence.

"Wait here." Blanche told Mattie in a voice that brooked no disagreement, not even from Mattie.

Mattie looked anxiously after them, but did as she was told.

Blanche and Tina settled Carol on the sofa. Blanche asked Tina to stay inside with Carol while she went out to talk to Mattie. Before she went out to the porch, Blanche took the note from her pocket and read it.

Sorry to leave you, old friend, it's just too much. I'm not sorry I killed her. She was a nasty bitch.
Tell Mattie it wouldn't have made a difference. I already knew.
Thank you for the best parts. I will love you always. H.G.

She put it back in her pocket before she went out on the porch. Mattie's lips trembled just a bit. She seemed to be holding herself in. When she once again demanded to know what was going on, there was a slight crack at the base of her voice. Blanche told her about the clothes and the note.

"Where is this note?"

Just as Carol had done, Mattie took the note from Blanche and stared at it for a long time before she read it. In the few seconds it took for her to read and understand it, Mattie seemed to collapse in on herself. Her mouth worked as if she wanted to speak but couldn't. Her usually clear, bright eyes turned cloudy. Blanche took a step toward her. Mattie raised her hand to hold Blanche back. Mattie leaned heavily on her walking stick as she opened the screened door and went inside to Carol. Blanche didn't follow her right away and beckoned for Tina to come out and join her. They stood in silence, listening to the murmur of Mattie's voice as she attempted to talk to Carol who was apparently unaware of everyone and everything around her.

Blanche sent Tina off to see to the children. "Tell them I'll be there soon as I can."

Tina gave her a pitying smile. "They already know, you know."

Blanche went inside and told Mattie she thought Carol needed a doctor and it was time to call Arthur Hill. Mattie stood up. She still held Hank's suicide note. She propped her walking stick against the cherry wood desk in the corner, dialed and demanded to speak to Dr. Sinclair, she didn't care how many patients he was seeing. When he was on the line, Mattie explained what had happened and Carol's condition. She listened, then with a firm, "Thank you, Doctor," dismissed him. She hung up the phone and looked at the note still in her left hand as if the paper were a disgusting growth that had attached itself to her. She grasped it with both hands and forcefully ripped the note into smaller and smaller pieces. She gave Blanche a challenging look. Blanche said nothing. Mattie put the scraps in the pocket of her slacks. She flipped open a door that released an electric typewriter supported on a shelf. She threaded paper from the drawer into the machine and typed a few lines. She took the sheet out of the typewriter, found a pen and initialed the page, Blanche assumed, with Hank's initials, then folded it before putting it in her pocket. She dialed the phone again and told Martin Tatterson to come to the Garretts' cottage at once.

Martin knelt before Carol and wrapped his arms around her with tenderness. There were tears on his cheeks when he took Mattie's trembling hand and leaned close to her. Blanche couldn't hear his words, but they seemed to strengthen Mattie. She told him Blanche had found Hank's things.

He listened closely when Blanche explained what had happened.

"On behalf of the family and Amber Cove, I'd like to thank you for looking after Dr. Harris and Mrs. Garrett," he said.

"May I please see the note?" he added.

Blanche looked at Mattie. Mattie reached in her pocket and pulled out the piece of folded paper.

Martin took it and read it. He shook his head slowly from side to side, "Poor man. I'm very sorry, Mattie."

Mattie gave him a short nod that reminded Blanche of a judge's gavel. Case closed. Do not bring it up again. If that was how Mattie planned to handle her grief, it was going to take her more time to heal than she likely had.

Martin went to the phone.

"May I?" Blanche took the note from his hand before he could respond. It said:

> Sorry to leave you, old friend, it's just too much. Thank you for the best parts. H.G.

She handed the note back to Martin and looked at Mattie, who avoided her eyes.

Martin called Arthur Hill who arrived breathless, stinking of anxiety and sucking on his bottom lip like it was pacifier. The police and the ambulance arrived next. Blanche stood aside and talked only when she was asked a question. She listened to the talk among the police about how bad it was for tourism to have these people keep killing themselves at Amber Cove Inn just a couple weeks before the village festival.

When the ambulance had taken Carol away and the officials had gone, Martin suggested he close up the cottage and take Mattie home. Mattie insisted that Blanche, not Martin, walk her to her cottage. Blanche said she would do it, although she hadn't really been asked. For Mattie's sake, she held her tongue.

Blanche settled Mattie in bed with a cognac and a cup of hot tea. "It was wrong to give Martin that phony note," she said. Mattie gave her such an angry look, Blanche thought she was going to get cussed out.

"Half of what was in it was a lie. You must know that!"

"What about Faith's husband? He has a right to know how his wife died."

Mattie clutched Blanche's arm with a cold and steely grip. "Believe me. If there is anything to tell Al J., I will do so. Until then, I beg you to keep quiet about this. Nothing will bring Faith back. Why ruin the memory of a fine but misguided, young . . ." Mattie's voice got caught in her throat.

"All right, all right. We'll talk about it tomorrow. You rest now. Is there somebody you want me to call?"

"Don't you understand?" All the fierceness that had been on Mattie's face was twisted into pain. "There *is* no one else. He was my last, my only. My lost." Her voice dropped so low Blanche could hardly hear her. "The only one left." Unshed tears made her eyes glisten. She reached down and pulled the sheet more closely around her. "I think I'll rest now." She promptly closed her eyes.

The children had finished eating their sandwiches and were cleaning up their dishes when Blanche got back to the Crowleys'.

"Did they find Mr. Garrett?" Casey asked her. "Maybe my mom and dad could have helped him."

Blanche put her hand on Casey's shoulder. "I don't think so, honey."

How to tell kids about suicide. How to make it make sense to someone who saw each day as a wonderful new adventure to shape to their liking. She looked at the children around the table, all of them watching her. "Sometimes . . . sometimes a person can get so sad inside, it makes them sick, real sick, so that they always got heartache that makes even the most beautiful day look bad. And even though they may have friends and people who love them, those people can't cheer them up, because it's a kind of sickness a person has to cure themselves and sometimes they don't think they can."

"But you said that bad things are going away at the same time they're happening. That change thing you told us about, remember? Why didn't he just wait for that, like you told us?" Taifa wanted to know.

"I don't know, baby. Maybe he just didn't think change was happening fast enough."

Tina and Blanche stayed in the kitchen after the children had gone out.

"God! You were just great, just great! The way you said just the right things to chill them out."

"How are *you* doing?" Blanche wanted to know.

"I'm OK. It shook me up at first. I mean, it was so eerie. The clothes and everything. But, it happens, I guess. What was he like? I never met him."

"I met him and it doesn't help. I think the man I met was the man in the corset."

Tina gave her a blank stare. Blanche explained:

"There was a man in my home town when I was growing up, Mr. Howard, who wore a corset. Everybody liked this man. At least, everybody said how quiet and nice he was, how polite and respectful. Then one day, he knocked out all the windows in his house, threw his wife and children into the street and played Little Esther records on his record player as loud as he could for twenty-four hours straight. Like to drove the whole street crazy. To this day, no one knows what really set him off. The next day he went back to being his regular old self. Only person I ever heard say anything that made sense about that day was Miz Minnie, she's the oldest black woman in Farleigh. She said the Mr. Howard who got drunk and tore up his place wasn't the same Mr. Howard we saw everyday. 'Didn't you notice?' I heard Miz Minnie ask my mama, 'The Mr. Howard who done all that damage wasn't wearing no corset.' "

Tina had tears in her eyes. Blanche hugged the young woman to her and got as much comfort as she gave.

That evening, after the children were in bed and Tina had gone to meet Durant, Blanche walked across the lawn to the water's edge. This was the first time she'd been near the sea since the kids found Hank's things. Earlier, there'd been boats out searching for Hank's body. The children, especially the boys, had been fascinated by them. At first, she'd wouldn't let them get any closer than the front porch. What if they actually found his body while the children watched? It was Malik who spotted the policeman on the beach keeping back the few onlookers who'd appeared. Blanche had then let the children go out and watched them hurry across the lawn toward the beach. The girls were only gone a few minutes. "It's too sad," Deirdre announced, to which Taifa added that the boys were stupid and gross. But the boys had straggled in not much later, more silent than usual, too. They'd all spent the rest of the day around the cottage. The boats wouldn't be back. Mother Water wasn't going to give Hank up, and he surely didn't want her to or he wouldn't have joined her in the first place. So that was that. It occurred to her that if, as the books said, the sea was where life had begun, it made a kind of sense to end your life here, too, to walk into Mother Water's arms and be rocked to death. She stared at the shifting, glistening blueness before turning to walk along the water's edge. But she needed something more.

She went back to the cottage and dialed the phone.

"Oh, Ardell," Blanche said and told her friend about Hank's suicide.

"Damn girl! Amber Cove is definitely the resort from hell. Lotta bad, bad vibes at that place. The kids OK? Musta been really scary finding his clothes like that."

Blanche told her about the suicide discussion with the children. "They seem to be OK, but who can tell? Casey reacted just like the child of doctors, but the others, who knows?"

"None of them seem like hiders." Ardell reminded her. "If stuff comes up, you'll know about it. Hummm. Young brother like that is bound to leave some broken hearts behind. I wonder if he cared? I know his people must be taking it hard."

"Not just hard." Blanche told her about Carol's state and then about Mattie tearing up the suicide note.

"No! She didn't! But why would he lie in his suicide note?"

"Exactly my question!" Blanche agreed, but was suddenly too tired to think about it. Even to her own ears, her voice sounded as though she were sinking fast.

"Hummm. Carol and Mattie ain't the only ones who had a shock." Ardell told her. "Get yourself a cup of hot tea with plenty of honey and lemon and a shot of rum. Drink it in bed."

"You sound just like Mama."

"Good. Pretend that I am and do as I tell you, for a change."

Chapter Seven

⌇

The morning after Hank's clothes and note were found, Blanche woke with Mattie on her mind. She'd fallen asleep remembering what Mattie had said about Hank being "her very last one." Something in the way the air had felt or smelled just after those words rode on it had reached inside Blanche and wrapped around her heart like a stout rope. She'd felt the pressure of it through the night. When her dream came, the consciousness of that rope round her heart had kept her aware of the world outside her dream, even while she was dreaming, which somehow seemed to have helped her keep more of the dream with her when she woke up. While she still didn't remember what happened in the dream, she now knew it wasn't what happened in the dream that frightened and depressed her, but what didn't happen. Even this paltry bit of information seemed important and she credited Mattie's comment with helping her get it. She felt she owed Mattie for that, especially since it grew out of Mattie's own pain.

She decided to take Mattie some freshly squeezed orange

juice and a small hoe cake—her favorite quick bread baked in a cast iron skillet in the Crowleys' oven, instead of on a hoe, over an open fire, the way the slaves made it.

First, she included Mattie, Hank and Carol in her daily communion with the Ancestors. She told Hank she hoped he was happier where he was than he'd been here. She reminded him that Mattie and Carol still needed him. She asked her Ancestors to help Mattie's people lay on the balm because the woman was in serious pain. She asked them to see about Carol too. She did all of this in the shower. She liked the combination of being wrapped in Mother Water, talking to her ancestors and getting ready for her day. Practical, she thought.

When the bread was done, she put it in a cloth-covered bowl and carried it and the juice across the still damp grass. She had to knock three times before Mattie opened the door.

She looked ragged as though parts of her had been torn away, leaving hollows beneath her eyes and under her cheekbones that had not been there yesterday. Blanche brushed gently by her and carried her offering to the kitchen.

The cottage was full of old oak chairs with wide wooden arms and adjustable backs. The walls were covered with paintings Blanche was sure were Mattie's on the basis of the piece she'd seen Mattie working on in the lobby. There was a large picture of a gourd that was also a woman rising from a tub of water; in another, multicolored circles in vibrant colors surrounded a small, deep, not quite black, not quite perfect circle. Blanche felt she could put her finger right into that darkness and that it would come out red with blood. She felt herself moving toward the dark space as if it called to her by name. From the corner of her eye she could see that even in her grief, Mattie was smiling. She folded her hands in front of her in a gesture Blanche had often seen proud mothers make when their children were under praise. After a few minutes of staring into the heart of the universe, Blanche turned to Mattie and bowed slightly.

"I'm glad you like it." Mattie turned and Blanche followed

her into the kitchen. It, too, was a study in old oak: a round table and four high backed chairs, a vegetable bin, smaller tables that acted as counter space; a pie rack and old ice box probably used for storage. The kitchen floor was painted to look like a blue, yellow and green rug with a fringed border. The kitchen was the only part of the cottage she'd been in that didn't smell of turpentine and oily paint. She set the bread and juice on the table.

Blanche was glad to see Mattie had some appetite and enough energy to insist on making coffee and cutting grapefruit to go with their bread and juice. Even so, this Mattie was smaller and slower. This Mattie looked less like old Queen Somebody and more like a very old lady in mourning. Blanche tried to decide if it had been a good idea to come. She wasn't sure she could handle the deep loneliness that clung to Mattie like a bad smell.

"I spoke to Sinclair," Mattie told Blanche. "Carol is in Forest Glen sanitarium outside Boston. She's in severe shock. No visitors. I've called her father, poor man. I'm not even sure he understood me. Alzheimer's. I spoke to the head of the nursing home where he lives as well. Carol's mother died years ago."

"What about Hank's people?" Blanche regretted the question at once.

Mattie's eyes clouded over. "His mother died on April tenth four years ago." There was a slight tremor in her voice. "His father . . ." Mattie stopped to gather herself. "His father died of cancer last January eleventh. Delia, his mother, was my best friend. Did I tell you that? She was very fragile. Very beautiful. But no cream puff. She was determined to have a child, even though her doctor said it could be dangerous. Complete bed rest, the doctor said. She and Jack were living in Virginia back then. He bought a lovely old place way out in the country, away from his medical practice and the noise that went with it. Delia and I were inseparable that year. Memories lit Mattie's eyes and made her smile. "Hank was the perfect child. Bright, inquisitive, funny. So endearing. You saw what a charmer he grew up to be. I used to love to come here summers. Just to see . . ." Mattie covered her mouth with her hand.

Blanche remembered Mattie talking about her sons' preference for their Caucasian heritage. Maybe she'd been trying to give her godson what her own sons didn't want.

The old Mattie suddenly glared at Blanche from beneath eyebrows drawn together like a ridge of snow across her forehead. "He didn't kill her. I don't care what he said in that note. He didn't kill her. Do you understand me?" She leaned forward over her walking stick, adding a wordless demand for a response.

"Ummhumm." Blanche shook her head up and down. She didn't agree with Mattie's opinion, but she understood Mattie's need to have it, to hang on to it until she could get accustomed to the extra weight of Hank's death. Blanche wrapped her arms tightly around herself to keep from reaching for Mattie. She recognized Mattie's posture, the defiance and will that kept her backbone stiff and made it possible for her to hold in the howl of pain Blanche could almost see clawing at her throat.

Mattie folded her arms on the table and lay her head on them. She was so still, she might have been frozen stiff. When she raised her head, her eyes were dry, her face composed. She smoothed the front of her shirt and slacks and picked at the crumbs on her bread plate. Blanche doubted she was aware of what she was doing, but she was deep in thought about something. She stared off into space for a bit, then leaned back in her chair and began talking. It was as if she needed to clear out great swatches of her memory to make room for Hank's death. She began with her girlhood life as a minister's daughter during the Depression—working the church breadline for the poor in her best Sunday dress and being spat upon by a girl her own age. She talked about being at university—one of two women, and the only black person in the school. She talked of meeting Carlton Syms after one of his lectures, of his obvious attraction to her, and the flattery in his attention; the way her dark-skinned father looked at her differently when it was clear this important white man was prepared to defy convention and his family to marry her.

"My mother begged me not to marry Carlton on racial grounds. She told me, 'Mattie, all we have is our people, our blood. We must teach them, provide them with moral and spiritual leadership. You have the makings of a fine teacher. You could help our women, be a model to them. You can't accomplish this as the wife of a rich white man. Our people won't accept you. His people won't accept you. No one will accept you.'

"But I didn't care about being one of the Talented Tenth. I didn't want to be a tightly laced proper Negro matron ministering to the minds and souls of my darker sisters. I wanted the world and Carlton Syms could give it to me. Anyway, Mother was wrong. There were plenty of our people who paid more attention to me because this white man found me worthy enough to marry."

Mattie laughed about her introduction to the physical side of married life: "I doubt I'd been kissed more than six times and Carlton was responsible for four of those times. I knew nothing of human anatomy or sexuality. My preparation for the physical side of marriage consisted of a lecture from my mother on the necessity of obedience to one's husband and keeping oneself clean 'down there.' Imagine my shock when this man insisted upon seeing me naked, insisted upon climbing into my bed! Lord! was I naive! On the first night of our honeymoon, I told Carlton to remove himself from my bedroom immediately or I'd call my father! A preposterous idea made more ridiculous by the fact that we were on a steamship headed for Italy.

"It took Carlton three months to break me in, and I use that term advisedly. In a way, I felt just like a slave—captured, taken to a foreign land and made to perform acts that certainly seemed unnatural—at least at first. And I was just as unwilling as I imagine the slaves were. But the analogy broke down in month four with the arrival of my first orgasm." She laughed and clapped her hands. "Carlton was a good lover, not magical, like some I've known. Oh yes, there've been others, including one that . . . and not all of them black. Or white, for that matter.

Mattie paused, caught by some memory. She'd said something in the bar that first night that made Blanche expect her to talk about a special lover, but she didn't. Maybe she had trouble letting somebody get close, too. She took up her story: "Of course, the lovers came later, after the children were away at school."

"My in-laws never accepted me, you know. My being black wasn't the only problem. My lack of any financial resources to bring to the union upset them almost as much as my race. Even so, they insisted on nannies for the boys from birth to boarding school at age eight. Of course, Carlton agreed. He wanted his children to have all the advantages wealth could provide, all the privileges that accompany white skin, since the boys were light enough to qualify. When my in-laws commandeered my children, I had nothing else to keep me from playing out the fantasies that ripped through me when Carlton made love to me." Mattie paused, her eyes turned inward. "From the moment of his death, I have done exactly what I pleased."

Blanche was fascinated. She'd never known a black woman who'd travelled the world, especially at the time Mattie had done; who'd never cleaned her own house; who only had to want something in order to have it. She pictured Rome and Paris and Spain through the eyes of a black woman and tried to imagine that black woman in the eyes of the people in those places. What had the Spaniards thought of this black woman caring for the wounded in the Spanish Civil War? Had it occurred to Mattie that she might not be welcomed by the French, or Dutch, or British people when she landed on their shores? But, of course, she had her passport—Carlton. Like the temporary Honorary White status apartheid South Africa gave to visiting blacks.

While she talked, Mattie's face took on her stories. Blanche could see the young Mattie being educated by her father at home and then being sent to university. She watched as Mattie, the girl, grew into the woman who buried Carlton Syms, new lines etching deep and forever into her face. Throughout her story, Mattie's eyes gleamed as though flooded with tears, but none fell.

At least five times, Mattie interrupted herself to turn her I-dare-you-to-disagree-with-me stare on Blanche and announced Hank's innocence. Blanche continued to nod in understanding, if not agreement. But, in the end, as she suspected, that was not enough.

"You don't believe me."

Blanche sighed. "Why would he lie, Mattie?"

"To protect someone."

Neither of them needed to name "someone."

Mattie rose from her chair and stood looking down at Blanche. "Don't you see? I knew him as well as I know myself. He was not a killer. He could not have killed Faith. It simply wasn't in his nature. I am more certain of this than I am of my own name. But he loved Carol deeply. There was nothing he wouldn't have done for her."

Blanche was still skeptical. "So what do you think happened?"

Mattie moved closer to her and leaned on the table. "It might have been an accident. Perhaps she didn't intend to do it. They argued. You've heard what Faith was like. Maybe she was going to expose something Carol didn't want known. She might have gone to Faith's, argued with her . . . Well, you see the possibilities." Mattie petered out.

"But Faith was taking a bath, remember? If I was going to argue with somebody I was planning to jack up, I'd get up and put on a robe or something."

Mattie shrugged. "Faith was always arrogant."

"So you think Hank killed himself to protect Carol?" Blanche couldn't hide her doubt.

Mattie paced slowly across the kitchen and back again. "I'm not accusing Carol of causing Hank's death. It's more com-

plicated than that." Mattie picked up her walking stick and
tapped it on the floor impatiently. "I never understood why
he was so unhappy. He was good looking, popular, smart. Yet,
he was fifteen the first time he tried. Fifteen! I didn't even
know what suicide was when I was . . . He saw a psychiatrist for
years after that. There was another bad patch when he was a
junior in college." She shook her head dismissively. "Some
girl was at the heart of it. I don't think he really meant to die.
Wouldn't he have taken all the pills if he really meant it? By
graduate school he seemed to just grow out of his . . . He met
Carol. She was the mate he needed, someone a little older,
wiser. She could lift him right out of his foolishness. We
visited, wrote, travelled together. Everything was fine, fine.
Until recently. There've been signs of the old distance, the
way he had of seeming to just move off to someplace no one
could reach. Carol tried to warn me, to make me see. I
wouldn't. I didn't want to watch him teetering there on the
edge of life, unable to help him, hold him. It hurt too much.
Now . . ." She stopped pacing, breathed deeply and pulled
her shoulders back as if throwing off an unwanted coat. "But
that doesn't make him a murderer. Perhaps he was planning
to . . . to die and then Carol told him what she'd done, and
he . . ." Mattie's nostrils flared. "I gave him everything,
Blanche. Every bit of approval and devotion and support.
Everything I could give. Every idea I thought worth repeating
I talked over with that boy. For the last thirty years, he has
been the only constant. The only one who . . ." The tears were
too demanding, even Mattie couldn't hold them back. She
covered her face as she sank into a chair. She doesn't want me
to cry, too, Blanche told herself.

While Mattie composed herself, Blanche was trying to decide what she needed to say to this woman whom she both
admired and didn't know, not in the ways that really counted.
Mattie talked about her life in a way that had made Blanche
see her in Spain, at sparkling dinner parties, and living the
mind's life with Carlton, but who had Mattie loved beside
Hank? How had she healed her heart when her sons first left

home? What had she done with her parents' deaths? It had not been heart talk. Too one-sided for that. But Mattie had offered not heart, but history—like a house with no furniture in it. Perhaps women who lived as she lived didn't need each other enough to announce their good intentions toward each other in this way. Was this the gap that couldn't be bridged— like the one that yawned between her and those few white women she'd worked for who'd called her Ms. White and invited her to sit at the table and eat with the family? Who kept insisting that she call them by their first names no matter how many times she refused to go beyond Ma'am? But Mattie wasn't a white woman, although the life she led, the privileges she had, were far from common to most black women or men. Was there a different definition of black for folks who had never known the struggle of most black folks? Did she have to spot Mattie points, because she didn't know the rules? Her mixed feelings about Mattie made Blanche even more determined not to lie. Mattie had already seen through her attempt to be noncommittal. Across the table Mattie's eyes looked as though she were watching hell; her hands clawed at each other like sworn enemies. Grief can make you crazy, Blanche thought. She'd learned long ago that the best way to communicate with crazy people was in their world. "What are you going to do?" she asked. "Are you going to the police?"

Mattie looked as though Blanche were babbling. "Why should I? Will it bring Hank back? Those idiots don't even realize Faith was murdered. Why involve them? They don't care, they never have."

"You think it's OK for someone to just get away with murder?"

"What does 'get away with' mean, Blanche? Not going to jail? I don't think anybody gets away with murder really, do you?"

And, of course, she didn't. Murder killed both parties. Neither one was who and what they were before the murder. And she shared Mattie's lack of faith in the police. In her experience, black people who called the cops stood a good chance of being abused instead of assisted. "Still, there's got to be some kinda balance."

Mattie nodded. "I'll solve that problem when I have to."

Blanche thought back to when she'd first seen Carol and Mattie together. There'd been a couple of uptight moments, but that wasn't all. Had she been totally wrong about what she'd felt between them? "I thought you liked Carol," she said.

"Of course I do!" Mattie snapped. "I don't want to sacrifice Carol for Hank's memory. And I won't." She looked directly at Blanche. "Whatever happens, I will stand by Carol. No matter what. But I know Hank didn't kill Faith. I know it in my bones. And Carol is the only person for whom he would tell such a lie."

Blanche wondered if Mattie was aware of the edge to her last words, as though she resented not having been on that short list of people for whom Hank would tell such a lie. Blanche was reminded of what Carol had said about Mattie not tolerating any serious rivals for Hank's affection. She was amazed at how complicated love could be.

"I didn't see Carol at all that day. Hank said she was in bed with a migraine." Mattie's eyes all but begged Blanche to see and believe as Mattie did. "You can see how it could happen. Carol went to see Faith while Hank was taking a walk or something. Afterward, she was in a panic. She ran to Hank." Mattie paused and looked off into space as though the scene was being played out before her. "He was probably relieved to be able to do this one last thing for her before he died." Her voice was almost wistful.

Mattie's certainty about what had happened to Faith was almost visible. Was it just a way of dealing with her grief, a way of keeping Hank's memory pure? Or was it, as Mattie said, a message from her bones?

"But what if Faith had something on Hank?" Blanche asked her. "Have you thought of that? Or maybe Hank killed

Faith because he couldn't stand the idea of her putting Carol's business in the street, even if he wasn't planning to be around when that happened."

Mattie flinched but didn't look away, or speak. She shook her head from side to side like a machine designed for just that movement.

"Even if you're right, there's no way to prove it." Blanche spoke as gently as she could, with her hands extended, palm up.

But Mattie had an answer to that:

"I don't need to prove it. I already know what happened. I simply want the evidence. I want whatever Faith was holding against Carol. It's existence in Faith's possession is what made Carol act as she did, and made Hank feel it was necessary to lie in the last words he wrote in his life. I want to know what it is."

"There may not be anything to find," Blanche reminded her.

Mattie raised her hand as if to ward off Blanche's words. "There's something to find." The steel was glinting in Mattie's eyes again. "I know it."

Blanche sighed. "So now what?"

Mattie reached for her walking stick and held it in both hands. "I want to take a look through Faith's things. But I don't feel up to doing it alone." She held Blanche's eyes with her own. "I'm not accustomed to having to ask for help. But from our first conversation, I felt a connection to you that transcends words. I know I can trust you. It's as though I was supposed to meet you here, now." Mattie sank back in her chair, as though it had taken the last of her energy to ask for this favor.

As Mattie spoke, a bridge seemed to suddenly span the gap between them. A current of something warm and half-remembered surged through Blanche, something older than memory. She thought about what women have always been and done for each other since the first human breath. She thought, once again, of what Madame Rosa had said about her making connections here. And hadn't Mattie used the very same word? Mattie, like Tina, was one of the connections Madame Rosa had said she was to make at Amber Cove. And there was more. Until now, Mattie had been a symbol of the kind of senior Diva Blanche's mama and Miz Minnie and all the other wise old girls Blanche had grown up around might have been under more privileged circumstances. Given Mattie's advantages, a small army of them could have changed the world. But Hank's death had made Mattie a symbol of Blanche's own future: She would not have Mattie's comfort, but, like Mattie, she would probably be alone. She might be closer to Taifa and Malik when they were grown than Mattie was to her sons, but that wasn't saying much. She could already see Taifa and Malik rounding a curve in their road that didn't exist on hers. Maybe Mattie was supposed to show her something that would help her get ready for her own time of being once again on her own.

Mattie slumped in her chair in a way that announced the end of her strength.

"We'll deal with this tomorrow," Blanche told her. "You get some rest." She left Mattie lying on the sofa.

Walking back to the Crowleys', Blanche could still feel the weight of her grief. Was it all the heavier because Mattie could be as icy as January? And what were they likely to find in Faith's cottage, because she didn't doubt that she was going to help Mattie—partly because she was sure it was what Madame Rosa intended and partly because she was how she was: nosey, she heard Ardell say in her mind.

But while she might be willing to help Mattie, she wasn't convinced, like Mattie's bones, that Carol had killed Faith. Still, bones were often smarter than brains. But she doubted it in this case. Poor Mattie.

Blanche suddenly felt the need to be in family—this temporarily enlarged one would do. She surveyed the pantry, fridge and freezer and found them all well stocked. She checked around for spices, utensils and so forth, then gathered fresh tomatoes, tomato paste, thyme, parsley, lemon and scallions for the kids' favorite lunch—cold tomato soup and garlic cheese toast.

Tina stomped into the kitchen and announced that she'd just had yet another fight with Durant about his mother.

"Maybe ya'll need something else to talk about. I don't recall doing all that much talking about the mamas of the men I was seeing."

"No, indeed, honey. We didn't hardly have time for mama talk."

"Sounds hot." Tina took a grape from the fruit bowl on the counter and popped it into her mouth.

Blanche stifled the impulse to tell her not to spoil her lunch.

Tina took another grape. "Sometimes I think men are so different from us we're like two different species who can't even speak the same language."

Blanche dunked tomatoes in hot water to loosen the skins. "Sometimes, and in some ways, I think you're right. Lord knows I've had enough conversations with men where I felt like I was speaking another language. Simple things—like how do you really feel?—scare the poor things half to death. I think we need to stop expecting men to be able to handle much beyond our behinds and a basketball."

"Blanche! You don't really believe that, do you?"

"Only when they piss me off."

"But what about when they don't piss you off?"

The question was asked in that earnest-young-woman tone of voice that told Blanche she couldn't kid her way out of answering it. She thought about Leo and her growing certainty that if she had managed him better, he would never have married Luella. She thought of Stu, and how much easier it was to deal with a man before he saw you naked.

"I ain't exactly an expert. I do know that relationships take a lot more work than anybody tells you about. Maybe the younger you are, the harder it is. The relationship is growing and changing and so are you. By the time you think you got things workin' between the two of you, you look up and one of you is a different person.''

"But if you love each other, you should be able to grow in your relationship, shouldn't you?" Tina sounded as though she'd been reading the how-to books.

Blanche shook her head. "It's more than a notion trying to love somebody, especially a man. Men say they want love the same as we do, but I ain't always sure we're talking about the same thing. Or maybe we don't know any more about loving than men do. Lots of times when women say love, we mean somebody to take care of us, or to make our lives seem worthwhile—things we ought to be doing for ourselves. Sometimes when men say love, they seem to mean they want to own you, or lock you in the kitchen and maternity ward or tell you what to think.''

"What I hate are these constant fights," Tina moaned.

Blanche shifted from the general to the particular. "Maybe you two need to fight." She juiced the tomatoes. "Sometimes a good fight or two helps. Clears things out so you can see what's really going on."

Taifa came into the kitchen and announced her need for water. She looked from Blanche to Tina while she filled a glass, as though she'd picked up some tension, but couldn't tell who it was coming from without some verbal cues. She watched them over the top of her glass as she sipped.

Tina slumped against the counter. "Our fights are making things worse instead of better."

Blanche ran the parsley and the scallions through the food processor, added the tomatoes and popped the container in the freezer to chill. She was aware of Taifa putting more attention into what she was hearing than what she was doing—a small, sleek, red-brown creature sniffing the wind.

"Durant wants me to be nice to his mother, to have lunch with her or something. Like she's going to stop hating the sight of me if I just put out a little more effort! I asked him what about her putting out a little effort? She's the one who's color-struck."

Taifa's head jerked up. She looked from Tina to Blanche and back again.

Tina's eyes flashed. "So, of course, he had to try to defend her. This was the way she was raised, and didn't I understand that it was really self-hatred that made her act so stupid about color, and blah, blah, blah." Tina turned and stared at Blanche, her hands on her hips and her pose challenging. "Does he think I don't know about slavery and white people's preference for people who look like them? I know that's how it all began. But that was then, and this is now. I told him I'm tired of having to understand why some black people act as racist as some white people! That really pissed him off!"

Blanche laughed. "Well, I guess I could see how a person could get pissed if you call his mama a racist." She sliced bread for cheese toast.

Tina opened her mouth to protest, but Blanche went on speaking.

"That don't mean I think you were wrong to say it. Maybe we don't get nowhere on this color business 'cause nobody's willing to say it out loud. Decent light-skinned folks don't want it brought up 'cause they're afraid they'll get lumped in with the Veronicas of the world. Us black-black folks don't bring it up 'cause it hurts more than anything any white person could ever do to us. When I stop to realize there are so-called black people who think I'm *too* black, it scares all hell out of me. I figure most brown-skinned folks either don't want to think about it, are trying to act like all our color hang-ups are disappearing on their own, or they think talking about it will just make us all more mad at each other. Course, the Veronicas—light and dark—do more than talk about it."

"Not talking about it hasn't helped," Tina said. "In Cleveland, where I used to live, there's a black church you couldn't join if you were darker than a paper bag! Can you believe that? And what about the light-bright preference at so many black colleges? Some of the so-called black frats and sororities are really sick around color, too, you know."

Blanche told her the story she'd heard last year from a social worker friend in New York, about a brown-skinned couple who wanted to adopt a child, but only a child with light skin. Taifa's recent words rang in her ears as well. She could feel Taifa looking at her, but didn't turn to face the child.

"Well, I'm sick of it!" Tina pounded her fist into her open palm, but there were tears at the edge of her voice. She turned her back to Blanche and Taifa.

Blanche went to Tina and put her hand on Tina's tense shoulder. This was the part that made her really mad. How can we keep on doing this to each other? Tina leaned back against Blanche's hand. Blanche began to talk to her in a low voice.

"By the time I was nine, I was always ready to be laughed at or teased for being so black. For a long time, I didn't trust nobody, nobody, but my friend, Ardell. You got a good girlfriend?" she asked.

Yeah, my homegirl, Karen. We been tight since grade school. She's always got my back." Tina told her.

"Good. Women like us need our girlfriends." Blanche told Tina about the time in grade school when Ardell had helped her tie fire to the butts of some classmates who had changed, "Inky Dinky Spider," to "Inky Stinky Blanche." She'd been surprised that a hardly brown girl like Ardell would feel strongly enough about the issue of color to stick up for her. She understood when she met Miz Maxine, Ardell's mother. She was light enough to pass for white. She was also the first, and for most of Blanche's life, the only light-skinned person who talked openly about why some light-skinned people looked down on blacker folks and the privileges that light-skinned people enjoyed because of their skin color. Blanche paused.

Tina waited for her to go on. And so did Taifa.

"When I was in my teens," Blanche said, "Boys made sure I knew that any girl dark as me was supposed to be an easy lay out of gratitude that they would even look at anybody black as me." Tina turned to face Blanche. Blanche crossed her arms over her chest. "A light-skinned girl once told me she liked walking with me 'cause it made her look almost white. After that, I figured any light-skinned person who tried to be my friend really wanted to use me in that same way. So I had an attitude. If anybody was going to get their feelings hurt, it wasn't going to be me. Mama was always telling me there was a princess in Africa who looked just like us. Ardell's mother kept reminding me there were some light-skinned people who hated color prejudice, too. But neither of them was catching the hell I was. I was the darkest one in the family."

Taifa was now making no pretense of setting the table. Blanche was careful not to make eye contact with her. The information wouldn't be half as valuable if Taifa realized the grown-ups knew she was listening.

Tina got juice and iced tea from the refrigerator. "Yeah. Like the first boy I ever really liked. As a boyfriend, I mean." She slammed the refrigerator door with a switch of her hips. "Russell. He was so fine, so fine. We all had a crush on him. I got to work with him on the class play. After practicing in the mirror for weeks, I finally got up the courage to ask him to the party after the play. He said he'd never gone anywhere with a girl as dark as me, so he had to think about it." Tina set the tea and juice on the table with a gesture so gentle, so careful, it nearly broke Blanche's heart.

Blanche could lip-sync it. She saw a chorus of black-skinned women, their mouths all moving to the words of this experience.

Tina cleared her throat and pushed back her dreads. "I remember thinking, if I was light-skinned, Russell wouldn't have to think about taking me to the party. I remember looking in the mirror wondering if despite what Mama said, I was really as ugly as so many people tried to make me feel."

Another memory they shared. Only the names and places

were different. She knew its aftermath: The feeling of being thin as a wafer, as though you could be seen right through; of being not just bruised, but totally crushed, as if words were clubs studded with nails—words that some folks thought went together—black and dirty; black and ugly; black and sneaky; black and stupid; black and lazy; black and easy.

"But you know it's not true, don't you? Not any of it." Blanche watched Tina's face for any twitch or shift in her eyes that said she held a doubt.

Tina bobbed her head up and down. "Definitely." She laughed a shy laugh. "Most of the time."

Blanche arranged bread slices on a cookie sheet. "I didn't get this color shit really straightened out until I was nearly thirty. This country's got so many ways to make us feel bad. Like these assless blue-eyed, blond anorexics who are supposed to be the last word in beauty." Blanche toasted the bread lightly under the grill.

"Yeah." Tina added, "It's everywhere. Notice how you never see really black women as stars in movies made by American black men? I bet if you lined up the wives of the most admired black men in America from all walks of life, very few of them would be our complexion."

Blanche laid slices of cheese on the toast, rubbed a cut clove of garlic over the cheese, sprinkled on some paprika and put them under the grill. "And it don't ever end. But you do learn, like you have already, that there's no sense being sick over somebody else's sickness." She thought of Leo and other men she'd known who'd made her feel as though she were the finest woman since the first sunrise; she thought of Ardell, Rosalee, Juanita and all the other women who loved her. "You find people who see the whole you, not parts of you, and love it all. You find you don't need the other kind. Or the pain."

Taifa moved slowly around the table putting spoons beside bowls, her eyes occasionally moving from face to face. When she came close to where Tina was standing she stopped and looked wordlessly up at her.

Blanche didn't expect that Taifa understood all that she'd heard. But she'd listened intently. During lunch Deirdre tried to get her interested in a story about a girl at their school who could do magic tricks, but Taifa was only partly present.

Blanche listened to the chatter, alert for any mention of Faith or Hank or anything that might mean they were upset by one death after another, but it didn't appear to be an issue.

Tina answered the phone when it rang. Blanche could tell from the way her shoulders drooped that it wasn't Durant.

"It's the same man who called yesterday. I forgot to tell you. Sorry" She handed the phone to Blanche.

"It's Tuesday." Stu made that fact sound like Christmas. "You did say Tuesday?" he asked when she didn't respond. "I called yesterday, when I heard about Hank, but you were out. I tried earlier today, too, but no one answered. You OK? About Hank, I mean?

"I'm OK. Carol and Mattie are both in a bad way, though."

"Yeah." He was silent for a moment, then: "I'll understand if you want to postpone, but I'll be damned disappointed."

Blanche laughed and told him to hang on. She went to ask Tina if she'd be around to keep an eye on the children.

"How about 9:30?" she asked him.

"Really? Great! Great!"

Blanche smiled at the eagerness in his voice. She was glad Tina was so absorbed in her own business she didn't ask Blanche how she planned to spend her evening. The children had disappeared by the time Blanche got off the phone.

"I been thinking about what you said." Tina told her. "About how it's not our problem that people are color-struck. I knew about Durant's mother before I met her. Durant told me she always pushed him toward light-skinned girls. I wonder sometimes if I'm just a way for him to defy her."

"If that's what's going on, why does Durant care so much whether you and his mother get along? Seems to me, if he wanted to defy her, he'd be happier if you two hated each other."

Tina agreed and added: "Well anyway, I've decided to do it,

to act like she's the one with the problem. I'll be nice to her the same way I'd be nice to any other mentally ill person." She grinned and ran her fingers through her dreds. "I was thinking maybe I'll bake a cake and invite her over for coffee and cake. That be OK with you?" She looked as though she wasn't sure she wanted it to be OK.

"That's fine, honey. Let me know if I can help." Blanche didn't bother to say she thought Tina was spitting in the wind. Some things you had to learn for yourself.

Blanche washed the dishes and wiped off the stove, counter and refrigerator. Someone would be coming to clean today. Blanche didn't want to make any work for her or him. She was eager to meet whoever it would be. She'd yet to see any of the housekeeping staff except from a distance. Her towels had been replenished, her room cleaned while she was out, as if by magic. She was looking forward to getting a worker's take on this place and these people. Then she'd take a walk, so he or she could do the job the way Blanche liked to do it: on her own, with no interference or so-called supervision. Despite the white bartender and the bellhop, she was surprised when a short, ruddy-faced white woman in her twenties showed up . . .

"The name's Rose."

"I'm Blanche." She stuck out her hand.

Rose looked both surprised and suspicious. She took Blanche's hand but dropped it so quickly she hardly touched it. She gave Blanche a sidelong glance from which a wall sprung up between them. So that's how it feels from the other side, Blanche thought. She left Rose to do her work. She wondered what kind of stories Rose and the other white help told their families and friends about the black folk who stayed here and ran this place? How were they different from the stories she told about her white employers? She obviously wasn't going to find out from Rose.

She spent the rest of the afternoon walking the beach and lolling in a chaise under a tree out back, reading and nodding. By the time a cool breeze roused her, Tina was organizing the children for baths before dinner. They had decided they wanted to eat at the Big House, which suited Blanche just fine, as long as she didn't have to go. She took herself out on the front porch before she got roped into the bath ritual.

She watched Durant walking toward the cottage.

"Hi, Mrs. White. How are you, today?"

Blanche hadn't noticed before what a nice voice the boy had, deep and soft and somehow trustworthy. "Hey Durant. I'm good. You?" She waved him to a seat on the porch. "You might as well sit down. Tina and the kids are still getting ready. How about some iced tea?" She brought the pitcher of iced tea and some glasses out to the porch.

Durant cleared his throat. Crossed and uncrossed his legs. "I've been meaning to thank you for asking Tina to stay with you. She'd have left otherwise. And as long as she's here . . ."

"They say you can't have your cake and eat it too." Blanche hadn't planned to say that and half hoped he wouldn't understand what she meant, since it betrayed a level of thinking about his business that was really none of her business.

Durant gave her a look that added a sharp determination to his soft face. "Sometimes you can. Sometimes you get lucky. It's already happened once."

Blanche nodded. "True, it's possible, but not easy."

Durant set his glass on the table. "It's not a problem if you know your priorities. For me, it's more like trying to have my bread and my cake at the same time. I need one to live, the other . . ."

"To live? That's pretty drastic."

"Yes, it is." Durant looked directly into her eyes. Everything about him was serious. "I've never known anyone anywhere near as wonderful as Tina. She's like fire and laughter. She's so deep, so alive. She's a necessity, like water. I can't even think about not having her in my life." He laughed. "Listen to me!" He was clearly embarrassed.

"Yes, I am listening to you." She remembered her concern about what Tina saw in Durant and was reminded of Miz Belle and Mr. Henry who'd lived down the block from her mother when Blanche was growing up. He was a little bit of a man, short, slight, soft-spoken. Every time Blanche saw a picture of the Statue of Liberty, she thought of Miz Belle. That's the kind of giant woman she was. She had a big everything— voice, laugh, heart, sense of humor, appetite. Young Blanche had often wondered what Miz Belle, who could have had any man in town, saw in puny, meek Mr. Henry. One day she'd seen Mr. Henry look at Miz Belle in a way that Blanche had never forgotten—as though Miz Belle were the sun and he a small, pale flower that could only bloom in her presence. Now she watched Durant's face as the children came tumbling out of the house followed by Tina. Yes, there it was. That look. She turned to Tina who smiled as though she knew a secret and wondered if being the sun was as good as being a real woman, but what the hell did she know? When they left she ate a can of tuna and sat on the porch. She watched the sun sink and the evening turn to indigo until it was time to meet Stu.

Chapter Eight

～

Stu was waiting on the stone wall that separated the lawn from the rocky beach. His skin glowed like old gold against the pure white of his shirt and slacks. His eyes gleamed a deeper blue than she'd remembered.

"I like your sandals." It was the only thing she trusted herself to say. He had nice feet, too.

Stu smiled. He held up a bottle of Moët Chandon and two champagne flutes. "It's such a great night. How about the beach? You game?"

They walked in silence under the near-to-full moon. It was just cool enough for the sweater Blanche had thrown around her shoulders. Bright, bright stars dotted the sky. The beach sparkled as though it had recently rained diamond dust. They settled themselves on one of the boulders Blanche had sat among her first day at Amber Cove. She pushed the sound of Carol and Hank's voices from her mind and the sadness that accompanied them. They were not her burden to bear. She held the glasses while Stu poured. Before she joined him in his toast to good friends and good times, she poured a few drops of champagne onto the sand.

"For the Ancestors," she responded to Stu's puzzled look.
"You believe in ancestor worship?"

"More and more." Blanche's voice was warm with enthusiasm. "It's taken me a long time to figure out what I needed.
I should have figured it would be something old and
African."

Stu's pale eyes seemed to darken. "What if your ancestors
were awful people?"

"I thought about that. I decided that only the positive parts
survive death."

Stu chuckled. "You decided?"

"Didn't somebody decide what stories to put in the Bible?
Didn't somebody decide that Mary was a virgin?"

Stu cocked his head. "I hadn't thought of it that way." He
held out his glass and let a part of his wine dribble to the
ground, then held the glass out toward her. "To the Ancestors
and their descendant."

Their clinked glasses sounded like crystal chimes.

"So, have you been here all along?"

"I only came back last year. I did a couple stretches in the
Army. Went to pharmacy school, ran a garage with a buddy
from Philly, hung out down in Mexico for a while. A wild,
fun-filled life."

Blanche was surprised. She thought men in his class started
for the top of something at age two and didn't stop until they
got there or dropped dead trying.

Stu gave her that soft, dessert-eyeing look she remembered
from the dance. "Tonight, I'm very, very glad I came back.
Especially glad." He raise his glass to her before he drank
from it.

It was the opening Blanche wanted. "I moved back to my
hometown a couple years ago," she told him. "But it didn't
work out. For one thing, I couldn't find enough work there."
She turned and stared directly into his eyes.

"What kind of work do you do?"

"Domestic work. Clean, cook, sew, wait table. I've been
doing some catering, too."

Stu laughed. "No, seriously. What do you do?"

Blanche didn't join in the laughter or even smile. "I told you what I do."

Stu looked into his glass, out to sea, into his glass again. He shifted about on his rock as though sand crabs had gotten into his drawers. Blanche didn't think she'd ever seen a black person go quite so pale. It was noticeable even in the dark. Didn't they call that blanching? She picked up the champagne. "Here." She poured some wine in his glass. "You look like you could use some more of this." A catch, just like she'd told Ardell. Were his lips always that thin? Or was shock pinching them? Stu suddenly stopped fidgeting. Blanche could see the awful possibility dawning in his eyes and nearly laughed at the horror that spread across his face.

"You don't . . . you don't work for Chrissy and Dave, or anyone, do you?" he asked.

She'd known what the question would be while it was still filtering down from his brain to his lips. She was tempted to say, yes, just to see if he'd go even paler.

"I don't work for any of these folks here, if that's what you mean. Although you work for them, don't you?"

Stu looked both relieved and puzzled.

"You mean it never occurred to you that you're a service worker? Not as invisible as my line of work, maybe. More like a shadow behind your counter." She got up and brushed off the back of her slacks. "Thanks for the drink." She began walking toward the Crowley cottage.

She could feel Stu behind her, but not close. His presence made her back rigid. She built a mental wall between them and began whispering to the sea about what a fool he was, and how glad she was to have expected a catch, regardless of Ardell. He called to her as she was climbing the porch stairs. She didn't pause or turn around. She tiptoed past Tina asleep on the sofabed and closed the bedroom door behind her. Her body felt very heavy; her head throbbed and her shoulders were tighter than a well-made drum. Why did she once again feel like the only kid in her fifth-grade class who only got valentines with something mean on them? I'm too old for this shit, she told herself. Too smart, the sea responded. Maybe that, too, she thought.

Even though she was weary to the marrow, sleep was not waiting for her in her room. She twisted and turned for an hour or so before she got up. She dressed and left the cottage by the back door. She walked toward the beach. There was no one about, although she could see puddles of light around some of the cabins. She sank down heavily onto one of the chaises near the Big House. She looked up at the stars and asked herself why she had agreed to see him, danced with him in a way that said she was interested, when all along she'd felt something off about him? Back in the pre–AIDS days, they'd have popped into the bed and got rid of that heat building between them. They might have left the motel, never to see each other again, without the subject of what she did for a living ever coming up. But she'd never really been big on quickies. And is that what she wanted? To hide what she did so some dickbrain would want her? She felt tears gathering. She told herself she didn't want him, either. That was true, right now. But would it have been true if he hadn't not wanted her first? That's what she didn't know, that's what hurt. "Oh, hell!" she hissed. This on top of Taifa's attitude toward her color was one more put down than she felt she ought to have to handle. Suddenly there was Leo shimmering in her mind like one of the stars overhead. The memory of his tenderness, of the pride in his voice when he'd introduced her to people as "my lady," even though it had irritated her at the time, was a stark contrast to how Stu had made her feel.

She held out her arms to the sea: "I sure could use some help here," she murmured.

A ribbon of moonlight lay across the water. The waves were hushed. Tears rolled down her cheeks and she let them flow. She replayed the evening with Stu from its hopeful beginnings to its hateful end. She sobbed a little, willing herself not to hold back, to feel the ache under her heart, the special kind of loneliness that came with being told you're not good enough by one of your own kind. She reminded herself that before long, the memory of this night would be just that, a memory. But she hadn't gotten to that point yet. Which was why, for a millisecond, when she felt someone coming and looked over her shoulder to see a man walking across the lawn, she'd let herself believe that Stu had come back to say she was right to think him a fool. She was still feeling the rush of relief and self-righteousness when she realized it wasn't him.

She wiped her eyes and watched the man approach. He hadn't noticed her yet. He walked slowly, with his head down and pulled into his neck. His shoulders were hunched as though against a frigid wind. He was a big man who'd probably once been imposing, now he was stooped; his footsteps were hesitant, as if he wasn't sure his legs could bear his weight. He stopped abruptly when he saw Blanche. Instead of veering off, as she'd expected, he moved closer to her. She stood to meet him, knowing intuitively who he was.

"I'm Blanche White," she held out her hand. His felt papery, as though she could squeeze it into a small ball without any effort at all. "My deepest condolences."

Al J. peered at her. She explained that they hadn't met and who she was.

"Oh yes," he said, as though her words made some sense to him, which she doubted. "I just came to say good-bye to this place. I always liked Amber Cove. But I won't be back. Not now." He turned his head away from Blanche and wiped at his eyes. "I just wish I could have given her some of the happiness she gave me."

"I'm sure you did," Blanche murmured.

Al J. shook his head in disagreement. "No. I didn't I couldn't. She was too mad to be happy, I guess. She had a lot of hard things happen to her, even though she was always well off. She really wanted people to like her, respect her, but she never seemed to fit in, somehow, never seemed to learn how to be liked, so she . . ."

Regardless, Blanche, thought. Faith had known better than she'd behaved.

Al J. went off in another direction. "Damn! She was good looking in the early days! She had a rosy glow, like a ripe peach. And a smile to break your heart. It wasn't until she got older, after the babies didn't come, and she started . . . She was never sweet. Not, you know, easy. But good to me, good to me."

Al J. went on for at least twenty minutes, recounting the time Faith made him a birthday cake from scratch, even though she was on crutches; the time he'd been depressed about being in bed for weeks with a bad back and she made her face up like a clown and danced and sang to cheer him up. The time she had his office redecorated as a surprise.

All the anecdotes were about how well Faith had treated him, which was wonderful, except there was no evidence Faith had ever done a nice thing for anyone other than Al J., Malik and Casey. Blanche wondered if Faith had a best friend. Who were the women who would step in and see to the feeding of the funeral goers on her burial day? "Well, if there's anything I can do . . ."

"There's nothing anyone can do, now. Nothing." He held onto Blanche's hand.

"I had another family, you know. Another wife. She died young. Left me with two girls to raise. They were about to go to high school when I met Faith."

Blanche thought about Deirdre's comment about Faith not liking girls.

"Raising kids is tough." Blanche paused. Al J. said nothing. "But they'll be a great comfort to you, now." She squeezed his hand.

"They hate her. Both of them. After all she did. Sending them to boarding school, college and all. They still can't see behind all her carrying on to the good, loving woman who made my life so, so . . ." Al J.'s shoulders began to shudder. He hid his face behind his other large, manicured hand.

"I wish I could tell somebody how it feels, how the world can suddenly be different, everything so far away, and cold."

Blanche immediately knew how she could help. She pulled her hand away from his and wrapped her arms as tightly around him as she could. Al J. hugged her to him so hard she thought she'd explode. His tears were hot on her shoulder. His sobs were deep and silent and almost made her glad she had never loved enough to generate this kind of pain. She remembered hugging Tina yesterday and wondered if hugging was one of the things Madame Rosa had sent her here to do.

"Al J.? Is that you?" A thin voice called out from the terrace stairs.

Al J. started. He jumped back from Blanche and quickly swiped at his eyes. "My sister. She brought me here to pick up a few things. Arthur will take care of the rest." He took her hand again and squeezed it gently. "Thank you." He looked at her a long time, as though wanting to remember her face. Blanche watched as he and his sister walked away. They didn't touch. She thought of the many times people she'd worked for had come to her in search of comfort. She'd generally withheld it. She didn't include solace in the parts of herself that she sold to employers. Even so, she felt sorry that they needed it. No one should have to go to the hired help for a hug. Until now, she'd associated this lack of a loved one to provide sympathy with rich white families who avoided showing affection for fear it would be seen as weakness. Now here was this black man needing from a stranger what he obviously couldn't get from his own sister. So, like Curdled Passion, this business wasn't just about being white. Maybe part of what happened when you had more than most people was that you fooled yourself into thinking you were independent. Until your wife died.

She stumbled off to bed to sleep a deep and heavy sleep.

Chapter Nine

〜

The morning sunlight lay in slivers on the bedroom floor, cut to ribbons by the bamboo blind. Birds twittered to the accompaniment of the ocean, but Blanche had none of her usual eagerness to rise and meet the new day. Stu's face popped into her mind as if from a jack-in-the-box buried in her brain. Son of a . . . No. She wasn't going to blame some woman for having birthed him when she had no proof that's how he came to be in the world. A sewer was more likely. She threw back the covers. She could hear the radio from the kitchen and the girls singing along with it. She called out a good morning on her way to the bathroom. The phone rang while she was brushing her teeth. Tina called to her.

"Is it Mattie?" Blanche wanted to know.

"No. It's a man. I'll ask who it is."

Blanche didn't hesitate. "No. Just tell him I can't come to the phone." She went back to her teeth. Wants to apologize, doing the polite thing, she thought. She'd be just as happy not to hear it. He wouldn't be making the effort if she wasn't connected to people he knew. He was no more sorry than a monkey with a stolen bunch of bananas. She'd seen his face. He'd been glad that he'd found out about her unacceptable work before they were seen together too often. Yes, she'd seen that on his face. She rinsed her mouth. She looked at the clock radio. Too bad. Ardell had already left for work.

Tina was reading on the porch when Blanche came out of the bathroom. The boys had gone to their fort and the girls were nowhere to be seen. Blanche made herself a cup of tea and got out her postcards. She never knew what to say, but she always promised she would send them, and so she did. "Having a fine time. Love, Blanche." "It's really beautiful here. Love, Blanche" "The ocean is wonderful! Love, Blanche." Her mother always complained about the skimpiness of Blanche's cards. She decided to give her a call.

"How's my grandbabies?"

"They're fine, Mama. We're all fine."

"Them folks got a nice place? Weather all right? What's the place like? Food good?" Mama asked in her usual run-on fashion that didn't allow space for answers.

"The cottage is real nice. It's very pretty up here. A little cool for our taste. But the ocean is as blue as I've ever seen it and the air's clear as crystal. Food's kinda on the white side, but well prepared. Fancy." It was her turn to ask a question. "You been doin' those exercises Ardell gave you for your arthritis?" And why do we mostly talk to each other in questions and answers, she asked herself. After she hung up and made herself another cup of tea, the phone rang again. She let Tina answer it. This time it was Mattie, calling to say she was ready. The phone rang again as she opened the screen door to leave. She didn't wait to see who it was.

Getting into Faith's cottage was no problem. Mattie told Arthur she needed the key to get some books and other things she'd lent to Faith. Arthur arranged to meet Mattie at the cottage. When Blanche and Mattie arrived, Arthur was already there and seemed to have been there for awhile.

"I just came, I just wanted to check on things, to make

sure . . ." His voice failed him under the pressure of Mattie's disapproving gaze.

She put out her hand. "Give me the key Arthur."

"I'd be happy to stay or come back and lock up later. Al J. asked me to . . ."

Mattie's only answer was to extend her hand further toward him. Arthur slowly pulled two keys on a small chain from his pocket.

"Good-bye Arthur," Mattie said.

"Really Ms. Harris, I am the manager. I really think I should . . ."

"Good-bye Arthur," Mattie repeated.

Arthur left. Mattie winked at Blanche.

Blanche didn't pay much attention to the living room. She got the impression of overstuffed fluff as she followed Mattie down the hall toward the two closed doors on either side of the bathroom. Blanche was glad the bathroom door was also closed. Mattie opened the door on the left into a good-sized bedroom.

"Up-scale cozy" was how she would later describe the room to Ardell. The large sleigh bed had a two-layered dust ruffle. The bed was covered by a lightweight quilt of octagonal patches made to look like flowers. A tall cherry wood clothes closet stood across the room. A skirted club chair was upholstered in the same rose-strewn pattern as one of the dust ruffles on the bed. There was a small blue-tiled fireplace. The mantle held a cut glass pitcher full of nearly dead flowers, an old clock and two large sea shells. A basket full of magazines stood beside the chair. There was a slim writing desk and a low chest of drawers. On top of the chest there was a row of antique windup toys: a tumbler suspended from two poles who did a flip when the handle was turned; a ballerina, all pink and white that twirled on one foot when cranked up; a clown that slipped on a banana peel; and a bicyclist who pedaled and tipped his hat. They were each less than a foot high, metal, with paint in various stages of fading or peeling.

Blanche and Mattie tiptoed around. There was still something of Faith in the place, a hint of scent, a tightness in the air common in the homes of the hard-to-get-along-with. Blanche noticed that someone had been sitting on the bed. "What do you think we're going to find?" Blanche wanted Mattie to be prepared for not finding anything.

Mattie looked around the room. "I don't know. I just know there's something here, something."

Blanche wondered why she didn't want to tell Mattie she'd overheard Carol and Hank talking about Faith. Maybe she just didn't want to add fuel to Mattie's fire.

"But if there was something to find, why would it still be here? Wouldn't the killer take it?" The word rang in the room like a machete striking stone. Blanche felt the flat of its cold blade along her spine.

"Maybe *she* couldn't find it. It won't hurt to look." Mattie looked around the room.

"OK. We're here, we might as well look and hope we know it if we see it." Blanche opened drawers and poked under piles of underwear and nightgowns, slips and sweaters that were not exactly jumbled, but not quite neatly stored. Mattie went through the drawers in the two nightstands. Blanche checked on top and under, as well as inside the closet. Mattie went through Faith's handbag. There was nothing, not even a speck of dust under the bed. Help clean like they live here, Blanche thought.

"Well, if there's something to be found, it sure is well hid." Blanche sank onto the ottoman at the foot of the slipper chair. "Maybe it's in some other room."

Mattie straightened up from having searched the desk and leaned back in the small desk chair "No. I'm sure it would be here. The other rooms are Al J.'s bedroom and his exercise room.

"Well, there's the bathroom." Mattie rose from the chair. "I have to use it anyway."

Blanche knew before Mattie returned that she hadn't found anything, she'd been too quiet. They'd already felt all over the fireplace for a loose tile or brick, lifted the rug around the edge of the room in search of an easily accessible loose board. Nothing.

"Blanche, where would you hide something you didn't want found?"

Blanche slipped off her shoe and rubbed her corn. "Depends on what it is. Now if it's something I don't need to have around, I'd maybe bury it, or maybe give it to a friend to hold. But if I needed it to hand, or just liked to look at it from time to time, I'd put it somewhere people could see it without knowing they were seeing it. Know what I mean?"

They both looked slowly round the room, then examined the lamps and under the chair cushions. They twisted the knobs at the corners of the bed to see if they could be removed to reveal a hiding place; they made sure nothing was taped to the back of the headboard or under the desk drawer. Blanche looked around the room again. What in it had they not turned upside down or poked inside of? She walked to the bureau and stood before the windup toys. Mattie watched her every move. Blanche touched the pointed fingers of the ballerina.

"When I was a kid, I once stole some money from a neighbor so I could buy my mother a music box with a spinning ballerina on top," she told Mattie.

"Did you get caught?"

"No. I took the money back. Halfway to the store I got cold feet. Not so much over what Mama would do to me, but how she would feel if she found out. I took the money back. It hadn't even been missed yet." She lifted the ballerina and turned it around in her hands. She held it over her head and looked at the bottom of the metal platform that held the toy's mechanical works. "Not as heavy as it looks." She sat the ballerina down and picked up the tumbler and then the cyclist examining them in the same way. Finally, she reached for the clown. "This one's heavier. Weighs 'bout as much as a small turkey." She looked closely at the box that held the toy's mechanism. This box was a bit larger than the boxes that held the other toys' works. She shook it. Something slid around inside. Mattie rose and came to stand beside her. Mattie's breath was quick and shallow. They peered at the toy itself, the clown in its faded red-and-white polka dot outfit, his peeling, bulbous blue nose, the splayed banana peel with hardly any yellow paint left on it. Blanche touched it. Pushed it. Something clicked. She tilted the toy forward and a metal box slipped from the base, like a drawer from a cash register. Mattie and Blanche exchanged triumphant looks. Blanche slipped the box from the toy base and handed it to Mattie. Mattie turned it around to show Blanche the slot where the key went. The box was securely locked. They pried at the inset lid and hairpinned the lock to no avail.

"Damn!" Mattie banged her walking stick on the floor.

"No need to use bad language," Blanche's imitation of Mattie's voice and autocratic tone were nearly perfect. Both of them laughed. Mattie plopped down in the slipper chair, holding the box in one hand and her stomach with the other.

"Someone's . . . ," Blanche began.

"Yoohoo! Mattie?" Veronica called.

Mattie looked at Blanche with surprise then down at the locked box in her hand.

"Mattie, where are you?" Veronica sang out in her most affected voice.

Mattie looked quickly around, then lifted some magazines from the jumbled basket beside her chair. She stuffed the box in the basket and pushed some magazines down on top of it.

Veronica poked her head round the door frame. "There you are! Didn't you hear me calling? Arthur told me you were here. I thought I'd come along and see if you needed any help." Veronica smoothed her hair. Her eyes devoured the room before she looked in Blanche's direction. "Oh!" she said as though she'd seen a mouse.

Mattie looked silently up at Veronica.

"Is something wrong?" Veronica approached Mattie's chair. "Are you all right, dear. I know the strain of Hank's death is . . ."

Mattie tapped her cane on the floor. "You remember Blanche, don't you Veronica?"

Veronica sniffed and tossed her head. "Oh yes, of course. Hello."

Blanche stared at her without speaking. Mattie did the same. Veronica fiddled with her belt, caught herself and put her hands down by her sides. She walked slowly around the room.

"We were just leaving," Mattie told her. "I need a rum and a rest."

"Did you find your things?"

Mattie gave her a blank stare.

"The things you came here to get. Did you find them?"

Mattie brushed past Veronica without a word. Blanche did the same. Veronica trailed behind them toward the front of the cottage.

"The place could use a bit of tidying up and I'm sure Al J. would want Faith's things sorted out and packed up. I think I'll stay and . . ."

"We are all leaving now, Veronica," Mattie told her.

"Well, I only thought . . . We could clear it with Arthur if you think that's necessary.

"Come along Veronica." Mattie's eyes were nearly as commanding as her voice.

Once they were all out-of-doors, Mattie carefully locked the door. They watched Veronica walk away.

"What do you think she really wanted? You think Faith had something on her, too?"

"Probably. Damn her! I'm tempted to turn around and go right back in there and look for the key to that box. I won't rest well knowing it's just sitting there in the magazine basket."

Blanche said she needed to see to the children, anyway. Mattie suggested Blanche call them from her cottage and let the Big House handle their dinner. That way, they could go back and look for the key. She seemed quite surprised to learn that Blanche actually wanted to fix the children's dinner.

"This evening, I'll go get the box and bring it to you, if that will help you rest better." A voice in the back of Blanche's brain told her this was stealing but she shushed it. Mattie handed Blanche the key to Faith's cottage.

When Blanche reached the Crowleys', the boys were squabbling over the outcome of their umpteenth game of checkers. Tina was talking on the phone with Durant—unless there was someone else who put that trapped-but-happy look on her face. The cottage smelled of just-baked cake. Taifa and Deirdre were sprawled on the lawn out back surrounded by magazines, cookies, Cokes, books, nail polish and tapes. They each wore a Walkman. Just two years ago, Taifa had refused to carry anything that didn't fit in her pockets. Now she dragged around a backpack that grew daily as she collected all the bits and pieces of soon-to-be teenager-hood. Taifa and Deirdre flipped Blanche a couple of waves and went on singing along with the song in their headphones.

Blanche decided they would eat out of doors and sent Casey to set the table on the front porch.

During dinner—Blanche's special marinated chicken, lemon broccoli, corn on the cob—Blanche and Tina debated the effects of various shampoos and conditioners, which led Deirdre to ask:

"Tina, how come you wear your hair like that?"

"You don't like my dreds?" Tina casually flipped her hair at Deirdre.

"It's not that I don't like them. It's just that its . . ."

Taifa screwed up her face. "Nappy," she said.

Tina laughed and poked Taifa on the arm. "Of course it's nappy. Most black people's hair is kinky. That's the way it grows. That's the way it's supposed to be! Helps to protect our heads from falling meteors and police batons."

"But you can't take 'em out, can you?" Taifa challenged.

"I can cut them off."

"But then you wouldn't have any hair!" Deirdre sounded as though she couldn't imagine a worse fate.

"Yeah, but it's only hair. It'd grow back."

"Then why don't you cut them off and get a perm?"

"Because I like nappy hair." Tina lifted a section of her hair and let it fall. "It does everything we've always wanted our hair to do. It doesn't shrink in the rain, it can be worn up or down, it blows in the wind, moves when I move." Tina swung her head from side to side so her dreds whipped about her face. "And I don't have to turn my head over to somebody else. I'm in charge of it. Why would I want to give that up for a permanent?"

The look Taifa and Deirdre gave each other said Tina clearly lived in a different world.

"Hair's always been a big thing with us black folks, especially us women," Blanche told them. "I can still remember how excited I was to get my hair straightened for the first time. Nobody had told me I'd be getting burned ears and a lot of threats about what was going to happen to me if I didn't keep my little behind still while my hair was being fried, let alone what it did to my poor hair." Blanche shook her head. "You should have seen me! Little skinny black child with two minutes worth of fried greasy hair plastered down on my head and scabs on my ears. It's hard to believe I thought that was cute, but I did."

"Is that why you won't let me get my hair straightened?" Taifa wanted to know.

Tina spoke before Blanche could respond. "I had hair just like you when I was a little girl, Blanche. Boy! I can remember praying every night that if I could just have long hair, I'd be good for the rest of my life. I'd have killed my baby brother for long hair, and don't even mention hair that moved like mine does now!"

"I bet your mom doesn't like it much," Casey said.

Tina laughed. "She's getting used to it. Especially now that it's long."

"When was the last time you straightened your hair,"
Mama Blanche?" Malik wanted to know.

Blanche thought for a few minutes. "I was seventeen, I
guess. It was the sixties. I was lucky enough to be in on the tail
end of a time when some black folks were saying our dark skin
and kinky hair have to be beautiful because they are ours. So,
there was a lot of nappy hair out there when I decided to give
up the straightening comb. It turned out to be more than a
fad for me."

"When I grow up, I'm going to have dreds too, like Dread
Rapper Dred" Malik announced.

"See Blanche, things are improving," Tina grinned.

Blanche didn't consider bunches of boys in dreds with their
pants hanging off their butts rapping about what bitches
black women were an improvement. Before she could say so,
the phone rang. Tina went to answer it.

Blanche followed her. "If it's Stu again, tell him I can't
come to the phone. No. Tell him I don't want to talk to him."
Why the hell should she lie? Tina gave her a questioning look.
Blanche went back to the kitchen and parcelled out the dish
washing chores to the children, then carried a glass of iced tea
out on the front porch.

Tina joined her. "It was him."

Blanche could feel Tina waiting for her to explain. When
she didn't, Tina told her Stu had left a message.

"I'll tell you what the message is just as soon as you tell me
who Stu is and what's going on. It's only fair. You know all
about me and Durant."

Blanche had to laugh. Why had she slipped into treating
Tina as though she were an older teen mother's helper instead of a grown woman? Did this happen automatically when
you hired someone to do something basic for you that you
turned them into someone not to be taken as seriously as
yourself? She told Tina the story of her brief connection with
Stu.

"He sounds like a real dickbrain," Tina announced with
the absolute certainty of an uninvolved party, which was not

to say that Blanche didn't agree with her. "I mean, what kind of person disses your living? It's stupid! God! Men!" She paused. "He's sorry, though. Know what he told me to tell you? He said, 'Tell her she can't possibly think worse of me than I do of myself and I'm going to keep calling until she gives me a chance to tell her so in person.' Kinda sweet, really, don't you think?"

"Yeah," Blanche replied. "For a dickbrain."

Blanche went inside and poured herself another glass of tea. In her mind, she played out a scene in which Stu told her he hadn't been able to sleep at all, he felt so bad for dissing her. What bullshit! He likely didn't mind if she went away mad, as long as she kept her mouth shut. He had a friendly relationship with Christine and David that went back to child-hood. He probably just wanted to keep her quiet, to keep her from telling Christine and David that he'd acted like a fool.

She left Tina a note on the kitchen table with marching orders for the children and headed across the lawn toward Faith's cottage. The grass was cool and tickled her ankles. Stu stepped out from behind a tree. Blanche walked right up to him, looked him in the eye and folded her arms across her chest. "Well?" It didn't appear to be what he expected. He sputtered and cleared his throat three or four times before he could get it together to speak:

"I don't expect you to ever forgive me for my rudeness and stupidity, but I am very sorry, sorrier than I can say. I acted like an ass." He gave her a bad-boy-in-remission look she was sure had gotten him over a hundred times before.

"What do you want?" she asked him as though he were a salesman at her front door.

"To start over again. To pretend last night never hap-pened."

She glared at him, struggling to keep her internal war out of sight. A part of her not only wanted but somehow needed to forgive him, to wipe out at least this one rejection by another black person. Another part of her was still suspicious of his motive in coming on to her in the first place. In yet another quarter his apology just added insult to injury and would never be acceptable. Other emotions, not quite so clear, made such a loud noise in her head, she knew she was about to lose it and show her natural ass.

"I gotta go." She walked around him and hurried back to the peace of the Crowley cottage, forgetting all about going to Faith's. In the distance she could see Durant and Tina throwing a Frisbee with the kids. When she reached the cottage she went straight to the bathroom, out of habit: It was where she always went for privacy from the children at home. She locked the door and perched on the edge of the tub. She concentrated on slowing her breathing. Don't think about anything, just breathe, just forget, stop thinking about him for a minute, just . . . She nearly fell over backwards into the tub when she felt, more than heard, him step up on the porch. He knocked, waited, knocked again.

"Blanche! I know you're in there. I'm not leaving until you come out."

"Shit!" She was too old for this mess. She looked at herself in the mirror and was reassured that she at least still looked like herself. She smoothed her hair, straightened her dress and went to the front door. Only the screen door was closed. She stared at him through it.

"Didn't you ever make a mistake?" he demanded to know. "Didn't you ever have a dumb reaction to something unexpected?"

Blanche opened the screen door and stepped out on the porch. Stu went on talking.

"I know we can't really pretend it never happened. And it's probably not the last mistake I'll make. But I really like you, Blanche, the way you handle yourself, the way you walk and look. Can't we be . . . can't we hang out together a little bit while you're here?"

Blanche searched his eyes and face for that unacceptable something else he wanted that a part of her insisted was there. She didn't find it.

"I'll think about it," she told him at last.

Stu grinned. "Fair enough. I'll call you tomorrow. OK?" He grinned again and waved from the walkway.

Blanche went inside and called Ardell.

"Hummm. I got to admit he don't seem like the man I hoped he was, but I like the way the boy apologizes. Anyway, he can't help how he was raised."

"Maybe not," Blanche told her. "But I bet there ain't a hell of a lot else he's still doin' 'cause his mama told him to."

Ardell sucked her teeth. "You are one hard sister! You only going to be there another week or so. Sunset walks on the beach, candlelight dinners with a good-looking man with reason to be extra-nice. Enjoy, girlfriend. You ain't signing on for life. You know how to play him."

"Well, I'll see. I just wanted to let you know that the catch wasn't just in my imagination."

When Ardell had agreed that Blanche had been right, Blanche moved on to tell her about going to Faith's with Mattie. "I had to help her, Ardell. On account of what Madame Rosa said, for one thing." Blanche explained, anticipating Ardell's attitude.

"Unh-hunh. And if Madame Rosa wasn't the reason why you had to stick your nose in other people's business, you woulda found some other reason, like the phase of the moon or the day of the year, maybe."

"Ain't nothin' wrong with bein' interested in people," Blanche told her. "Sure ain't no better way to learn what not to do in life. And you don't exactly hang up the phone when I start telling you what's happening up here."

"Hummm. You just watch your back, Blanche, you ain't exactly among friends, you know." Ardell hesitated a beat or two before asking, "You think maybe Mattie knows what she's talking about?"

Blanche grinned. She might not know much, but she knew her Ardell. "I don't think so. Now, if I was to get real bad cancer or something else that's killing me fast, I maybe wouldn't mind strapping on some dynamite and paying a visit to the Grand Dragon or one of them other crazy-ass crackers.

So, I can see how Hank could kill Faith, I just don't see no proof Carol had anything to do with it. The police and everybody but Mattie thinks Faith had an accident," Blanche told her. "But I saw Hank's note. He said he killed Faith."

"Hummm. That's got to count for something, don't it?"

"Not with Mattie. There's no question her in mind. She's positive Carol did it and Hank covered for her in his suicide note."

"Damn, girl! That's deep!"

"Ain't it?" And there's more. She told Ardell about the box in the windup toy, but not about her plans to go get it later on—no sense plucking on Ardell's last nerve, "From the sound of that box when we shook it, I'm bettin' more folks than Hank and Carol got reason to be glad Faith's not around."

"Hummm. Like I said, Blanche. You best be careful. You remember the last time you got mixed up in this kinda mess."

Blanche sucked her teeth and rolled her eyes to the ceiling. "This ain't nothing like that, Ardell. Here, I'm just doing what Madame Rosa said I'm supposed to do. I ain't really involved."

"Hummm. That's what you think," Ardell told her. "You just do like I say and be careful. And keep me posted," she added with a laugh.

Blanche felt better when she got off the phone. She whistled a little while she altered the note she left to tell the children to put themselves to bed at the usual time without making Tina's life a misery. She called Mattie and told her she was on her way to Faith's to get the box.

It took her a few seconds to unlock Faith's door. Her fingers were clumsy with thoughts of Stu and Ardell. It was darker inside the cottage than it was outside. She finally found the light and headed down the hall toward Faith's room when it registered that one of the shadows she'd passed was not a chair or a lamp. She turned toward the living room. The light went out. As she opened her mouth to shout. She didn't so much feel the blow as she heard the sound it made as her skull was jarred. The sound echoed through her body and loosened her joints. Her knees and ankles and back turned to gravy.

Chapter Ten

~

Mattie was a *café con leche* moon hanging full over Blanche's head. Blanche smiled or thought she smiled. Maybe the smile was on the inside of her face. Mattie didn't look like she was being smiled at.

"Thank God! I was just about to call Sinclair. No! Don't try to get up! I'll get you some water, some . . . just lie there a moment."

"There" was Faith's living room floor, and this was one of those rare occasions when Blanche was delighted to do as she was told. She wasn't sure she could get up if she wanted to. Her body felt more like an idea than anything over which she had control. When Mattie came back, Blanche propped herself up on her right elbow. She felt like she'd been riding a merry-go-round on the fast track. How did she get here? Oh yeah, the shadow. She sat up to a headache that began high on her forehead and pierced deep inside her brain. She gently touched the front of her head. There was a large, hot lump, like a small, taut, water-filled balloon attached to the front of her head, but there was no blood. Mattie handed her a glass of water. Blanche's hand shook so badly she spilled part of it but managed eventually to get it to her lips.

"I think you need to see Sinclair. I'm going to call him this minute."

Blanche tried to shake her head but her headache put a stop to that. "No, Mattie. I don't need a doctor. I need some ice."

Mattie hesitated, eyeing the phone. Blanche understood Mattie's impulse to call a doctor immediately: Mattie'd always had the luxury of help—doctors, nannies, lawyers, housemaids, while Blanche needed to be sure it was necessary to pay a doctor when some ice and rest would be enough.

"Come on, now. We've both treated enough knocked heads to know I'm all right. Get me some ice."

Mattie opened her mouth as if to protest, but didn't. "All right. Then I'll call Sinclair."

"Bring a flashlight, too." Blanche called after her.

Mattie brought ice in a dish towel and a small, black flashlight. Blanche applied the ice to her forehead.

"Why'd you come looking for me?"

Mattie sat on the coffee table close to Blanche. "I got tired of waiting. I called the Crowleys'. No answer, so I came here." She flashed the light in Blanche's eyes. "Yes, both pupils contracted. Did you see him, Blanche?"

"No."

Mattie looked around the room. "I wonder if he took anything, or if you frightened him before he could steal? I'll call Arthur. One of those private security people should be on the premises until Faith's cottage is secured. The word is obviously out that it's unoccupied."

It took Blanche a little while to understand that Mattie thought Blanche had interrupted a burglar. That wasn't Blanche's guess. Of course, Mattie was one of the owners, like the sort of people she worked for. They were always expecting someone to steal their stuff, as though they understood they

shouldn't have so much more than other people. At least
Mattie didn't suggest calling the police. They agreed about
that.

"What about the box?"

"Of course. I should have thought of that!"

"Close the curtains first," Blanche told her. She pulled
herself up from the floor and into an armchair. Mattie went
down the hall.

"Good God!" Mattie came hurrying back to the living
room. "Someone's been in there!"

Blanche eased slowly down the hall, careful not to aggra-
vate her headache. The bathroom door was open. From the
breeze blowing from the bathroom, it was likely that whoever
had broken in had used the bathroom window.

Faith's bedroom looked as if someone had picked it up and
shook it. The blanket and sheets were jumbled together like
unfolded wash. One pillow hung over the side of the bed. The
nightstands' drawers were ajar. The closet door was wide
open. Dresses lay on the floor. The book basket had been
knocked on its side. *House and Garden, Home Beautiful,* and a
Laura Taylor catalog spilled across the floor.

Mattie righted the basket. The metal box was still lodged
firmly inside. Blanche grinned and offered Mattie some skin.
Mattie hesitated, then shook Blanche's hand, instead.
Blanche stifled her chuckle and thought again about spotting
Mattie points.

"I hope he didn't do all of this while I was conked out in
the hall."

"What if you'd come to? He might have . . . !"

"Exactly." Anger began to roll in Blanche's stomach. Some
motherless fucker had hit her. Hit her! And could have killed
her! This wasn't the first time she'd been attacked. She'd been
raped and mugged. She was too familiar with the feeling of
separation from herself that came with having been rendered
defenseless, but she wasn't taking responsibility for shit that
wasn't her fault. Rage was beginning to burn holes in her
belly.

"We keep saying 'he,' Mattie pointed out. "Why?"

Blanche closed her eyes and remembered the loud intake of breath that had accompanied the loud thump from inside her head. She'd turned her head and there had been the breath and a shape. Was the face covered?

"You're right. It could have been a woman. I didn't see enough to tell. The light went out just before I was hit."

"You rest, my dear." Mattie set the metal box in Blanche's lap. "I'll take a quick look around for the key and if I can't find it, we'll take the box and blast it open if we have to."

"Are you sure there's no small key on her key chain in her handbag? Let me see."

Mattie fetched Faith's handbag from the floor where it lay in the closet with its contents scattered about. She looked at the key ring, then put it and the rest of Faith's things back in the bag and handed it to Blanche. "I'll check all of her pockets," Mattie said.

Blanche set her ice pack on the floor and the metal box on the hassock. She turned Faith's handbag upside down and dumped the contents into her lap: compact, wallet, change purse, pill box, lipstick tube, tin of Altoids Peppermints and a leather-covered notebook with attached pen. She examined them all, opening, probing, shaking. She took up the bag itself. A good bag, a Carrie Henson, glove leather, lined with heavy canvaslike material. There were two inside zipper compartments. In the upper one Blanche found a Band-Aid; a pack of matches from the Occidental Grill in D.C. and a couple of safety pins. In the lower one was a folding toothbrush, a very small tube of toothpaste, a container of dental floss and a couple of safety pins. Blanche scooped out the contents and examined the toothbrush case and the dental floss. She checked the bag to make sure she hadn't overlooked anything. There was a safety pin still in the top zipper compartment. When she looked closer, she could see it was pinned to the lining in the bottom of the compartment. She lifted the handbag and shook it. Something that sounded like a small pebble bounced against the side of the bag, but

Blanche could see nothing inside but the safety pin. She reached in and unfastened it from the lining. The pin both held together the edges of a hole in the lining and had a piece of strong brown string attached to it.

"Mattie?"

"Yes?" Mattie hurried to Blanche's side.

Blanche slowly pulled the pin and the attached string up out of the bag. Mattie gasped when the other end of the string appeared with a small, sturdy key attached to it. She clapped her hands and laughed. "My dear, you are damned clever!"

Mattie picked up the box and sat on the hassock facing Blanche. She cradled the box protectively on her lap and held out her hand to Blanche for the key.

The peppery smell of old paper rose from the box. There were a number of folded sheets and a small book inside. Mattie's gnarled hand shook as she lifted a piece of paper and unfolded it. It had the slick surface of cheap copier paper. Mattie said it was a letter from the African-American Heritage and History Society addressed to Veronica. She read it aloud.

"Dear Mrs. Tatterson:

This is in response to your inquiry regarding your ancestors, the brothers, known as Moses and Cyrano, documented to have been the property of Gardner Hancock in 1702. As you indicated in your letter, Cyrano and Moses were both on the Hancock Plantation at the time a major slave revolt was planned which would have likely involved hundreds of slaves on at least ten major plantations in the eastern South Carolina area.

Our records, unfortunately, do not show why these two brothers were kept together when most kidnapped Africans were separated from their captured kin at the time of sale.

While our data indicate that your research is accurate about many of the events that took place around this aborted revolt, there is one discrepancy. It was your great-great-great-uncle Cyrano, who was alleged to be the major planner and organizer of the planned revolt. His brother, whom you identify as your great-great-grandfather Moses, is reported to have told Gardner Hancock, the plantation owner, about the planned revolt. Cyrano and his collaborators are reported to have been skinned alive and left to die in the slaves' quarters as a lesson to other such plotters. Our records further indicate that Moses was rewarded for his loyalty by being given his freedom and safe passage to Nova Scotia.

If we can be of further service, please call upon us.

Sincerely yours,

Rushell Harris

Rushell Harris
Director"

They both screamed with laughter.

"So that's why she suddenly stopped boring us to death about the book she was writing about her family of noble black savages and upper-crust white colonialists!"

The next piece of paper killed the laughter in Mattie's throat. She seemed to tremble with excitement. She looked like a child at Christmas. "This is it!" She handed the paper to Blanche. There was a picture in the right-hand corner and an array of fingerprints across from it. There were three columns beneath the picture and prints: Date, Charge, Outcome. There were three dates and three crimes, or rather, one crime—prostitution—repeated three times. The first two incidents, on July 27, 1972, and April 17, 1974, each had a two hundred dollar fine and a year's probation listed in the Outcome column. The final entry ended in an eighteen-month sentence. The name on the sheet, Lena Guy, was unfamiliar, but the picture was not. It made Carol look hard and old—not in years, but in worldliness. Her hair was blond; it made her face look dirty.

Mattie's eyes glittered in triumph. Blanche took the paper from her and examined the picture more closely. It was Carol all right. Busted in Seattle. Blanche chuckled to herself. Carol had said she'd known a lot of powerful people. Blanche hoped that meant she'd been working the high end of the john pool, if there was a high end.

"Hank once told me they had no secrets from each other," Mattie said. "I wonder if Carol's disclosure was a full one. Hank was very straightlaced in some ways."

Blanche remembered the conversation she'd heard between Carol and Hank. "Now that I come to think of it, of course he knew, or at least he talked as if he knew." She finally told Mattie what she remembered of Carol and Hank's conversation.

"Why didn't you tell me this before? It all falls into place. Carol wanted to get this back from Faith. She came here and . . ."

"Mattie, hold on. Being a prostitute don't make you a murderer. That's exactly why I didn't tell you, because I knew you'd jump to conclusions. Let's see what else is in the box before you call Hank's wife a murderer."

Mattie stiffened. Her eyes flashed for a moment, but once again, she held her tongue. She unfolded another piece of paper, also a reproduction on slick copy paper. "Well, well, well," she said.

Blanche held out her hand. It was a birth certificate on a Commonwealth of Pennsylvania form dated May 17, 1989. It said that a female child named Artura Hill-Martinez had been born to Maria Elena Martinez. Written on the line entitled, Name of Father, was Arthur Hill.

"Arthur has gone up in my estimation. I wouldn't have thought he had the initiative." Mattie was clearly amused.

"Who is she? Do you know that name?"

"Not exactly, but it sounds . . . What was the date again?"

Mattie thought for a while. "The child would have been conceived about July or August of the year before. I was on tour that spring. Carol and Hank joined me in San Francisco.

We went up to Ventana, at Big Sur, then came up here in late July." Mattie sat silently, with her eyes closed.

"Now let me see. Oh, yes. That was the year Clothilde—she's Arthur's wife—was in Atlanta looking after her mother. Broken hip, as I recall. Their children were at camp and Arthur was here on his own, something he hates and does not manage terribly well, as you may have noticed. At any rate . . ." Mattie's face took on the satisfied look of someone who's had a good belch after a good meal. "Of course! Maria! One of the maids. Lovely girl, damned lovely. Like a fawn. Only worked here that one summer." She gave Blanche a look that was as seriously sad as it was amused. "Arthur must be half-crazed knowing Faith had this. It would ruin him."

Blanche gave Mattie a skeptical look. "Only people I ever knew to be ruined by an unplanned child were women who birthed them."

Mattie shook her head. "You don't understand. Clothilde's a Coghill. Her family built Amber Cove. It's hers and she is not the sort of woman who could forgive this level of betrayal." Mattie stared down at the birth certificate and then up at Blanche.

"I wonder if he loved her," Mattie said.

Blanche sucked her teeth. "I wonder if he pays child support," she replied. Did he love her indeed! Didn't Mattie say it was men who were romantic?

Blanche lifted the book from the box. It had a hard, marbled gray cover bound by a black leather spine. It was slim and about the length and width of a small diary. The title was spelled out in simple red letters set in a rectangle of white with a black border. *Lovers,* by R. B. R. Lynch. Blanche opened the cover. Beneath a tissue paper sheet was a black and white drawing on heavy, stiff, cream paper. It was of two men inclined together on a chaise lounge, their arms and legs wrapped around each other. Beneath it was a scrawled inscription in thick, black ink:

"MDT, I'll never forget you. Or us." The initials, RBRL, and May 1991, were written beneath the initials.

Blanche handed the book to Mattie. "Did you know about this?"

Mattie's eyes widened. "Ah." She nodded her head in a confirming way. "There was talk when he was younger. Veronica has a brother, you see. Some people thought he and Martin . . . It all died down when Martin and Veronica married and had children." She laughed with self-deprecation. "I suppose we were naive to assume that one apparent sexual preference precluded any other."

"Does Veronica know?" Blanche asked.

"If she does, she doesn't. It's not real to her if it's not public, if it isn't affecting her public persona."

Blanche thought about Martin's children. Would they have been better off if Martin had come out, left Veronica, maybe? Would Veronica be better off? And who was to say whether Veronica knew or not? When Blanche was growing up, all the black folks in Farleigh had known that Mrs. Carter had a more intimate relationship with her roomer, Charlotte Moore, than that of landlady. Everybody, including Mr. Carter, who'd been heard to remark that he was getting tired of sleeping in that cold little back room of theirs. Maybe if Martin had got it together, he and Veronica could have had a real old-fashioned Carter kind of marriage, although Martin had better not bring home no dark-skinned honey, the way Mrs. Carter did!

"What else is in there?" Blanche wanted to know.

Mattie lifted the remaining plain white envelope from the box. It held a small, ragged newspaper clipping. At the top, in faint pencil were the words Philadelphia Daily News. The date was 21 June 1978:

Mary Lacy, aged nine, of Upper Darby was fatally struck by a hit-and-run driver near the intersection of Kelsey Road and Pier Way. Witnesses report seeing a dark blue sedan in the area of the accident. Police are seeking

The bottom edge was ragged and the rest of the article was missing. Mattie passed it to Blanche who read it and passed it back.

"No ideas on this one," Mattie said. "Could be anyone. And what's this?" A gold bracelet or anklet made like an identity bracelet glowed in the corner of the box. Blanche picked it up by one end of its chain and let it twirl in the light from the nearby lamp. The name tag was gold filigree, as delicate as lace. The name plaque was a thin, slightly curved, oval wafer of thinnest gold held in place by the lacy filigree. The gold glowed like trapped sunlight.

Mattie leaned forward and examined it. "Exquisite! I wonder who it belongs to?"

Blanche held the name plaque to the light and read the inscription out loud: You are my Sun and my Moon. May our love last forever. July 17, 1974.

There were no initials or names. Mattie took it and draped it across her palm before putting it on the arm of the chair.

"How'd Faith get this stuff?" Blanche asked.

"I wondered about that. You know, every year, one guest or another complains about their cottage having been broken into. Even me. Nothing missing that I could find. Years ago, some village boys were seen running from the place, so we always assumed it was them. As long as nothing was stolen and it wasn't a regular thing . . . Now I wonder. If Faith did steal some of these things, people might be reluctant to mention it." Mattie pointed at the folded papers in the box. "Those are all copies. She could have taken the originals, copied them and put them back."

"Why would Arthur have this child's birth certificate lying around for someone to steal?" Blanche wanted to know. "And what about Carol's rap sheet? You think she had that laying on the coffee table or even in an unlocked drawer? Faith may have stolen some of this stuff but not all of it."

"You mean a detective?" Mattie's voice made it clear she didn't want to believe it, but couldn't avoid the possibility.

Her mouth drew down at the corners. "Awful, awful creature," she muttered.

Blanche looked at each of the items again, then handed them to Mattie who also examined each one, before putting them back in the box. Blanche felt as though she were taking part in a ceremony.

"Arthur Hill!" Mattie hooted. "And poor Veronica! She must have been mortified by that letter. Of course, that's nothing compared to how she'd feel if she knew about Martin's love affair."

"Any one of them could have hit me," Blanche said. "Anybody except Carol."

Mattie was silent for a long time before she said: "No. Carol certainly couldn't have done that. But I now know why Hank lied for Carol."

Blanche gave her a get-real kind of look.

"He did lie, he did! I know it, Blanche. Hank simply couldn't have killed Faith. It just wasn't in him."

Blanche knew there was more to be said on this issue, but she couldn't think. Her body seemed to be sinking into the ground and dragging her mind with it.

"You've overdone." Mattie handed Blanche her walking stick. "Here, lean on this. I only carry it as a weapon."

"Don't make me laugh Mattie, it makes my head throb."

Mattie picked up the box, locked it and tucked it under her arm. "I have a safe," she said.

Blanche hesitated when she stepped out of Faith's cottage. She looked carefully around, conscious of a slight vibration in the air, as though someone had just passed by, was still nearby. There was no movement, except the leaves high in the trees. She stepped off the porch. Her uneasiness dissolved as they moved farther away from Faith's cottage. Blanche walked Mattie to her cottage, just beyond the Crowleys'. Mattie insisted she come inside for a moment. "You look quite done in." She left Blanche sitting in the living room and returned without the box. "What can I get you? I haven't a thing for a headache. I never get them. You shouldn't take any alcohol."

Blanche asked for water. Mattie brought her a glass with ice. "Here. Take this with you." She handed Blanche the heavy crockery bowl that had held their morning hoe cake. "And use it to bop anything that moves out there!"

"Mattie, didn't I tell you not to make me laugh? The shape I'm in I sure hope there's nobody out there. I'm lucky to be keeping my feet on the ground instead of my behind!" She saluted Mattie with the bowl and left. She could feel Mattie watching from her porch. Mattie called good night when Blanche reached the Crowleys' porch.

Durant and Tina were building up bad vibes on the porch. Blanche said good night to them and blew each of the children a kiss from the doorway of their rooms. Once guilt sharp as a knife would have pierced her because she hadn't been home to see the children to bed, but she'd been a parent long enough now to know that if this was the worst thing she ever did to them, she'd be a perfect mother. Anyway, it gave the children something to complain about. They needed to understand she wasn't perfect, either. She gulped down three extra-strength Tylenol and slid into bed. The memory of her attack threatened to keep her awake, but her body had other ideas. She tumbled into a deep and untroubled sleep.

Chapter Eleven

∽

Blanche reached out and answered the phone ringing at her bedside. Without opening her eyes or sitting up, and before Ardell could say, "Hello," she blurted out the story about the lump on her forehead.

"What?! Blanche, grab the kids and get your ass out of there!" Ardell's voice got so loud Blanche had to hold the receiver away from her ear. She sat up and leaned against the headboard.

"What should I do with Deirdre and Casey? Lock 'em in the house until their parents come back? It's the box, Ardell. It's not me somebody wanted to hurt. I just showed up at Faith's at the wrong time. I coulda been anybody." She was amazed by how calm and reasonable she sounded. Ardell was neither impressed nor fooled.

"Whoever bashed you over the head has a funny way of not meaning you no harm! And don't tell me you ain't mad about it, 'cause I can hear it in your voice. You wouldn't leave now if you could, not 'til you find out who bashed you. I know you, girl!"

"Ardell, did I say anything about not being mad? All I was trying to say is that it ain't me, personally, that somebody wants to get at."

"Then tell Mattie to do her own dirty work, or do like Faith and hire somebody." She paused. "Aw shit. I forgot about the Madame Rosa thing. Maybe you should call her. See if you can get an update on whether what you supposed to do there is worth endangering your life."

Blanche didn't answer.

"I think maybe Mattie's right!" Ardell told her. "There is some murdering asshole running around up there and you look to be right in his path." Ardell stopped. Blanche could hear her breathing; she waited for it to slow down a bit before she spoke.

"I'm doin' just what you'd do in my place, Ardell. Now that I know this business is likely to include being knocked out, believe me, I will be more careful. I ain't concerned about nobody breaking in here, cause I don't have what he's looking for."

"But you seen it, didn't you? Maybe he don't want nobody else to know about it."

Blanche had no answer for that and didn't try to find one.

"Hummm. I see you ain't gon' pay me no mind, as usual. At least I hope you have some fun before you die. You talk to that pretty man, yet?"

Blanche remembered that Stu was supposed to call her yesterday. She couldn't swear he hadn't because she hadn't been around. Ardell was confident he would call and reminded Blanche once more to keep her posted.

There was a phone message for Blanche tacked to the refrigerator: Stu had called three times. Tina came in the kitchen.

"You should have heard the relief in his voice when I told him you were really out, not just refusing to talk to him. I think he likes you a lot. Maybe you should forgive him."

Blanche laughed at how much Tina sounded like Ardell. She'd already decided to forgive Stu, or at least lay aside his first fuck-up because it was fun being sought after. But that's all. They weren't building a relationship, they were carrying out a short-term flirtation. She wondered who she was reacquainting with that fact, since neither Tina nor Ardell could hear her.

Her headache was a vague memory but the bump at her hairline was tender and obvious. "Wow!" was Tina's first response. Blanche made up a story about a run-in with the medicine cabinet in the dark and hurried on to ask Tina if she needed any help with her cake and coffee get-together with Veronica.

"Durant says she's really looking forward to it, which shows you how easily he can be lied to."

"Maybe she is," Blanche started breakfast. She could hear the children bouncing around in their rooms. "Maybe she means something different by that than you mean." Blanche could tell from Tina's expression that she didn't get it. At least not yet.

"Durant's going to take us for a ride this afternoon," Malik announced immediately after "Good morning."

"He has a convertible," Deirdre and Taifa said in unison.

"I haven't been in a car since we got here!" Casey added.

When Stu called again, Blanche was braiding Taifa's hair, but talked to him anyway. He invited her to lunch at the seafood place in the village. She accepted.

She had coffee with Mattie first.

"What I would like to know," Blanche responded, "is who hit me over the head. Carol's in the hospital a long way from here. She wasn't the fool who knocked me out."

Mattie took another tack: "Maybe what happened to Faith and you getting hit on the head don't have anything to do with each other. Anyone with something in the box wants it back. As you said, any one of them could have hit you, but it doesn't mean that person killed Faith, that's what matters, and we know why poor Carol killed Faith."

Blanche ignored her. "I been thinking about all the folks we know who have belongings in that box. Everyone of them, except Carol, has already tried to find the box once without hitting me on the head. The day after Faith died, I saw Martin slinking around Faith's cottage. Arthur was at Faith's waiting for us the first time we went to the cottage, remember? When I went through Faith's drawers, I was surprised how jumbled a couple of them were. Maybe we weren't the first to go through her things. Then Veronica showed up and tries to get you to let her stay behind. Of course, it could have been one of them giving it a second try, but I don't think so. I got a feeling it's the unknown person who hit me."

Mattie tossed her head impatiently. "But who could they be? Practically everyone here is implicated already."

"Not everybody. Just you Insiders. What about the so-called Outsiders? Faith messed with them, too." Blanche paused to make sure she had Mattie's full attention. "Maybe she had an even nastier surprise for one of them. Or one of the help. I want to know who hit me. I got a right." Blanche hoped she wasn't going to have to come right out and remind her that she wouldn't have been in Faith's cottage if she hadn't been trying to help Mattie. She attributed Mattie's attitude to her being consumed with Hank, but that didn't help Blanche like it any better.

"Yes, of course you have a right." Mattie didn't look happy, but she didn't argue. "Very well. I have a journalist friend who should be able to find out if there was anything more to the hit and run story, although I doubt anyone here would do such a thing."

"I want to take another look at that anklet," Blanche told her.

Mattie went off to another room and returned with the box, opened it and handed it to Blanche. Blanche took out the anklet and held it close to her eyes, examining the back of the plaque and the clasp. "You got a magnifying glass?"

"At my age?" Mattie snorted. "I could probably supply a small city." She opened a drawer and handed Blanche one.

"What are you looking for?"

Blanche held the anklet under the glass. "There it is!" She

looked up at Mattie. "Mr. Adamson, a jeweler I worked for in New York, told me some jewelers put their trademark or some kind of number on all their jewelry so they always got record of who bought it and for how much."

Mattie leaned over the glass. "There's one on there?"

"There's something on the back of the clasp, but I can't quite make it out." Blanche handed the glass and anklet to Mattie. "See it? I'm going to call him right now."

"Why?"

"Maybe he can tell from that number or design or whatever it is where this came from and who bought it. It's a good piece of jewelry. Eighteen carat."

"How do you know?" Mattie sounded as if she didn't believe Blanche did know.

"Mr. Adamson, of course. See how deep the color is, and you can tell that it wouldn't take much to bend it. Eighteen carat gold is soft like this."

Mattie waved her to the phone.

Mr. Adamson was still listed on the Upper East Side. He was, by his own account, delighted to hear from Blanche and to help her. She didn't tell him why she needed the information and he didn't ask. He told her she could send the piece to him and he'd return it quickly. "Don't hold out too much hope. Some of the bigger jewelers' codes are well known. If it's one of them I'll be able to help, but otherwise . . ."

Mattie produced a small box and an overnight mail service envelope and form for the anklet. "The driver comes directly to my cottage. I receive a great deal of mail and send a great deal as well. Hank always makes sure I have . . ." A quick flash of pain distorted her face for half a second. She took the package to a basket by the front door.

"Now it's your turn," Blanche handed Mattie the phone and the article from Faith's box. She watched and listened while Mattie phoned her newspaper friend and asked for his help. She only had a few days left at Amber Cove. She wanted to find out who hit her before it was time to leave.

Blanche left her and took the path to the village. She waved to Stu heading toward her.

"What happened?"

Blanche had forgotten about the knot on her forehead until she saw Stu's anxious stare. She told him the medicine cabinet story. She wanted to tell him the truth. She wanted to tell him what she and Mattie were up to and ask his advice; he'd known these people all of his life. But that was part of the reason she held her tongue. Stu asked her about Carol.

"Mattie's told everyone to hold off on the memorial service a little while longer, to see if Carol improves, poor thing. Mattie's not in such great shape herself."

Stu shook his head. "Sad, really. But in a way he was lucky. To have two women who loved him so much. I wouldn't mind that. But I'd happily settle for one."

Blanche looked away. She knew that line of conversation wasn't going to take her anywhere she wanted to go with this man.

"Did you play with Hank when you were kids?"

Stu slowed his steps. "My dad was his godfather, you know that. He was at our house a lot in the summers. Dad used to call him his 'Little Brown Bomber.' Dad was real light, like me."

"Were you surprised when he committed suicide?"

Stu shook his head. "This wasn't the first time he tried. He just didn't succeed before."

"You didn't like him," Blanche stated, rather than asked.

"You met him. What was there to like? He had the personality of a cardboard box. I never understood what everybody saw in the guy. One thing we had in common, that's how I'd do it too, if I were going to commit suicide. Right out to sea."

"Why do you think he did it?"

Stu shrugged. "Too sensitive for his own good. Too inward, maybe. People like that get easily bruised. Especially men. Both his parents died within months of each other, about four years ago. That probably didn't help."

"Both of them? I thought Mattie said his father died recently."

Stu stopped and turned to her. "She told you that?"

Blanche was no longer so sure. Mattie had told her so many things. "I'm probably mixing him up with someone else."

Stu started walking once again. Blanche got the impression he was deep in thought. She didn't interrupt.

They ate lunch at a wooden table on a pier not too far from his shop. She could hear the waves sucking at the piles as though they were lollipops. Blanche loved the taste of the lobster just cooked in sea water, but was not so delighted to learn the restaurant was part of the lobster pound. The idea of hundreds and hundreds of lobsters being held in pens beneath her, waiting to be sold in the winter when the price was higher reminded her of prisoners waiting to be executed. If she let her mind linger there too long, she knew she'd never be able to enjoy another lobster. Large gulls wheeled over a fishing boat headed toward shore. She breathed in the smell of brine and freshly caught fish and marvelled at the beauty of the sea and the cliffs far to her right, gray and glistening like fortress walls.

"It must have been wonderful growing up here, seeing this every day of your life."

"Not every day. I was sent to boarding school through high school, so I only got to spend my summers here after the age of six, although I begged to go to the local school. My dad wouldn't even consider it." Stu paused and looked out to sea. "I think it's the most beautiful place I've ever seen." Emotion deepened his voice. "I ached to come back here to live. Dad wanted me to be a doctor. I always wanted the shop. At school, I'd put myself to sleep at night pretending to be measuring out pills and giving elderly ladies advice about how and when to take them. I memorized the placement of every jar on the two back shelves." He shrugged. "Of course, nowhere's perfect. The winters get lonely. Sometimes I drive down to Portland just to walk around among black people.

That surprises you," he told her in response, she was sure, to the look on her face.

"Yeah, I guess it does."

Stu waited for her to go on.

"I'm surprised because I didn't think someone who looks like you and went to boarding school would necessarily want to hang with everyday black people," she said.

He took her hand. "Don't confuse me with the light-skinned creeps you've known, Blanche. OK, I messed up about the work thing. But that doesn't necessarily make me an Oreo." He grinned at her. "Or maybe you think vanilla wafer is a better comparison?"

Blanche had to laugh but she wasn't ready to let him off the hook. "Well, you can see how I'd come to the conclusion that you weren't the type of person who'd want to hang out with people who make their living doing things not too different from what I do."

She watched Stu's eyes go from teasing to somber. He leaned further back in his chair. "Yeah, I can see how you might think that." He looked directly into her eyes. "But here I am. Maybe my instincts work better than my brain sometimes."

Yes, there was definitely more to this man than showed on the surface. Something you, of all people, should have suspected, she chided herself. She looked down at his pale hand lying close to hers. "What would your people say if they saw us sitting like this?" she nodded at their hands lying side by side.

"You mean my family?" Blanche nodded and Stu went on. "Mixed reviews. My mother would be accepting but pained, since no woman could possibly be good enough for her one and only bouncing boy." He grinned. "My dad would be delighted. He was into Garvey, you know. Loved everything black—including my mother. She was about your complexion, maybe darker.

"I once brought an Asian woman friend home. I thought

Dad's teeth would fall out. He made it very clear what would happen to my inheritance and relationship with him if I dared think of marrying outside the race."

Blanche was truly surprised. It was the last thing she'd expected. She wondered how much of a part color had played in Stu's parents' marriage.

"Color nearly tore our family apart," Stu said, as if answering her question—something that happened to her so often she was no longer surprised.

He looked out to sea, although Blanche doubted he was really seeing it. "My mother never really fit in with my father's family, or most of the folks at Amber Cove. She was just as smart and well-educated as any of them, and from as fine a family, too. But, well, she was just too dark for them."

Blanche smiled at the way he announced this, as though he could hardly believe his own words and was afraid she might not believe them either—which was pretty funny, given what she and his mama had in common.

"Dad was always making Mother go places they both knew she wasn't really comfortable or welcome—parties and dinners with the Amber Cove set, for instance. I never heard anyone say anything nasty directly to her, but I overheard plenty, the way children do. It's amazing the way adults act as though kids are too stupid to understand what's being said in front of them. A lot was said in front of me. As I got older, I began to wonder how much of it was being said on purpose. Certainly, the teasing I was getting about Mother's color from my playmates was based on what they were hearing at home. Maybe their parents didn't insult Mother to her face, but even I could hear the ring of phoniness in their voices when they told her how glad they were to see her. And at least once every summer, someone would make some remark about having been in the sun too long. All eyes would then automatically shift to Mother. I'm sure there were people who wanted badly to cut her more directly, but my Dad's family has always been big in this state."

"How did your parents deal with it?"

"Mother was miserable and Dad was always after her not to let stupid fools spoil her fun, as he put it. When I was very small, he constantly harangued her about it. Then, I guess he gave up. I wonder if Mother didn't give him an ultimatum of some kind, but who knows? She seemed happier once she stopped socializing and so did he. But she became more and more withdrawn over the years until she would hardly leave the house at all. Dad seemed to need other people more and more. He was hardly ever home evenings or weekends. When he was, he paced a lot."

Blanche listened to the feelings in his voice and heard a lonely boy whose parents were more involved with themselves than they were with him.

"And what about you?" Blanche asked.

Stu turned his head so that their eyes met. "Me?" he snorted. "I was just the shadow. You see, Dad was very disappointed that I didn't inherit Mother's coloring. It was as if he felt less black because he was light-skinned, you understand what I mean?"

Blanche nodded.

"All my life he was saying things like, 'Boy! Why don't you get some sun,' or, 'Boy, you don't have as much color as a vanilla shake!' "

And Hank was his Little Brown Bomber, even though he had hardly qualified as brown, Blanche thought. Another variation on the color fuck-up.

Stu stretched and smiled at her. "So that's my sad story, what about yours?

Blanche obliged with a quick version of growing up in a small, southern community of little or no means and the costs and benefits of that. "Nobody may have said anything to your mother, but plenty was said to me," she told him. "If I had a nickel for every time I've been called ink spot, coal bin or little black Sambo; or for the times a playmate's parent made it clear they didn't want anyone as black as me playing with their child, I'd have enough money to buy my own country, not that being comfortably off makes any difference, as you know from your own mother."

When she got to the part in her story where she decided to stick with domestic work instead of taking up nursing, like her now dead sister, or clerical work, or some other career, she expected some comment from Stu, but none came. He was obviously on his best behavior. "So, when my sister died, I became Taifa's and Malik's guardian," she told him.

"And what about marriage?" Stu wanted to know.

"Never has interested me all that much," Blanche told him and slammed the door on Leo in a cutaway jacket and spats.

"Too independent," he said without a bit of doubt.

"I could be a bit set in my ways," Blanche argued. "But that goes with the territory, don't it? You're single. You know what I'm talking about."

"Yeah, I'm single all right. Not that I expected to be at this age. I turned forty last year! By now I thought I'd have a family, a couple of kids. At least you've got that."

They'd finished their lobsters and were working on their second glasses of iced tea. Blanche looked at her watch. "I really enjoyed this," she told him. Once again, his eyes brimmed with pleasure.

"How about coming out on the boat with me tomorrow? She's a real beauty."

"Let me think about it," she told him. "I haven't spent much time with the children and so much has been happening around here. I just want to feel them out, make sure they're OK." Blanche was aware that he hadn't suggested bringing the children along.

"And what about your shop? Isn't Saturday a big day for you?"

Stu's mouth tightened. "There aren't any big days in the ye old prescriptions and ice cream business when there's a forty-flavor franchise down the way and a cut-rate pharmacy chain in the shopping center down the road." Stu knocked back the last of his tea. "Like they say, be careful about what you ask

for, you just might get it. I did and look at me—up to my butt
in debt and competition growing like Topsy. What the place
needs is a face lift, a gourmet coffee bar, maybe. But that's
another story."

When they parted, Blanche hurried back to the cottage.
She wanted to be comfortably settled near a window when
Veronica arrived. The tea things were already on the porch
when she reached the cottage and Tina was hovering over
them, as if she were afraid the sugar might escape. Veronica
arrived about ten minutes after Blanche.

"I thought we'd have tea out here on the porch." Tina
didn't ask Veronica what she thought about the idea. Blanche
chuckled to herself and admitted she didn't think Durant was
good enough for Tina. Too concerned about what his mama
thought to be mate to a strong, smart woman. Blanche
couldn't decide who was more nervous. Tina definitely
showed it most. Her voice had a serious tremble in it, and
Blanche could tell Tina was smiling too much. She'd regret it
later. Veronica was icy. It might have been on purpose but
Blanche thought it was tension, the same tension that made
her clear her throat again and again. They discussed the
weather, the beauty of the Maine Coast, the tastiness of Tina's
box cake and the uniqueness of Blanche's apple-spice iced
tea. But when Veronica said "Tina, my child," Blanche knew
the heavy stuff was about to begin. She leaned forward in her
chair.

"Tina, my dear, thank you so much for providing us with
this opportunity to talk to each other woman to woman, as it
were."

Blanche could feel Tina waiting for the punch line.

"My son tells me that he wishes to marry you."

Tina was silent.

"His father and I are very proud of Durant. He's going to
make a fine biochemist. But to do that, he needs to concen-
trate on his research before settling down and taking on the
respons . . ."

"Didn't he also tell you I don't plan to marry for at least five years?" Tina's voice was louder than it needed to be, but the tremble was gone.

Now Veronica was silent.

"Didn't he tell you that? Didn't he?"

"Well, yes, he did say . . ."

"Then what is it you really want? It's not to keep us from getting married too soon, because you already know that's not going to happen."

There was a long silence in which the waves on the beach were the loudest sound.

"All right. It's true. That isn't what I want." Veronica's voice had a sharp edge. "Frankly, we wonder if you and Durant are really suited to each other at all. We just don't want Durant, or you, to do anything foolish. Believe me, we have both your interests at heart."

Blanche wished she could step outside and pitch Veronica off the porch, and to think she'd had some sympathy for that cow. But Tina didn't really need Blanche's help.

"Please do me the courtesy of telling me why you think I'm unsuitable for Durant."

Blanche admired the question. It sure wasn't what Veronica expected and definitely not a question she'd want to answer.

"Well, you come from different backgrounds. You have different, er, ah, manners, ways of being in the world." Veronica's uneasiness made her voice go nasal.

"You mean I'm poor and black and he's rich and light-skinned? I don't think that's such a barrier. Don't worry, I won't make him poorer or blacker. As far as money is concerned, it'll be the other way around. And the black doesn't rub off, except on your future grandchildren, of course."

Veronica's intake of breath was sharp and loud.

Blanche had to clamp her hand over her mouth to keep from screaming with laughter. Damn! that girl had guts. She'd be a super-Diva by forty-five.

"How dare you . . ." Veronica began, but didn't get any further.

"How dare I what? Be more honest with you than you are with me?"

"I think perhaps I should leave."

Blanche heard the rustle of Veronica rising from her chair.

"Good idea. I'm sure you're eager to tell Durant about our little discussion about his future."

Blanche gave Veronica some time to get away from the cottage before she went outside. Tina was looking furious, frustrated and defeated all at the same time.

"I won't cry! I just won't!" she insisted as tears gathered in her eyes.

"Well I would," Blanche told her. "Best thing in the world for getting bad chemicals out of your body and a nice shower will get the last of that bitch off your body." Blanche put her hand on Tina's shoulder.

The young woman reached up and covered Blanche's hand with her own. Tears slipped down her cheeks. "Oh, Blanche! I meant to be nice! I tried to stay on subjects people don't fight over. I wasn't even going to mention Durant. He'd really convinced me to try to make her like me, see me as a person, not as her future dark-skinned daughter-in-law. How could I have been so stupid?"

So they are planning to marry, Blanche thought. Too bad. On this one thing, she totally agreed with Veronica.

"Love and sex, honey. Either one can make you do the damndest things. The two combined will make you a sure 'nough fool. And stop blaming yourself for Veronica's meanness. She came here to say her say. Wasn't too many other ways it could have ended. You won, girlfriend, trust me."

Tina tried to smile but didn't quite make it. "You know what really makes me mad? A part of me wants to believe people like her can be made to see how stupid it is to look down on other people."

Blanche patted Tina's shoulder. "Well, I got to admit that's right up there with believing in Santa Claus. Still, you were trying to do the right thing. Myself, I can't decide if you should get a medal or have your head examined. I am sure of two things: I wish I could have seen Veronica's face when you told her about those possible black grandbabies!"

Tina laughed with Blanche. Their laughter had more vinegar than sugar in it.

"What's the second thing?"

"The other thing I know is that Durant can't possibly deserve to have you in his life."

Tina grinned from ear to ear. But later Blanche had to convince Tina that she should join her and the children for dinner at the Big House. "What you hidin' from? She's the one ought to keep her head down."

"No. It's not her, it's Durant," Tina confessed. "I haven't had a chance to talk to him about what happened. When I do . . . well, I just don't want him to have to choose between me and his mother."

The quaver in her voice and the uncertain look on her face told Blanche that Tina wasn't at all sure which choice Durant would make and that she cared very much. Blanche wished she didn't.

"Listen girlfriend, this ain't about Durant. This is about you, about whether you're woman enough to stick by what you say and what you feel, regardless. If Durant can't handle it, you might as well know that now."

While Tina took a shower, Blanche called Mattie and gathered from her response that dinner with four children was not exactly Mattie's idea of a treat. They agreed to meet for dessert.

The dining room was nearly empty when they arrived. The girls had decided to weave multicolored beads into their hair. Every time someone came near them, they arched their slender necks, preening, sure their matching beadwork was being noticed. Blanche sighed. Another one of the things women had confused. All you had to do was look at the rest of the animal kingdom to see who was supposed to be dolled up for whom. She gave Malik and Casey a looking over. They had surprised her by wearing ties and jackets. Blanche didn't argue with them, although she did mention that if she were a man, they'd never get her to slip one of those nooses around her neck.

"We're not babies," Malik said with as much disdain in his voice for infants as Glenda had shown for Outsiders. Blanche had one of those moments when her heart nearly stopped at the thought that this child she was raising was growing up to be a prime aged male. She focussed on the affectionate, good natured, individual person Malik had always been. Would puberty turn his entire personality around? She knew she didn't have much control over whether he'd develop into a man she'd like to know. No matter how often she told him to treat girls and women with fairness and respect, and about the importance of knowing and understanding his own feelings, even if he and his buddies didn't think it was cool to show them, there was still a whole world of other boys and men out there telling him that being a butt-fondling troglodyte was not only OK, but all right. She was already talking to the Ancestors about him.

Carol and Hank's table, as well as Faith and Al J.'s had been moved, probably down on the lawn. The Insider side of the room now had only a couple of tables. The Outsider tables were nearly full. A middle-aged man in an Armani suit, complete with loafers without socks escorted a much younger woman to a remaining Outsider table. Blanche hadn't seen them before. From the way the man was looking at his companion's breasts, she assumed the young woman wasn't his daughter. The jogging couple was there. Blanche had seen them exercising together but they didn't seem to talk much. The Hot Couple was sitting near them. She didn't think she'd ever seen them when they weren't touching. Now both of them sat with a hand beneath the tablecloth and a look of being elsewhere on their faces.

Veronica looked startled when she saw Tina but quickly recovered. She gravely nodded in Blanche's direction, without making eye contact. Martin waved. From the corner of her eye Blanche could see Veronica shooting them quick, sly looks.

Durant hesitated when he entered the room, finally deciding to approach Tina first.

"Meet you on the beach after dinner?" he asked her when the greetings were done.

"Not until after I put the kids to bed." She shot Blanche a look that asked for back-up.

"We can put ourselves to bed, at least Deirdre and I can," Taifa told them.

"And so can we," Casey chimed in.

"OK, OK. Let's just say you need an organizer to help you," Tina told them.

"I'll help," Durant offered. He looked around the table. "See you later," he said when no one disagreed.

Taifa watched Durant walk away. "When I have a boyfriend, I want him to have a convertible just like Durant's and I want us to come here on vacation."

"I'm never having a girlfriend," Casey announced.

"Me either," Malik agreed. "You have to dance with 'em and kiss 'em and stuff. It's stupid."

Tina winked at Blanche who didn't care to know what "and stuff" meant.

"You'll change your mind, I bet. You'll have a girlfriend, sometime," Deirdre told her brother.

"Yes. You might meet someone on vacation," Taifa added with a sidelong glance first at Deirdre and then at Blanche.

The girls covered their mouths and giggled in unison. Blanche was sure they were kicking each other under the table. In case I thought I was getting away with anything, she thought, and decided the less said the better. Tina was watching her with a mischievous grin on her face.

Malik looked from Taifa to Blanche and back again. "That's stupid! Just 'cause you meet someone on vacation doesn't mean they're your boyfriend!" He glared at Blanche, letting her know this was all her fault.

"That's not what she said." Deirdre told him.

More giggles followed by a squabble about Taifa's exact words that left Blanche and Tina out of the action.

"Anyway, what if your girlfriend dies or something?" Casey asked.

Blanche tuned back into their conversation.

"So what if your boyfriend dies? You get another one." Taifa's answer was quick and easy.

"First you have to cry and wear black clothes." Deirdre reminded her. "I'd wear a veil and long black gloves, and carry a handkerchief with black lace." She shifted her face into fake sadness.

"And keep a piece of my loved one's hair in a locket around my neck forever," Taifa added, her hands resting on her imaginary brooch.

"What kind of junk have you two been reading?" Tina wanted to know, which opened a discussion of books that had nothing to do with death and boyfriends.

Blanche looked at their bright faces. How easily they molded what they were given into something they could use and understand. She'd meant to question them about how they were feeling about the deaths that happened here, but had never gotten around to it. She realized how little time she'd actually spent with her two since she'd been here. There'd been no pileups in her bed; no complaints about what his or her sister or brother had done; no whispered secrets. Not even any real demands for her time and attention. Was that due to being here and having Tina at their beck and call? Or were they suddenly beyond that already?

By the time Mattie arrived, the children were having ice cream on the terrace and Blanche had told Tina her moment of joy was approaching. Tina gasped like a groupie at the sight of Mattie.

"Mattie, I believe this young woman would like to meet you. Mattie Harris, Tina Jackson."

Tina stood up and held out her hand. "It's truly an honor Dr. Harris. We read *Woman as Warrior* in our feminist theory course my last term. I felt like I could go out and take on the world after I read it. I just want to thank you for writing it."

Mattie fiddled with her shawl. Her eyes were misty when she

looked up. "You're a dear and generous young woman. I thank you. Quite frankly, I was in need of a few kind words."

"I'm sorry about Mr. Garrett's death. I know he was your godson."

Mattie nodded. "Thank you, dear."

Tina waited for Mattie to sit before she sat back down herself. "When I was reading *Woman as Warrior*, I fantasized about meeting you, about being able to ask you something."

Mattie leaned forward slightly. "What would you like to know?"

"Well, I wondered about your idea that there can never be equality of early childhood parenting between biological heterosexual parents. It was kind of hard to accept."

"You're not alone. I still get letters from women protesting my premise. However, they tend to be childless women who hope to share parenting with a man. Many more women have written to thank me for corroborating the reality of their lives. As I said in the book, no matter what the parents may wish or do, the child instinctively knows which parent lactates and which, therefore, can provide life-giving sustenance. The child has a parent preference that transcends our desires for equal parenting and the yeowoman efforts of many fathers. None of my critics have been able to refute this. Can you?"

Tina shook her head.

"Don't let this discourage you, my child. You can do the lion's share of parenting and still run the world, if you make sure your partner understands the need to make up for having less intense parenting responsibilities by taking care of other necessaries generally left to women."

Tina nodded her agreement. Mattie went on.

"We women would be wise to remember that we have always done all the important things, grow food, raise children, develop social groups, all the things that sustain human life. In my new book, I try to understand and explain why it is that we won't accept the power and ascendancy this gives us."

Blanche grinned to herself. While she agreed that women did most of the work that really mattered in the world, she had a hard time picturing Mattie out in the fields picking apples and berries, helping a neighbor birth a child, tending the village fire. But, writing a book that convinced a young black woman that she has an important part to play in the world was certainly a kind of midwifery and planting and sowing and mothering.

"Maybe we don't appreciate ourselves because no one else does," Tina said.

"Not good enough, young woman, not good enough. We can easily prove our power. For example, what if every woman in the country refused to prepare dinner Thursday evening. Just the thought of it makes our power clear. And what if every secretary or waitress in the world decided to take the same day off. We don't need other people to know our power, we need ourselves, ourselves." Mattie's eyes were brilliant, her voice strong and certain.

"You mean organize," Tina said.

"Exactly, my dear, exactly. That's when the change will come, when women organize and declare it time for the boys to make way. I don't mean the insipid women's organizations out there today, fooling around trying to reform the system using the boy's rules. Ridiculous. No risk, no gain. We want equality, but we're no longer willing to get hurt in order to get it. Today's national movements, women's and blacks', seem more interested in being players in the white male club than challenging the white male patriarchy.

Tina cleared her throat. "A bunch of sisters started getting together after the Anita Hill thing to work against violence against women. Black men who didn't even know us called us man-haters and dykes, and talked about how we were siding with the white man, like Anita wasn't even black! Those of us who didn't immediately drop out, ended up spending most of our time trying to figure out how to deal with the way black men were treating us."

Mattie shrugged. "So what? Some white person has probably called you a nigger in your life. Did that stop you?"

"No! It made me push harder."

"Exactly my point," Mattie said.

Tina nodded again. "But it's different when it's a black man who puts you down, especially if you're a straight woman."

"Ah yes," Mattie sighed. "It always comes back to that, doesn't it? Our need to be loved by our torturers. I can only suggest that young black women put a great deal of time and energy into pulling men back from where the only way they see to be whole is to assume a position over women. I wish you luck, my dear. I can't imagine what it will take to make men feel it's all right to be human before they're male or black. I suggest you not ally yourself with any man in a serious way until you're very sure he's got some of that straight."

The three women were silent. Blanche could almost see Tina thinking about what Mattie had said, trying to figure out how to use it to find her way through the mine field of being young and sharing control of your life with your hormones. But how different was it for her, at her age—feeling the loss of Leo and the heat of Stu?

The children had finished their dessert and were clearly ready to leave. Tina rose. "It's been really wonderful talking to you. I hope I see you again before I leave."

Mattie nodded as though a future audience might just be possible.

Durant rose from his family's table and followed Tina and the children. Mattie watched the two of them descend the stairs to the grounds. "I'll bet you five dollars he loses her."

"I ain't got that kinda money to lose, and quite frankly, it's a bet I'd like to lose."

Blanche relieved Tina and Durant of their bedtime responsibilities. They left and the children settled down for the night. The only sounds came from the creatures in the trees and grass and from the waves. Blanche settled into the living room and slipped first into her book and then into a sound sleep. Tina waked her when she came in later that night and they both shuffled off to bed.

Chapter Twelve

～

An overcast sky and the sound of the waves breaking
more furiously than she'd heard before told Blanche her boat
outing with Stu was off hours before she got a call from him.
She could tell he was about to suggest something else. She
headed him off by telling him something had come up that
she needed to do today, anyway. Mattie had called her earlier:
"Carol's been asking to see me," Mattie had told her. There
was a long pause. "I'm not eager to go, as you might imagine.
Nevertheless, she was Hank's wife. I do have a duty. But I can't
see her alone, I simply can't. Would you . . . could you possibly
come with me, Blanche? I'd be very grateful."
"There are nurses, I'm sure someone would be glad to . . ."
"No, I couldn't bear some stranger."
A hired car picked them up at the Big House and took
them up to a small airstrip. Blanche had never before been in
a commuter plane. The experience was one she hoped never
to repeat. She tried to keep in touch with the Ancestors during her flight to lend some weight to the flimsy plane.
Forest Glen Sanitarium was a tall, old brick building with

a high, black, iron-railed fence. It could have been mistaken for a private estate, until she noticed the heavy screening on the second and third floor windows. A nurse in a starched uniform and perky cap sat behind a large desk inside the door. "May I help you?" was written on her face before she spoke. When Mattie told her how she could help, the nurse made a phone call. Another starched nurse came to escort them to Carol's room.

"How is she?" Mattie asked the nurse as she ushered them down a long corridor of closed doors.

"Improving, we think. Slowly. She's still deeply depressed. Doctor is hoping a new medication regimen will help. But so far . . ."

Carol's room was near the end of the hall. She was sitting up in bed near a window dominated by a tree just outside. She looked like an old child. A dated, yellow bed jacket helped that impression and made her look jaundiced. Her eyes were dull when she looked up to watch them enter the room. The nurse had knocked, Carol hadn't answered. Her face changed when she saw Mattie. Her mouth opened in a silent cry, she lifted her arms and held them out to Mattie. Her eyes were flooded with yearning and she reeked of loneliness, Blanche had to turn away. Mattie leaned heavily on her stick as she crossed the room. Blanche could feel Mattie's conflict, recognized it in her stalling-for-time gait. Little mewling sounds were coming from Carol now.

The nurse took six giant steps to her bedside. "Now dear, don't excite yourself."

Carol strained forward, her hands outstretched toward Mattie. Carol nearly lifted the older woman off her feet as she pulled Mattie's hands to her lips. She showered them with kisses and washed them in tears.

"Don't, my child. Don't," Mattie was trying to pull her hands away.

Blanche was sure they weren't going to get any sense out of Carol. The nurse pushed a button and a woman in a pink striped uniform and white apron entered the room with a tray on which there was a hypodermic and vial of clear liquid. The nurse filled the hypodermic, pushed up Carol's sleeve and slipped the needle into flesh. Carol relaxed immediately. She slumped back against the pillows.

"She's been doing so much better, really." The nurse straightened the sheet over Carol. "Could you possibly stay a few hours? Perhaps after lunch she'll be more coherent. She's been asking to see you for two days. Doctor thinks it would do her good to talk to you."

Blanche could tell Mattie didn't want to stay. "Let's do it, Mattie," Blanche took Mattie's arm. "We've come all this way, we might as well."

"We have quite a nice dining room and I'm sure you'll find the solarium very comfortable." The nurse directed them down an adjoining hallway.

The stuffed chicken breast and rice pilaf were bland but at least the string beans were fresh. Mattie was distracted. Blanche knew Mattie was afraid Carol might tell her something that made it impossible to continue to believe Hank was innocent. Blanche wanted to say something comforting, but nothing came to mind. When the nurse appeared, Blanche gave Mattie's hand a quick squeeze.

"Thank you, my dear." Mattie picked up her walking stick, straightened her back and preceded Blanche down the hall to Carol's room. The nurse ushered them in.

Carol's eyes looked slightly glazed, but she was relaxed and smiling. The nurse showed Blanche how to operate the call bell and left them.

"Mattie. Oh, Mattie." Carol held out her hand. Mattie took it in her own for only a moment before letting it drop to the bed.

"Hello, Blanche. This is a nice surprise." Her eyes filled. "I'm sorry." She reached for a tissue on the table by her bed.

"Don't upset yourself," Mattie told her. "I'm not going to stay long, too tiring for you. They said you wanted to see me."

"Yes, but . . ." Carol looked from Mattie to Blanche and back again.

"You two talk, I'll be outside," Blanche offered.

"No!" Mattie's voice was tinged with panic. "No need, Blanche." She turned to Carol. "Blanche and I have become fast friends. She's been wonderful to me since . . ."

Carol pressed the tissue to her eyes for a second. "Oh Mattie, I can't believe he's gone. I knew he was depressed, but I didn't think . . ." She raised her head and looked at Mattie, who spoke with urgency:

"My dear, tell me what happened the night Faith died, please! I must know, I must. You know he couldn't have done this thing. Not Hank."

Tears pooled in Carol's eyes. "Faith had invited us in for drinks. I didn't want to go. Neither did Hank. We knew she . . . I was so angry, I'd given myself a massive headache. Hank insisted I lie down. He said he'd called Faith. I lay down and fell asleep. It was around ten when I woke. Hank was gone." Carol stopped to blow her nose. "I went by the Big House. Someone told me Hank had been there earlier and left. I decided to look for him, to find out what happened with Faith. I had a feeling he'd gone to see her without me. I walked down the beach to his favorite spot. He wasn't there. He often walked back and forth between here and the village, so I decided to get my flashlight and check there. I don't know what made me stop at Faith's. There were no lights on, although it was dark outside. Only the screen door was closed. I knocked. No one answered. I went in. I thought she'd gone to the dance. I had my flashlight, of course. I thought maybe I could find . . . I don't even know why I went in the bathroom."

Mattie's head snapped up as though Carol had given her an uppercut.

"I know I should have called someone, should have . . . I ran. Hank wasn't at the cottage when I got back. When he came in he looked tired, forlorn. He said he'd been at the Big House. I told him I'd been out looking for him. It was as if we were trying to wait each other out, force the other one to mention Faith first. After awhile, I couldn't take it any longer.

'Did you go see Faith?' I asked him. He looked at me for a long time, almost as though he'd never seen me before. 'In a manner of speaking,' he said. 'Although I'd hoped for a less radical solution.' I'll never forget the look on his face. I tried to tell him that I'd seen Faith, too, that I knew what had happened, but he cut me off. 'It doesn't change anything between us, you know that don't you?' I asked him why should it? I tried to get him to tell me what happened. 'What's there to say? It's done now,' he said, over and over again.

"The next day, we argued about it on the beach. I was angry. At Hank for doing something so stupid and at myself for not having the courage to just ask him, ask him . . . I tried to let him know how much I hated her, how glad I was that she was dead, so he'd know it was all right. But I was mad, and he, he wouldn't . . . he . . ."

Carol was sobbing and shaking. Blanche pushed the call button.

Mattie was as rigid as stone on the return trip. Blanche didn't try to make conversation.

"You think I'm a deluded old woman. Caught up in some fantasy, unwilling to accept the truth, don't you?" Mattie asked as they walked toward her cottage. She didn't give Blanche a chance to answer. "But I'm too old to deny what I know, and I know Hank didn't have anything to do with Faith's death. If I knew how I know that, I'd explain, but I don't. Carol could just as easily be lying to protect herself, couldn't she?"

Blanche stopped listening to Mattie go on about how Carol had helped ease Hank into suicide by giving him another reason to die. She realized it was grief, not intuition, that was driving Mattie. She needed to hold Hank in her mind as she'd thought she'd known him because that memory was all that was left. If he hadn't been the person she'd thought, had her relationship to him been any more real? Mattie wasn't going to rest until Hank had a halo. Instead of helping Mattie hang on to her belief, maybe what she was supposed to do was to help Mattie let go. She had no idea how, partly because she had the feeling that she didn't quite understand all that was driving Mattie. She looked at Mattie's stony face and shining eyes. I need to talk to somebody about this woman, she thought. It was four o'clock. Ardell didn't get home until nearly midnight.

When she left Mattie's the wind off the ocean was brisk. The sun hadn't been out all day, but none of that seemed to matter to Malik and Casey who were working away on their fort. They had sweaters on. Tina's doing, no doubt. The girls were in the kitchen with Tina. They were playing a game of Jeopardy. None of them seemed particularly impressed to see Blanche.

"There's some pasta salad in the fridge," Tina told her. "It's good, too," Taifa added. "We made it."

Blanche got a plate, but was careful only to take a small amount until Taifa was proven correct. Too much mayo, but it wasn't bad. Blanche carried her plate out to the porch.

Tina came to the door. "I forgot. Stu wants you to call him." She grinned at Blanche. "He's really on your case."

"I guess so." Blanche smiled back, not bothering to pretend to Tina or herself that she wasn't getting a kick out of all the attention. "What did he say?"

"Well, he was very disappointed when you weren't here. He left his number. I put it by the phone. And he said to please call him when you come in."

Blanche finished off her salad before she went to the phone. As soon as she heard Stu's voice, she knew she wanted to see him.

"You ashamed to be seen with me?" Stu asked her when she hesitated over his suggestion that he have dinner with her at the Big House. Blanche flushed. He was right in a way. She didn't want to advertise that they were seeing each other, and she didn't know all the reasons why. She'd have to eat alone if she didn't invite him. Mattie had already said she was having dinner at her cottage. The children were looking forward to having their own table and Tina was off somewhere with Durant. She couldn't think of any reason to say no.

The girls were no longer enamored of their own table when they realized they could have been sitting with Blanche and Stu. He winked at them over his shoulder. They giggled. Veronica Tatterson stopped at their table on the way to her own.

"Stu! Why haven't you been to see us?" Veronica brushed her hair back with her customary gesture.

Stu stood up. "You know Blanche, of course," he said.

Veronica reminded Blanche of their old dog, Maizie. Maizie had never mastered house training, no matter how many times she'd had her nose rubbed in her leavings and been spanked with newspaper. They'd finally built a house out back and retired Maizie to it. Now it was Veronica's turn. Blanche looked up and gave Veronica her shark's tooth smile. "I love your hair Veronica. Just this morning, I was telling Tina how natural your hair looks."

Great spots of red developed around Veronica's collarbone and crept up her face. The stream of venom that poured from her eyes was so strong Blanche expected her clothes to be drenched. Veronica turned with the smartness of a drum majorette and went to her own table.

"Did I miss something?" Stu asked.

Blanche widened her eyes. "When?" she asked with a grin she couldn't suppress.

Dinner was lovely. Her sautéed scallops were perfect, but Blanche was only aware of them at the edge of her mind.

"What's wrong, Blanche? I can tell something's bothering you." Stu gave her a shame-on-you smile. "You didn't think I'd notice? Or didn't you think I'd care? Is it Mattie? I saw the look on your face when you mentioned her at lunch. Hank's death must be really tough on her. I know she was crazy about him. Maybe she'd be better off if she left, got away from where it happened."

"I know you didn't like him, so . . ."

"So you thought I wouldn't be sympathetic to someone who did? Like I told you, I envied him that love." He laid his arm on the table so his hand was just touching hers. "You're wonderful for worrying about the old girl, but what about you, Mama Blanche? Who's looking out for you?"

"I am worried about her, but I don't want to talk about it here."

After dinner, Blanche offered him a drink at the cottage. Taifa and Deirdre took charge of him the minute he stepped inside. They showed him the drinks caddy, switched and grinned and generally showed off for him. Malik and Casey talked with him about boats. At bedtime, he offered to help, but Blanche declined. While she was overseeing lights out, there was a crash from the kitchen.

"Just dropped a glass!" Stu called out.

"I'll be right nearby. I'll look in on you in an hour," Blanche told the children. "I expect everybody to be in bed by then. OK?" No one was foolish enough to disagree.

When she passed through the kitchen, she checked for signs of broken glass. She found the glass all swept up and in the trash. Good boy! she thought. She walked with Stu toward the beach. An occasional cloud blotted out the moon and turned the landscape black as pitch. Blanche shivered, although she wasn't cold. Stu put his arm around her shoulders.

"OK, talk," he told her.

"If you repeat a word of this, I'll swear you made the whole thing up. I wouldn't be doing this if I wasn't worried."

She didn't tell him about Hank's real suicide note, only that Mattie was fixated on the idea of Carol's being involved in Faith's death because Faith had information about Carol that Carol didn't want known. Blanche didn't mention that Faith had information on other guests as well, although anyone who knew Faith at all would guess as much.

"But Faith's death was an accident," Stu said.

Blanche realized she was going to have to fudge a little to keep from mentioning Hank's original note. "Not to Mattie."

"But why would Carol do such a thing?"

Blanche shrugged. "Even if she's wrong about Faith being murdered, something is going on that involves Faith." She

liked the way Stu's eyes flashed when she told him about what
had happened when she'd gone to fetch the box.

"You could have been killed!" There was shock and anger
on his face. "Get rid of whatever you and Mattie found and
let it be known it's destroyed. Keeping it can only cause trouble and it's too dangerous. I've heard about Faith being a
snoop and a gossip, but it sounds like she was really sick. I
wonder if Al J. knew?"

Blanche told him about her meeting with Al J. "I doubt
whether he'd believe it even if someone told him about it."

Stu stopped and turned to face her. "You know, it's not just
you who might get hurt by whoever's trying to get what you've
got. There's also Mattie. Alone. You're a good and loyal
friend, Blanche. But it's no good. Maybe you ought to think
about destroying the stuff, whether Mattie likes it or not. I can
see how you would want to know who hit you. What I worry
about is whether that information is dangerous for you to
have. If this person cares enough about his or her reputation
to knock you out, what would happen if you decided to announce who hit you? Please, Blanche, leave it alone. Get rid
of the stuff."

Blanche continued walking. It was not a bad idea. She'd
been bothered by having seen it, by knowing about it. More
than once since they'd found the box, she'd fantasized using
what she knew against Veronica in some way.

"Maybe you're right about getting rid of the stuff." As soon
as I find out who hit me she added to herself. "I'll talk to
Mattie about it." But she didn't say when.

He took her hand. "Poor baby! You're supposed to be on
vacation, not playing Watson to a grief-crazed Sherlock! You
need some R & R. A day trip. Shit! I forgot. I've got to run
some errands early tomorrow. I won't be back until late afternoon. We'll leave as soon as I get back. I'll show you some of
the spectacular spots. Deal?"

Blanche gave him her usual let me check with the kids and
think about it response. Stu pulled her to a stop. She turned
toward him. His lips were soft and firm and careful. It was not

a deep kiss and there was only the one. Blanche wanted both more and less.

"I better get back."

"It's only been twenty minutes since we left. You keep running like this, Blanche, I'm going to start thinking you're afraid of me."

"Should I be?"

He moved closer. "Maybe. Depends on what scares you. Does this scare you?" He stroked her arm with the tip of one finger. "Does this?" The next kiss was deeper and longer. A murmur started in Blanche's throat, like the creaking of a cold stove warming up. She pushed at his chest. He moved back immediately. His eyes were hungry.

"Come to my place later." The urgency in his voice was a promise of pleasure.

Blanche shook her head. Stu put his hands on either side of her face and played his tongue over her bottom lip. "Don't say no. Think about it. No strings attached." He kissed her again, even more briefly. "Promise."

Blanche laughed, "Sure. I can see us sitting down for a bit of polite conversation."

Stu laughed too. Blanche wouldn't let him walk her back.

Tina and Durant came in a couple hours later. They seemed to have managed an evening without fighting and were winding it up on the front porch. Tina had one of those post-orgasmic smiles that Blanche couldn't handle at the moment. She went to her room to read. She couldn't, of course. She couldn't do anything but think of that sweet, cool tongue passing across her bottom lip. She got up and took a shower. She put on her robe and walked to the front door. Tina and Durant were kissing on the moon-washed lawn. She went back to her room and dressed. She put a couple condoms in her pocket then put in her diaphragm on the assumption the more barriers the better. She took the flashlight from the kitchen counter and propped a note against the sugar bowl: "In emergency: 691-7672. Love, Blanche." She slipped out the back door, all the while watching herself heading to bed with a man she'd known a couple of days. She watched herself, but she didn't dare talk to herself about it. She just kept that kiss going in her mind. It carried her halfway to the village, her flashlight playing over the path in front of her. Then she stopped. She was ready for some serious sex, but she wasn't ready for Stu. Ardell was wrong, it wasn't about his color. Maybe she was just scared to let somebody get close, like Leo said. She hoped her decision now didn't have anything to do with Leo. Maybe she really believed the only safe sex she could have was with her vibrator. Whatever the reason, she was back at the Crowley's cottage in less time than it seemed to have taken her to get halfway to Stu's. Tina and Durant had hardly moved. She went in through the kitchen without turning on the light and picked up her note from the kitchen table. She heard a sound and walked down the hall toward the children's room. She was nearly at her own door before she realized that was where the sound was coming from. Malik's had a bad dream, she thought. He still sometimes came looking for her when that happened. She went to the door. "Here I am, Hon . . ."

The shove sent her flying back and out against the far wall of the hall. She struggled to catch her breath. The bedroom door slammed shut. Blanche was immobilized. Her lungs lay in her chest like two deflated balloons. Tina turned on the light in the living room and peered down the hall. "You OK? We heard a loud bang." Durant was leaning over Tina's shoulder. They both came running. Blanche was panting for breath and pointing at the door and shaking her head "No" at the same time. If Durant understood that she meant for them not to open the bedroom door, he didn't act like it. He flung the door wide and switched on the light.

"Holy shit!"

Blanche's room looked as though it had been tossed in the clothes dryer. The curtains had been torn down. The screen was knocked out of the window.

Blanche checked on the children. They were still sound asleep. She called Mattie. "Are you all right? Yes, I'm sorry I woke you, but someone's broken into my room. Nothing's missing, so I figure . . . I just wanted to make sure you were all right. Yes, OK. Good night."

Tina and Durant had listened to every word. Blanche didn't have enough energy to make up a good lie, so she told them the vandals story, the same one Faith had spread around when she was ripping people off.

"Yeah," Durant chimed in. "Kids from the village do this stuff every year. It was dark inside. They probably figured everyone was out. We should at least leave the porch light on, I guess."

She agreed to notify Arthur Hill in the morning. Tina brought her a large brandy, and Durant helped her straighten up her room. Blanche sat in the chair in the corner and wondered how long the intruder's vibe was going to saturate her things. She couldn't sleep here. She didn't argue when Durant suggested he spend the night. She gladly gave him and Tina her room and camped out on the sofa in the living room.

Chapter Thirteen

～

She hadn't expected to sleep at all, but sun was warming the room when the phone woke her. She could hear the children trying not to make noise in the kitchen. She picked up on the second ring. She'd expected it to be Stu, then remembered he was away.

"Blanche? Are you all right, my dear?"

Blanche told Mattie she was fine. "Except I'm getting pretty tired of being knocked around!"

"Well, I'm afraid my reporter contact hasn't helped any. I was right. Nobody in the article has anything to do with Amber Cove. I never heard of any of them, and I doubt whether Faith knew these sort of people—poor whites. They found the driver, one Mort Snarkey. No, I am not making up his name. His license had been previously revoked for drunken driving. He was tried and convicted of the hit and run."

Blanche was sure the article had to have something to do with someone at Amber Cove. Why would everything but this item be related to this place?

"I think you should tell Arthur about your attack." Mattie said. "It can't be tolerated twice! I should have insisted on security when you were hit over the head."

"My attacker could *be* Arthur Hill," she reminded Mattie. She told Mattie she'd come by so they could talk about what next as soon as she'd bathed and dressed.

Blanche climbed into a full tub of hot water, enriched with Christine's bubbling bath salts, and prepared for a long, restful soak. Her back was sore where it had made contact with the wall. She cushioned it with her washcloth. She had an all over ache. The nonphysical part of it was because she was mad and didn't have any place to put her anger. She punched the water with her fist a few times, then tried to relax. She talked to Mother Water, trying to find a peaceful place in herself. It didn't work. She was too wound up. Taifa and Malik both had to pee while she was in the tub. Tina knocked on the door to ask how Blanche felt and if she wanted anything from the village. All the children gathered outside the door to tell her their plans for the day, then thundered down the hall and out the door. End of soothing bath. End of thoughts of Stu and the cost in back pain of not having spent the night with him.

She didn't notice the note until she went to the refrigerator for lemon for her tea. It was stuck under an apple-shaped magnet:

Blanche: Thurs. Adamson called. Sorry, can't identify.
sending anklet back fed ex today. T.

Blanche's disappointment was a chill that radiated out from her stomach to her limbs. She was going to have to give it up. Christine and David were due back day after tomorrow. She wasn't going to have time to find out who had attacked her; and she wasn't sure she could figure it out even if she had more time. One thing she could do was follow Stu's suggestion and put people out of their misery.

* * *

The dulled brass box sat in the middle of Mattie's kitchen table. Blanche sat across from Mattie at the table.

"Why did he think I had the box instead of you?" Blanche asked.

"Good question!" Mattie sounded like a school teacher. "Who knows there's any connection between you and the box?

Blanche snorted. "Everyone, probably. Arthur and Veronica saw me with you at Faith's. Maybe she told Martin, maybe not. But don't they all know you have a safe? Wouldn't that be the logical place for the box to be?"

Blanche thought back to the night she and Mattie had taken the box from Faith's. With the memory came the feeling of helplessness that she'd felt as she was sinking to the floor after being struck. She'd had a similar feeling when she left the cottage—a feeling of being a target and not being able to do anything about it. Yes, she remembered now.

"He saw us!" she said. "He was still outside when we left. Maybe he was planning to go back to Faith's after we'd gone."

"But he couldn't have been following us," Mattie protested. "There's too much open space!"

"And a lot of deep shadows." The more Blanche thought about it, the more certain she became. It was being knocked on the head that had confused her, otherwise she'd have realized at the time that someone was following them.

"But what if he did follow us? Why would he assume you had the box and not me?" Mattie wanted to know.

Blanche saw herself and Mattie leaving Faith's, walking to Mattie's, then . . . Yes. She turned to Mattie. "I left with the bowl! I tucked it under my arm, the same way you carried the box from Faith's to your place."

She decided to take the children home as soon as the Crowleys got back. Regardless of whether Faith was murdered and whether Hank or Carol killed her, there was a sneaky person around here willing to hurt people. As for Hank and Carol, until she'd heard what Carol had to say, Blanche had believed Hank's note. As she'd said to Mattie, why would he lie? But if Carol was telling the truth—and she didn't seem to be in good enough shape to make up a good lie—Mattie could be right about Hank lying because he thought Carol killed Faith. Stupid! Why didn't he just ask her? Maybe he wasn't prepared to believe her, no matter what she said. Maybe he needed to think his dying would be useful to her.

Blanche pulled the box toward her. "Mr. Adamson was no help either. He didn't recognize the marks. He's sending the anklet back."

Blanche dove into her planned speech: "Mattie, remember when you asked me to help you I said there may be nothing to find? That's not exactly how things turned out. We did find the box. But I don't think we're going to find what you're looking for. I don't think there's any way to prove Hank lied in his suicide note and that Carol killed Faith. And frankly, I don't think Carol had anything to do with what happened to Faith." Blanche lifted the article and envelope, the folded papers and the book from Faith's box and spread them out on the table. "I'm leaving day after tomorrow. Let's have a good-bye burning and get rid of all this stuff."

Mattie's face was closed. "What about the person who struck you? I thought you were anxious to know who it was?"

"It really galls me to leave here not knowing which one of these people thinks it's OK to knock me out and push me around. I would like to get in the face of that bastard! And it was a man. Veronica isn't big enough to shove that hard. But Christine and David are back day after tomorrow. I'm not staying once they come back. Neither are the children."

Mattie was still quiet but she was watching Blanche closely. Blanche took a deep breath.

"I think we should destroy this stuff. I think you should let Hank go. Blaming Carol won't bring him back. Whether he killed Faith or not, he wanted to die. He wanted it."

"The hospital called. Carol is asking for me again." Mattie looked at Blanche with eyes that seemed even deeper than usual. "I miss Carol."

A moment later, Blanche could feel Mattie's temper flair.

"Damn Faith and her viciousness!" Mattie swept her hand across the items from Faith's box, scattering the folded pages and envelope and sending the article floating to the floor.

Blanche leaned down to pick it up. It had flipped over on its back side.

"Look at this. There's another article on the back. Why didn't we look at the back side?"

"We assumed the side with the date on it was the important side. A logical assumption, I think." Mattie's voice said she still thought their approach was right.

Blanche read the article aloud:

The body of an Asian woman was found in a dumpster behind 177 Drake Street. The cause of death is currently unknown. 177 Drake is also the address of an alleged Chinese gambling club said to be owned by major figures in the growing Chinese criminal underground.

"Curious," Mattie said without much interest. "Who here could possibly have anything to do with someone in Chinatown?

Blanche left Mattie for a walk on the beach. After lunch she took Taifa and Malik aside and broke the news about their leaving.

"But why, Mama Blanche? Why?" Malik asked. Taifa squinted the way she did when she was trying to figure something out.

Blanche didn't have a ready answer she wanted to share. She could have told them they needed to be protected from the worst in themselves and this place and these people weren't helping; she could have told them there was somebody here who had tried to hurt her twice and she didn't want her children around such a shit; or, that the Christine and David who'd left them might not be the ones who'd return day after tomorrow. "Families need to be together sometimes just to keep their family thing going. I think we could use some of that right now, and so could the Crowleys."

Neither Taifa nor Malik had anything to say. They went out on the porch to join their friends. Blanche heard disappointed groans from that direction.

Tina was in the kitchen. "What's all that groaning and moaning about?"

Blanche told her.

"Durant and I are thinking about leaving tomorrow instead of waiting 'til Monday when the Crowleys come back. Would that be all right with you?"

Uh-oh, Blanche thought. "You and Durant are leaving together?"

Tina grinned and held out her left hand to show Blanche the square cut ruby with small diamonds surrounding it. "His grandmother's engagement ring. She left it to him to give to his fiancée."

Blanche admired the ring for longer than it merited. She needed a little extra time to let her disappointment drain from her face. "Well, this is a big change from the woman who didn't want to get married!"

Tina brushed back her dreds. "I know, I know. But I made Durant promise not to hassle me about a wedding date for at least a couple of years."

Like trying to slow down a mule headed for the barn after a long day in the field, Blanche thought. Had Tina listened to anything Mattie had told her? Was it possible to listen to sound advice when you were deep in a love affair spiced by evil parents?

"So what happened?" Blanche asked.

"I just took a good, hard look at him. He's decent and responsible and kind, and I think he really loves me. How can I ask more than that?" She looked as though she was sorry she'd asked that question. "Anyway," she went on, "at least my children won't have to go through the kind of color crap you and I had to put up with."

Blanche thought about Stu's mother becoming a prisoner

in her own house, she thought about the families she knew where there was a dark child and a light child and what happened to them.

Tina seemed to read her thoughts: "I know it's not going to be easy with a color-struck mother-in-law, but I'm not marrying her and don't intend to waste any time on her."

"Well I think he's damned lucky!" And I hope you are, too, she added to herself. "Congratulations to both of you!"

When Tina left with Durant, Blanche decided it was time to call Ardell.

"I told you to get your ass out of there!" Ardell told her. "I hope whoever is messing with you is walking in front of fast-moving truck right now. I'm glad you're takin' the kids too. That place definitely has a bad vibe. In the meantime, if I was you, I'd call that big fine man and tell him to wrap me in his arms and protect me!"

"Not only is you a fool, you're a lying fool, Ardell. You'd choke to death before you'd let some mess like that come out of your mouth!"

"You wouldn't have been there to be pushed around if you'd gone on and given the boy some."

"There is nothing more disgusting than a middle-aged horny female. You better go take a cold shower, girl."

They laughed their way off the phone.

By way of announcing her leaving to the children, Tina fixed them a wonderful stir-fried chicken and rice dish and one of the best green salads Blanche had had in a long time. The girls were particularly disappointed about Tina leaving. The boys did a guy thing and pretended to ignore the whole business.

"But you promised to let us help you twist your hair!" Taifa reminded her.

"And what about my cornrows?" Deirdre added.

"OK, OK. A promise is a promise. One more day won't make a difference."

Blanche spent her evening walking on the beach, listening to the news on the radio, reading and pretending to watch

Taifa and Deirdre teach, or try to teach, Malik and Casey to dance. None of it kept her mind off the phone and the fact that she still hadn't heard from Stu. Tina was in her room trying to figure out how much wash she needed to do before she left. Blanche read for awhile before she went to the phone, but she didn't call Stu. He'd said he'd call her when he got back. He hadn't. She also hadn't taken him up on his invitation to a night of hot fun. Were those two things related? Too bad if they were, but no harm done. She was almost gone from here. But she wished he hadn't turned out to be another typical pussy hound who couldn't stand to be turned down. She chided herself for falling for romance under the stars. She locked the front door and made sure the children's windows were open from the top instead of the bottom.

She tossed for what felt like hours before she slept. When she finally did go under, her dream was waiting for her:

She was walking the streets of a pretty city with pink and blue buildings and palm trees. It was a warm and beautiful day. She could just glimpse the ocean in the distance. She was the last of a group of people laughing and talking as they walked down the middle of the street. She quickened her step, but the group grew further away instead of closer. She speeded up, but so did they, until they were nearly out of sight. Now she passed stores and a movie theatre, all open, but no people, only those in the distance, moving further and further away. She could still hear the buzz of their voices, although she could hardly see them now. She called out to them to wait, but the sound curled inward, ringing through her body, unheard beyond the walls of her skin. The day grew white and hazy, the buildings dissolving into gauzy mist. She could see no one ahead. She hurried after the voices growing more and more faint until they were hardly a rustle. Faster and faster she ran, straining to hear them, to at least hear them. But it was as quiet as falling snow. The people were gone; even their voices were gone. And in the way of dreams, she knew that they were gone forever. That she had seen and heard her last human being; that she was alone in a way that made her understand the word as she had never done before. Grief seeped from her marrow into her bones and guts and heart and eyes until she was drowned in sorrow, drowned in alone. She looked down at herself, but couldn't see her body. She felt her insides drain away until she was hollow. Empty and alone.

She sat straight up in the bed. Warmth poured over her at the sight of the room around her, the solidness of her breasts hanging heavy on her chest, the golden glow of the morning outside her window. But the hollowness was still there. She got up and peed. She was back in bed again before she realized that she'd remembered her dream.

She lay in bed thinking about it, examining it in relationship to recent events in her life—like the growing knowledge that her children were not all that far from being on their own and their potential for moving away from her. And there was Mama, and Miz Minnie, Aunt Cora and Uncle Johnny, and all the old folks she was lucky enough to have in her life. That wasn't going to last for much longer. At least some of them would dead before Taifa and Malik were gone. She was momentarily paralyzed by the remembered loneliness of her dream. Al J. had talked about the world becoming different when his wife died—cold and far away. She saw Mattie's empty eyes and heard Carol repeating "no" over and over again as if she could reverse death by denying it. Maybe the strongest of us is a fool in the face of that hollowness, she thought. She got out of bed and rang Stu's number. There was no answer.

Chapter Fourteen

∽

All the children had something they wanted to do before it was too late. The boys wanted to finish their fort, which now had three and a half walls. Taifa and Deirdre were deep in debate about zig-zag parts and which way they wanted their braids to fall. Blanche began packing and sorting their things and grew increasingly depressed. Mr. Adamson called to say he'd left the anklet at his office and totally forgot to mail it. He'd make sure it went out in today's mail. Blanche took his call as a reminder of her failure to identify her attacker, let alone protect herself. She leaped at Mattie's invitation to come over for coffee.

"My young friend at the *Post* called. There was a follow-up piece on the article." Mattie told her when she arrived. She read from a notebook:

"Susan Moon, aged 35, Vietnamese. Autopsy said natural causes, heart attack. But the way they found the body makes the police wonder if somebody didn't cause her to have a heart attack. Aggravated assault, or maybe even manslaughter." Mattie held up her hand for emphasis. "The police are seeking a man, possibly African-American or Hispanic with whom the dead woman was seen in the area."

Mattie shrugged. "No one from here, I'm sure. Unless, as you suggested, one of the Outsiders. Of course, a person like Faith . . . What is it, Blanche?"

Blanche ignored Mattie and went to the kitchen. The box wasn't on the table, but Mattie seemed to know what Blanche was looking for. She·hurried into another room and returned with it. Blanche opened it and removed the contents until she found the envelope the article had been in. She looked at it closely—a small, plain white envelope, nothing on it. At least nothing written. She looked at the way the envelope bulged in one corner, although there was nothing inside, the way her shoes held the shape of her feet. She turned the envelope over. It was a two-sided dimple, like something lumpy had lain in the corner of the envelope for a long time, with other things pressed on top. She picked up the article and held it up to the light. One corner of it was waffled slightly. She'd bet money the anklet and the article had once been in the envelope together. Belonged together. She lay it slowly down and looked up into Mattie's inquiring face.

"Philadelphia," she said and asked Mattie if she could make a long-distance call. When she got Mr. Adamson on the phone she asked him if he'd mailed the anklet, since she hadn't yet received it. She flashed Mattie a triumphant fist when he gave the right answer. "You know any jewelers in Philly?" she asked him. She also asked him to tell her what the anklet said, although she was pretty sure she remembered it exactly. She hung up and turned to Mattie.

"You are my sun and my moon—Susan Moon," she said.

Mattie got it immediately. "Susan Moon! Very well could be," she said in her aren't-you-more-clever-than-I-thought voice.

But Mattie couldn't hear the conversation playing in Blanche's brain—the one in which Stu told her that he'd lived in Philadelphia, that he'd brought an Asian lover home to meet his parents. Maybe it was Mattie's tone that stopped

Blanche from saying what she suspected; maybe it was because she didn't want to believe it herself.

"I'll be back." Blanche was out the door before Mattie
could speak. She needed air and room to think. She walked
along the beach at a near run, away from Mattie, away from
Susan Moon, away from the anklet. She told herself she could
be jumping to conclusions. Even if she'd made the right
connection between Susan Moon and the anklet's inscription,
there were a lot of Asian women in the world. It didn't have
to be the same woman, but she knew it was. She knew. She
turned around and headed for the village.

Stu's shop was closed. Blanche banged on the door with her
fist. The door to the living quarters was next to the shop. She
tried it. It was open. She climbed a steep set of stairs and
banged at the single door at the top. "Stu? Stu, are you in
there. I want to talk to you! Stu?" She gave up. He'd said he
had a boat. Where was it? She put a big friendly smile on her
face and played Stu's pal well enough to get the man in the
craft shop to walk down the pier with her to point out Stu's
boat, since he couldn't remember the name and she didn't
know one kind of boat from another. But there was no boat
to point out. She thanked him and headed back to Amber
Cove Inn.

She thought back to when she'd first met Stu, when she'd
thought her sense that he was half-hidden had made him all
the more interesting. Fool! She whispered to herself. Fool!
She made a harsh sound that might have been mistaken for
a laugh. Stu had kissed her like he meant it. He had looked
at her as though he saw and appreciated who and what he
saw. He had also hit her over the head hard enough to knock
her out and pushed her with enough force to give her a
backache. She didn't want to have to make a place in her
mind for all that he had done to her.

She abruptly turned back toward the village. She would
wait. She called Tina from the convenience store, then made
herself as comfortable as possible on the shallow step outside

Stu's shop. She didn't know how long she waited. The memory of her helplessness and fear at being attacked kept her sitting and waiting beyond any length of time she would have thought possible.

Stu laughed and shook his head when he found her sitting there, as though he were both delighted to see her and regretted her presence. He looked older, more angles and shadows in his face. Blanche rose. She concentrated on the litany of all that he had done to her and to others. They stared at each other for a moment more before he spoke.

"I'm sorry, Blanche. I keep having reasons to say that to you."

"Oh, you're sorry all right. What I want to know is how sorry."

He moved to go by her, to open the door.

"No. We talk right here." He sat on the stoop at her feet. Passers-by looked at them, some nodded.

"Now what?" he asked.

"Everything, that's what! Everything." She stepped onto the pavement in front of him. She looked down on him and was nearly overcome by the urge to kick him and to kick him and kick him until she had kicked out every thought and memory of him. He looked up at her. His face and eyes were sad.

"I never meant to hurt you, never. I never meant to hurt anyone."

Blanche's laugh was full of disbelief. "That's why you hit me, pushed me, because you didn't want to hurt me, you rotten liar, you shit! You coulda killed me!"

Stu shook his head from side to side, as if to throw off her words. "If I'd wanted to really hurt you, Blanche, I could have. Easily. You just kept showing up in the wrong places. If you'd told me in the beginning that you were mixed up in this mess with Mattie . . . By the time I realized you were helping her, it was too late."

"How did Faith get the anklet?" Blanche asked him.

"Stole it, of course. I hadn't looked at it in so long I didn't even know when it went missing. Don't ask me how or when she took it. It wasn't hard. The back door hasn't been locked for years.''

"How'd you know she had it?"

"The last thing she said to me, about a week before she died. She complimented me on my taste in jewelry. It was on the terrace at the Big House. Dave or somebody pointed out that I wasn't wearing any jewelry. Faith laughed and said it wasn't my jewelry she meant. That night, I looked in the desk where I'd left the anklet. It was gone and the article, too. Then Faith was dead, and I had to have them back before Al J. sent someone down here to pack up her things, before somebody started going through her stuff and wondering."

"But what made you think I had the box instead of Mattie?"

"The box? I never thought you had the box. I gave up on finding the anklet at Faith's place when you told me you and Mattie had found the box. I knew Mattie has a safe. I figured that was that. Then I saw the note on your fridge."

Blanche was blank for a moment, then remembered the note from Adamson. "That could have been about my anklet."

"No. Not once I knew you'd found Faith's misery box."

"But I didn't have the anklet when you pushed me," Blanche told him. "Adamson forgot to send it back."

Stu made another of those unfunny sounds. "Of course, of course. That's my luck. Always has been."

"You mean the luck you started making when you dumped Susan Moon's body in . . ."

"But I didn't kill her," Stu interrupted. "I didn't! I loved her. She was already dead. I was drunk! I panicked! I loved her!" Stu sunk his head into his hands and rubbed them across his face before he continued.

"I met her in 1966, in Saigon. Back then, her name was Thuy Duong. Her people were shop owners. Pretty well off and all dead by then. She was able to get out. I couldn't believe it when I met up with her again in San Francisco. She was alone in the city. So was I. She wasn't used to it. Neither was I. We got married. We honeymooned crossing the country from San Francisco to Philadelphia—with a side trip up here, to introduce her to my folks."

Blanche could almost see memories swirling around him.

"She was so beautiful." He raised his hands and stared at them as though the words to describe her were written on his palms. "So delicate. So . . . I knew Dad would love her, even if she wasn't black. You know what happened. He was furious when he saw Thuy Duong. When he told me I'd never get the shop if I married outside the race, I couldn't tell him we were married! Still, we were happy. I thought she was happy. But I came home one night and she was gone, clothes, tooth-brush, everything. Not even a note. I almost went crazy look-ing for her. I finally found her in Chinatown. She was living in a disgusting old building, working for dimes in a sweat-shop, but she wouldn't come back to me. She was calling herself Susan Moon. Said she wanted a new name to go with her new life. She even bought herself some papers in that name. I tried to get her back, courted her as if we'd just met, dinner, drinks. That's when I bought the anklet. The night I gave it to her, she said she didn't want to be married to a man who was ashamed to tell his parents she was his wife. I guess I drank too much. I kept asking her to come back to me. She kept insisting I tell my family about her. Finally, she just got up and walked away. She left the anklet on the table. I sat in the bar for a couple minutes before I realized she hadn't gone to the bathroom. I caught up with her about a block away. I didn't call out to her, I just ran up behind her and grabbed her, just grabbed her. If there was something wrong with her heart, she never told me, I swear! She pulled away, pulled away and clutched at her chest. It was over almost before it began."

"But why dump her body like she was a bag of trash?"

Stu stood up and paced the pavement. "I told you, I pan-icked! I didn't know what had happened, why she'd died. I couldn't get involved. What if Dad found out? I told you what he said! I've wanted this shop all my life. What if they investigated, found out she was Thuy Duong. I was a drunken black man in Chinatown . . . The alley was right there. We'd only been in Philly a couple months. She'd made no friends and my friends knew her as Thuy Duong. There was nobody to care, nobody to ask . . ."

Blanche walked a few steps away and turned so that she could only see enough of him to know if he made a sudden move. She forced herself to feel only her rage and the possibility that this man was dangerous. Everything else would have to wait. She turned back to Stu.

"What about Faith? She didn't have a heart condition."

Stu jumped up. "I never touched Faith. I was on the path from the village, headed for the bar at the Big House. When I was close to Faith and Al J.'s place, all the lights inside went out at once. Then I saw Carol hurrying toward Faith's. She went inside. She was really running when she came out. I walked over to the cottage and called out. No one answered. I could see the door was open. I was tempted to go in, but I told you about my last encounter with Faith. I didn't want her to catch me snooping around her place, so I left."

"What did you tell Hank?" she asked him.

Stu stopped doing whatever it was that he did with his eyes and body that had once made her want to lean closer to him or maybe she just didn't feel it anymore. He suddenly seemed extremely tired and anxious to get this conversation finished.

"I saw him later, at the Big House. I told him I'd seen Carol come charging out of Faith's like she was being chased by the devil. I thought he was going to pass out. He gulped his drink and took off. I followed him. You should have seen our Little Brown Bomber when he came out of Faith's. Like a guy who'd just been sucker-punched. I knew then that Faith was dead in there somewhere. And it was pretty obvious what he was thinking. I could have told him Carol wasn't in Faith's long enough to do Faith any harm. But he brushed right by me when he came out, as if I didn't exist. Just like he did when we were kids."

Blanche made a disgusted sound. Stu searched her face.

"You think he killed himself because he thought Carol killed Faith? Stu laughed at the idea. "He'd have killed himself, anyway. He was too weak to live. Too righteous, too pure and decent. He could hardly wait to die."

Blanche couldn't, didn't want to speak. Everything about him looked phony to her now, that endearing little smile, those eyes that could by turns be sad enough to break your heart and hot enough to melt it. That pillow-soft voice that had wrapped itself lovingly round her now seemed to suck all the air out of the place. She wondered if his tiredness was contagious. All she wanted to do suddenly was sleep, to be unconscious.

"It's not over," she told him. "Mattie deserves to hear what you have to say, too. And I want an apology. In front of her. And I want reparations. Yes, that's what I want. I don't know what kind, but reparations." She moved in closer to him. "And I want this." She put the force of all her rage and betrayal, the weight of her entire frame behind the fist she drove into his stomach. Air whooshed out of him as though he were a released balloon. He staggered back, gasping for breath. Shock and pain twisted his face. Blanche turned and walked away. "Tomorrow morning at nine. At Mattie's," she said over her shoulder.

Mattie waved to her from her porch and quickly ushered Blanche inside. She demanded to know what was going on, but couldn't seem to comprehend what Blanche told her.

"You mean Rudolph's son, Stu? Have you talked to him about this? No son of Rudolph's would ever marry . . . There's really no proof, you know. Unless your jeweler can identify that anklet." She looked at Blanche as though she'd never seen her before and was not pleased by what she saw.

"Do you know how much Stu disliked Hank? He told Hank he saw Carol coming out of Faith's. He didn't mention that Carol wasn't in Faith's long enough to do anything or that the lights went out before Carol went in. They probably went out when Faith dropped her radio into the tub."

Mattie flinched. "I told Rudolph that boy wasn't wholesome. He took something that belonged to Hank once, something Rudolph and I had . . ."

She told Rudolph? She and Rudolph? Lord! What was there about this place that blinded her to what was right in front of her? Didn't Stu tell her he'd had his father's pharmacy since last fall? After his father died. And hadn't he done a doubletake when she'd told him Mattie had said Hank's father had died last year? "Delia and I were inseparable that year," Mattie had told her. Of course they were, how else could they pass Mattie's baby off as Delia's? It was like Miz Minnie always said, most times, you didn't have to ask people much, you just had to listen to what they told you.

"Did Hank know you were his mother? Is that what he meant in his note, about already knowing? I'd forgotten about that. Is that what freaked you? The possibility that your secret might be in Faith's possession? That Hank might have killed her to protect you, too?"

"What I did, or did not do, and why, is none of your business."

Blanche was glad Mattie didn't lie, at least she hadn't done that. All along she'd told the truth. What was important was which truths she'd decided to tell. A retractable bridge, she thought, remembering those few moments when she'd felt that she and Mattie had come together across all that divided them. It had never really happened.

Mattie hadn't reached out for a friend, even a temporary one. She'd reached out for someone to help her cover her tracks, to keep her image pure. She'd reached out to someone who was not a part of her set, not likely to be hanging out with folks she cared about, someone who would be excited by stories of a life she would never, ever lead, and pleased to be in the company of a black woman who had. It hadn't been necessary to spot Mattie points, they weren't even playing the same game. Blanche laughed, Old Queen Somebody or Another. And whenever there was Queen, there had to be an image to keep up. "Were you afraid people would find out that the warrior woman had a child she didn't have the courage to claim? I can think of a whole lot of things worse than that. At least you loved him. Or say you did."

Mattie's eyes flew open. She leaned toward Blanche. "How dare you! How dare you question my love for him! You couldn't possibly understand. I loved him more than life and I will not allow . . ."

"I'll tell you how I dare! You used me like I was one of your pens or paintbrushes. All that talk about "our sort!" I see why nobody's ever called you girlfriend before. You don't even know what the word means. I guess you figured I was used to cleaning up other people's dirt and keeping quiet about it, so why not yours?" Blanche's hands flew to her hips like soldiers to their battle stations.

Mattie's mouth tightened. "I will thank you not to repeat what you think you've learned here. It concerns no one beyond these premises."

Blanche remembered what Mattie had said about Amber Cove Insiders closing ranks. Rudolph might not have been an Insider in the strictest sense, but he was one of their set. And Mattie's lover. And Stu was his other son. Blanche suddenly saw a woman, small and very dark, sitting alone in a quiet room. "Did Stu's mother know? Did you and Rudolph make her ashamed to show her face? Or was she smart enough to turn her back on all you phonies? And what would all those women who think you're the last word in womanhood have to say about this shit, I wonder?"

The air was suddenly chilly as a November day.

Mattie banged her walking stick on the floor. "I will not be spoken to in this manner by some poor, uneducated, ignor . . ."

"There's more than one way to be poor, more than one kind of education and a whole lot of ways to be ignorant," Blanche told her. "And you, honey, with your books and pictures and money, your cottage and so forth are poorer, dumber, and more ignorant than I'll ever be. Too bad you can't live what you write." Blanche stared at Mattie until Mattie averted her eyes. Her voice was different when she spoke.

"If I have offended you, it was unintentional, I assure you." Mattie's voice and manner were now strictly under her control.

Blanche could almost see Mattie painting over the spot where Blanche was standing, eliminating her from consideration.

"I'd appreciate it, Blanche, if you would be decent . . . if you would be kind enough to hold what you've learned here, what you've learned about Hank, about me, in confidence."

Blanche savored this small victory, the closest thing to an acknowledgment of Mattie's maternity and an apology that she was likely to get. She hesitated a while before she answered, enjoying Mattie's obvious discomfort.

"I'll promise you this," Blanche finally told her, "I'll never tell any of it to anyone who gives a damn." She was careful not to slam the door as she left.

She dragged herself back to the Crowleys'. Tina took one look at her and told the kids they wre going to town for fish and chips, so they could just munch some fruit for lunch. She moved her hair braiding out back and told the boys they'd have to play Nintendo with the sound turned down. Blanche fell face down on her bed and cried until she felt as dry inside as an overbaked flounder. When she woke, it was dark and no one was home. She peed and climbed back into bed, thankful for Tina and glad to know she'd be out of this particular nightmare tomorrow. If she dreamt that night, she didn't remember it in the morning.

Chapter Fifteen

⌁

The house was quiet when she woke. She didn't need to look at the clock to know it was quite early: The birds' songs had that practice quality, as though they were just warming up for the day. The last tendrils of sleep slipped from her brain, leaving her mind at the mercy of memories of the events that had driven her to hide so deep in sleep. She thought of the recurring dream she'd come here hoping to remember. She understood it now in ways that she hadn't the night she'd finally been able to recall it: It wasn't just a way of reminding her to prepare for the future—when the children's adulthood and the likely death of Mama and other old folks would change the contours of her world. The dream had also been about now. She hugged herself against the memory of people in her dream moving further and further away from her, against that feeling of hollow loneliness that could kill a person. She thought of Mattie and Stu and how they'd both seemed to rush toward her at first, only to have moved so far from her she could hardly see them. And didn't want to. And won't, she thought, suddenly positive that she would never see either of them again. As well as getting her Mattie-witnessed apology, which was out since her blowup with The Queen, she'd also planned to pressure Stu to get in touch with Carol. She reached for the phone and called his number. She wasn't surprised when he didn't answer. She'd foolishly expected Stu and Mattie to be a part of setting her mind at rest since this whole mess started with them. Once again, she'd been wrong. Is that what Madame Rosa had in mind for her, to try to make connections where they couldn't exist? Maybe she'd misunderstood Madame Rosa. Maybe Madame Rosa had said rejection, not connection. She struggled against the weight of unfinished business and pulled herself out of bed.

She showered, dressed, ate a pear and tried Stu's number again. No answer. When the children got up, she fed them, corralled them into the last of their packing, then released them into the out-of-doors. She waited until Tina was in the shower before poking her head in the bathroom to say she was going out and where. She also made herself tell Tina how long she should wait for Blanche's return before sending Durant to the village after her. Tina peered around the shower curtain with a face full of questions. "I'll tell you about it when I come back," Blanche responded. "I promise." She was aware of having to force herself to tell Tina to send Durant if she was gone too long. She still didn't want to believe that Stu was dangerous. Yet, one of her children could have opened that bedroom door; or she might have had a bad heart like Susan Moon. He was at least reckless, which was always dangerous.

She didn't expect him to be in his shop or to answer her knock. She also didn't expect to find his boat. She was right on all counts. She went around the building and climbed the stairs to the back door. It was locked, too but there was a small cardboard box propped against it with her name printed on it. The sight of the box made her so mad she couldn't open it until she was halfway back to Amber Cove Inn. How dare he know that she'd go to the back door? There was a note in the box:

Dear Blanche, I'd do anything to change what's happened.
I can't face you again. Or Mattie. I'll contact Carol, I
promise. This is the best I can do in the way of reparations.
It was my mother's. Stu.

The large oval brooch was made up of a ring of brilliant
emerald green stones nestled between an inner and outer
ring of twinkling diamonds. She turned it over and over in her
hands. Excellent taste in jewelry, Faith had said of him. Had
he carefully gone through his mother's jewelry case looking
for just the right piece for her? Or had he figured that any
piece would melt her heart? After all, it did belong to his
mama. It wasn't fair that a man like him didn't throw off a
scent that warned people off. Or maybe he had. She thought
back to the first days. Why hadn't she heeded her first mind
when it told her there was something off about him? Was she
so determined to prove she could get a man to replace Leo
that she had stopped listening to herself? Now here she was,
a few kisses later, all turned around because Stu wasn't who
he seemed. And since she was on the hard questions, what
part had their complexions played in all this? Had his daddy's
love for dark skin rubbed off on him? Or did he really hate
black people because his dad dissed him for not being dark
enough? Maybe all along he'd planned to hurt or embarrass
her in some way. Well, he'd certainly done that. Her face grew
hot at the thought of how he'd used her own body to lure her
out of the cottage. Maybe he'd planned to ransack her room
and then run home and throw her across his bed. Or maybe
not. She could see herself standing outside his locked door
with damp panties, her mouth sour with self-loathing. She
stomped on the possibility that he had simply been attracted
to her. Dragging along behind it was that which fueled much
of her rage at him and made her want to hang her head in
shame: her attraction to him. Her attraction to a man who'd
knocked her out, pushed her. Shit! She didn't mind stepping
wrong, that was only natural, but this was part of that woman-
thing, where the man in your head has little to do with the

man in your bed. She'd thought she'd grown beyond that. And where had he gone? Was his note to her a lie like Hank's note? She put the brooch back in the box and slipped it into her shirt pocket. It was time to talk to Ardell.

"I'm back!" she called out to Tina and slipped quickly into her room and closed the door. She reached for the phone. "I got caught in the catch." She told Ardell about making the connection between the anklet, Susan Moon and Stu's having mentioned bringing an Asian friend home to visit. "It was all down hill from there," she said, then backed up. She couldn't tell the story of what had happened to her without beginning with what had really happened to Faith.

She began with Mattie and the note and worked her way through what Stu had told her about the night Faith died. "No one touched the woman! It was an accident, just an accident."

"Damn!" Ardell said, when Blanche stopped talking. "Do you think Stu really meant to let Hank believe Carol killed Faith?"

Blanche didn't hesitate. "I know he did. I told you what he said. That business about not telling Hank because Hank ignored him like he did when they were kids is so much bullshit. They ain't been kids for a long time. Stu saw how upset Hank was. He could have stopped Hank and told him Carol had only been in Faith's for a second, but he didn't. Because he liked hurting Hank. Although he probably didn't expect Hank to kill himself and leave a note saying he'd murdered Faith. But it's what Stu didn't tell Hank that made Hank think he needed to tell that one last lie."

"Hummm. But why was Hank so sure Carol would be blamed for killing Faith? Didn't everybody think Faith had an accident?"

"You know how it is when you got a big run up your stocking," Blanche reminded her. "It's so obvious to you, you know everybody else sees it, too. Hank knew, or thought he knew Carol had killed Faith. And Stu knew about it so naturally Hank thought other people must know, or at least would come to find out somehow."

"Hummm. I guess you're right. The whole thing's just too crazy for me. The antics of people with too much pride and money and not enough melanin. I called that color thing, didn't I?"

Blanche agreed that she had. From the very beginning Amber Coveites had told her this was a place where none of the color codes could be ignored, including Stu's attempts to play against the rules with her.

"I'm sorry it's been so rough for you, Blanche."

"I know you are, honey, and that helps, believe me."

They were silent for a moment in which Blanche felt her friend as close to her as her heartbeat.

"I wish I could stop feeling like I shoulda figured something was seriously wrong with him," Blanche sighed.

"You *did* figure something was up with him, Blanche! I'm the one who pushed you to give him a shot."

"Yeah, but you never saw him. If you'd been here, maybe . . ."

"This is stupid," Ardell told her. "He's the one in the wrong! Why we keep trying to find ways to blame ourselves for what men do to us?"

"Maybe it's because we know we wouldn't get hurt so much if we paid more attention to who the man is and less to what we'd like him to be."

"Hummm. I can't argue with that. But don't beat up on yourself. It was an honest mistake."

"Yeah, but I still keep feeling like there's something more.

"Like what?

"I don't know. Something that'll put paid to the whole damn business."

"What about taking your ass home? That's one thing you can do, girlfriend. Just leave that place. Time'll do the rest."

"There's got to be something more."

"It ain't that simple, Blanche. You're up in Maine, not out

in Hollywood. Life don't work like the movies. What you want
to happen? For him to drag his tired ass to your door and beg
your forgiveness? For Mattie to come to you with tears in her
eyes and goodness in her heart? For the whole thing to never
have happened, so you can be different from all the other
women in the world who've been fooled and knocked around
for even less reason? I don't think so! That's what makes it
tough. It's like gettin' shit on your shoes, no matter how you
scrape, there's always enough left to stink, until you just walk
it off. That's what you got to do, walk it off."

Tina was waiting for Blanche when she got off the phone.
When she heard the story, she wanted Blanche to press
charges: assault, breaking and entering, bodily harm, she
rattled off charges like a lawyer. "No way you can let him get
away with this Blanche, no way!" Tina's eyes were angrier than
Blanche had ever seen them.

Blanche thought about her conversation with Ardell. Neither of them had even thought of the police. She reminded
herself that she had about twenty years on Tina. Maybe their
worlds were even more different than she'd realized. But she
didn't really think so. Time was the difference. She kept her
voice as neutral as she could when she spoke. "He's already
gotten away with it, honey. Nothing can change that. Throwing him in jail don't change a thing he's done to me. No. I'm
not going to put myself through that. Not enough payoff."

Tina looked at her in a way that made Blanche want to
flinch. "How can we stop men from battering women if we
don't press charges?" she demanded to know.

Blanche felt a wave of regret as she watched Tina's mouth
set in a line of disapproval but she wasn't about to betray
herself or lie.

"No," she said, "I'm definitely not going to press charges.
Far as I'm concerned, teaching self-defense to girls starting in
the first grade has got a better chance of stopping men from
beating us up than pressing charges. I'm not going to add
insult to injury. Anyway, he wasn't my boyfriend punching my
lights out on a daily basis. He didn't rape me. I don't think he

knocked me out because I was a woman. How do you think I'll be treated? How seriously do you think the police would take me? Not only am I an outsider, but the inside folk would shoot me down. It scares me half to death to think of ever having someone do something to me that I can't avoid going to the police to get fixed. I'm glad this ain't it." She remembered the look on Stu's face when she'd punched him in the gut and smiled. "Besides, I'm sure Stu has at least one tender spot for me." She explained.

"Yes!" Tina shouted, her fists in the air. "At least that!"

But Blanche's account of her moment of retaliation wasn't enough to lessen the distance that now stretched between them. Ah well, Blanche thought, ah well. Maybe we'll run into each other in ten years. She didn't tell Tina about the brooch. She hadn't mentioned it to Ardell either.

By the time Christine and David arrived, Blanche, the children and Tina were ready to go. Deirdre and Casey had the droopy look of those left behind.

At a superficial glance, Blanche might have believed Christine and David had managed to patch their marriage together. But when she listened closely she heard the brittle edges of over-politeness, like the thin crust over hot lava. Neither of them seemed much in the mood for talking, which suited Blanche. She only had a moment alone with Christine, who said she'd be in touch.

While the Crowleys went off with the children to say goodbye to the fort, Blanche walked up the beach away from the Inn. It was time to take her load of Amber Cove to the sea. Out of sight of the others, she squatted on the beach and gathered a small heap of stones—larger than peas but smaller than eggs. As she recalled each hurtful event of her stay at Amber Cove, she picked up a stone. She rolled it between her palms and fingers coating it with what she could see and feel, smell and hear of the moments she hoped to leave behind: Taifa's color complex; the knot on her head and the bruise on her back; Tina's disappointment in her; Mattie's acting like Mattie and Stu being Stu; the pale, cold, color-conscious attitude of Arthur Hill, Veronica and others; and the haint in Hank's eyes. She rolled each of them round and around a stone then threw the stone and it's worrisome new shell as far as she could out into the sea. She felt freer when she was done. Not free, but freer, now that the hurts were outside of herself, rolling back and forth and back on the floor of the sea where the sway of Mother Water was already rubbing them away to sand.

She held out her arms and thanked Mother Water and the Ancestors for safe passage and lessons learned. She took Stu's brooch from her pocket and raised her arm to throw it out to sea. But in the last moment, something told her it might best be put to a different use. She slipped it back in her pocket and went to collect the children.

Epilogue

~

She was only home a day before David called to say he'd forwarded a package that had arrived at the cottage for her and that Adamson wanted her to call him. A part of her wanted to tell David to call Adamson and say she'd left the country unexpectedly and would call him in a year or so. But, of course, her curiosity wouldn't allow it.

"It was my old friend, Abby Greenbaum's signature. That's how I got it so fast. A fine piece of work, isn't it? Someone lost it, hunh? She'll be glad to get it back. Let's hope this fella's her husband. Could cause a problem if this is his doxy's bauble!"

She assured him she'd be very careful.

"The guy's name is Stuart, Robert Stuart."

As if she didn't know.

The postcard from Christine came a week later:

Blanche,
Here's my new add. & #. Please be in touch. I have C. &
D. on weekends. Let's get the monkeys together. Poor Stu.
They found his boat, but not him. How much do you know
about this? Why didn't you tell me?
Love,
Christine Crowley
12 Catherine St.
Cambridge, MA 02139
866-2656

Blanche called Ardell.

"Do you think he's dead?" Ardell asked her.

"I don't know."

"Do you care?"

Blanche laughed. "I always care. That's just the problem, ain't it?"